Plains Crazy

Also by the author

The Grey Pilgrim
Mad Dog & Englishman
Prairie Gothic

Plains Crazy

A Mad Dog & Englishman Mystery

J.M. Hayes

Poisoned Pen Press

First U.S. Edition 2004

10 9 8 7 6 5 4 3 2 1

Library of Congress Catalog Card Number: 2004108170

ISBN: 1-59058-132-6 Hardcover

Poisoned Pen Press
6962 E. First Ave., Ste. 103
Scottsdale, AZ 85251
www.poisonedpenpress.com
info@poisonedpenpress.com

Printed in the United States of America

For Chuck, Eric, Sallie, and Clay.
Sometimes eccentric uncles
leave you their fortunes.
My fortune is being able to dedicate
a book to you.
Don't spend it all in one place.

Some kind of love starts as friends,
that kind of love never ends,
for it comes on as slow
as a flower in snow…
—John Stewart. "Some Kind of Love"

…the girls are prettier than those across any of the
bordering state lines and only slightly less willing
than those up in the hills on the Missouri side, and
virginity before marriage—or puberty, for that matter—
means less than regular church attendance.
—Earl Thompson, *A Garden of Sand*

Michael Spotted Elk wasn't sure what woke him. He lay in the dark of the Cheyenne lodge and listened. He was getting used to his father's gentle snoring, that wasn't it. His mother and little brother breathed deep and steady, comfortably wrapped in their dreams and buffalo-skin blankets.

Something moved outside the lodge. Something big. It spooked him.

Everyone had assured him there were no dangerous animals roaming the Kansas prairie anymore, but he wasn't sure he believed them. He'd seen those buffalo over in the nearby pasture. And they said the guy who owned them had a pet wolf.

He heard the noise again. He wanted to get up and turn on the lights and find his baseball bat, then maybe peek out a window to see what it was. Only he was in an Indian lodge, a tepee, in the middle of the Great Plains. They didn't have electricity or windows here, and he wasn't allowed any modern artifacts.

He did have a lance, though. He pulled on his moccasins and crept to where the skins had been drawn tight over the opening that made do as an entrance to the lodge. He fumbled in the dark, found his bow and quiver of arrows, and passed on them. He couldn't hit the broadside of a billboard from ten feet. He wasn't much good with the lance, either, but if there happened to be a ferocious mountain lion, or even a testy prairie dog, out there, he wanted something to put between him and it.

It took Michael a few moments to work the unfamiliar leather straps. When he pulled the hides apart enough to peer out, he could tell it was still before dawn. The moon hung just over the cottonwoods at the west side of their patch of pasture, still bright enough so he could reassure himself no prairie monsters lurked out there, waiting to pounce. He pushed the lance through ahead of him, just in case, and followed it silently.

Their encampment was a quiet little circle of conical tents. The motor coaches, semi truck, and other vehicles that were part of the Public Broadcasting System's production crew sat, equally silent and encircled, a few hundred yards away. No one seemed to be about. That was nice. At least he would have a few private moments without the camera following his every humiliating failure to properly recreate the lifestyle his ancestors had lived a century and a half ago.

Why had he let his folks talk him into this? Just to be on TV? He scratched a chigger bite and wished he were snuggled into his bed in Phoenix.

It was cool in the moonlight, but not cold. A soft breeze brought fragrant, earthy scents up from the south, something musky and curiously erotic. What isn't curiously erotic to six-teen-year-old boys?

A shadow emerged from behind the nearest tent and Michael practically impaled himself on his lance as he tried to get it pointed in the right direction.

"It's only me."

Daphne Alights on the Cloud stepped into the moonlight, leading one of the band's ponies. "I couldn't sleep," she said. "Thought maybe I'd ride down to the creek. Wanna come?"

Daphne was hot. She was almost two years older than Michael, and so *Sports-Illustrated*-Swimsuit-Issue stacked that she'd become the subject of all manner of his fantasies in the few days since they'd started filming *This Old Tepee*.

"Uhh, sure," he said. He was surprised she wanted anything to do with him. Every time he'd tried to hit on her he'd turned into such a fumble mouth that he'd been certain she'd assigned him the role of last dork on earth to be caught dead with.

"Want a horse?" she asked. "Or do you wanna just double up with me?"

The idea of riding next to her, letting the horse's gait rock their bodies against each other, was enough to put a strain on the fabric of his breechcloth. He couldn't ride well. He didn't want to show her what a nerd he was by falling off the great beast. Worse yet, let her realize exactly how excited he was to be anywhere near her.

"You ride, I'll run." It wasn't far. "I need the exercise."

"OK." She grabbed a handhold of mane and swung onto the horse's back. Getting her legs around its girth caused her deerskin dress to hike up enough to send a whole new series of signals inside his breechcloth. He started trotting ahead, leading the way so she wouldn't notice that, at the moment, he was equipped with more than one lance.

The run to the creek helped rein in his raging hormones. By the time she slid down and tied up the horse, then led the way along the little path through the trees and scrub down to the muddy stream, he was presentable. The relative dusk of moon shadows provided cover.

Just short of where sand had piled up along the near bank and formed a perfect beach, she stopped suddenly and turned to face him.

"Maybe we can take a dip." Before he could stammer a wildly enthusiastic answer—hey, what was she gonna wear? She couldn't get in the water in that buckskin dress—she continued. "But first I've gotta pee. Wait here, Michael, and don't look."

Michael fought the temptation to peek. He didn't want to mess up this chance. He would have waited forever, as long as there was a possibility he might go skinny dipping with the delicious Daphne.

He kind of needed to pee, too, but when he managed to extract himself from the unfamiliar confines of his breechcloth, he discovered he was far too excited to do any such thing. Just the thought of Daphne, hiking up her skirt a few feet away, was almost too much for him. He knew he'd better tuck himself safely away before she came back and his state of arousal scared her off.

The creek gurgled invitingly…and there was something else—sand grinding, as if something was coming their way. It wasn't coming from the direction Daphne had taken. He dropped to his hands and knees and peered toward where the road cut off the east end of the pasture that housed their encampment, at the old wooden bridge over the stream. The sound came from there. A silhouette appeared atop the bridge. It was a motorcyclist, idling along with the lights off. Was this someone else who couldn't sleep, or someone following them? The shadowy biker rumbled across the old wooden structure. Michael stood and watched and made sure it disappeared behind the brush on the far side of the creek. The sound of its passing was soon inaudible.

"What was that?" Daphne was straightening her leather dress as she stepped back onto the path. And then she was looking down at him and he realized he had forgotten to stuff himself back inside his breechcloth. And she was saying, "Oh! I know what that is," and reaching down to pull up the hem of her leather skirt again. He forgot all about the motorcycle when he realized she wasn't wearing anything underneath.

Talk about a quickie, Daphne thought. He was already done before she could more than prop herself against the trunk of a cottonwood. Good thing she hadn't gotten her dress all the way off or the bark might have scraped her back.

"That was fast." She couldn't keep the disappointment out of her voice. He was breathing too hard to answer. It didn't matter. She had yet to meet a teenage boy who wasn't multi-orgasmic, and they were usually desperate enough for what she'd just provided to do anything to have it again. She was sure Michael would perform as asked for the promise of more.

Maybe finding a young kid like him wasn't such a bad deal. She could teach him the things *she* enjoyed. It wasn't like, out here playing Cheyenne, she had many other ways to entertain herself. What with young Lancelot here, and the untested promise of the cute guys on the camera crew, this might turn out to be an amusing way to spend her spring after all.

The Cheyenne wouldn't do it like this. Hell, from what the old chief had told them, what they'd just done might have gotten them tossed out of the tribe. If they really were mid-nineteenth century Cheyenne, the rules demanded she kept herself pure for marriage. Her very chaste courtship could have gone on for years. Daphne knew she wouldn't have made a good Cheyenne. Not since she was thirteen.

Michael was leaning against her and breathing hard. From the way he was moving, she thought he might be ready for more even sooner than she had expected. She pushed him back and stepped away from the tree so she could finish pulling off her dress. This time, she would control the action.

Then she heard the noise. "What's that? Is there someone over by the road?"

Michael muttered something about a motorcycle. His mind was elsewhere.

It wasn't a motorcycle. What she heard sounded like footsteps, fast and regular, like someone running. She stepped away from Michael a little and moved to where she could see the bridge. Sure enough, it was a jogger. He was a big guy, moving smoothly, out running with his dog. Neither the man nor the animal seemed to notice them. Not surprising, she thought, since they were well back from the road in deep shadow, and what little breeze there was wouldn't have carried their scent toward the bridge. She watched until the pair disappeared. Michael began giving some none too subtle attention to her backside. She reached around and pulled him in front of her and started whispering very specific instructions in his ear.

Something whistled through the underbrush. An early bird, maybe, though she had to grin to think how badly she had beaten it to its prey. The thought slipped from her mind like quicksilver. Michael was doing his best to follow directions and she was rapidly losing focus on everything else.

To her surprise, Michael dropped to his knees in front of her. She hadn't expected him to get to the advanced stuff nearly this fast. His head came forward, brushed her belly, moved down... And then he crumpled between her legs and the only shaft he pointed at her was the arrow protruding from his back.

Mad Dog showered and shaved after his run. Shaving, of course, meant his head as well as his face. His hair was naturally curly and couldn't be coaxed to produce the braids he would have preferred. If Benteen County's only Cheyenne shaman couldn't wear braids, he wasn't going to settle for anything less than bald. It might not be a traditional Native American look, but it had worked for Yul Brenner and Patrick Stewart. It was dramatic, so it worked for Mad Dog too.

It was unusual for him to skip his post-run exercises, but his left knee was pretty sore from the fall he took when Hailey knocked his legs out from under him. He was still surprised about that. She'd never before even brushed him when they went running, and they'd been doing it almost every morning since she'd come into his life, a wolf-hybrid rescue. It was a puzzle. Maybe she'd been trying to protect him from that motorcycle that came bursting out of the brush up the road a few seconds later. That was another puzzle.

Mad Dog and Hailey shared their normal breakfasts—ground sirloin and kibbles for Hailey, a couple of chocolate chip cookies and an apple for him, washed down with flat Dr. Pepper. He liked it that way, and was constantly doing unplanned kitchen clean-ups when he failed to get the twist top screwed back on tight while he was releasing bubbles from the bottle after a bit of wild shaking. What most folks shook was their heads, when they witnessed Mad Dog's efforts to decarbonate his favorite beverage. Not that they were surprised. They expected weird behavior from the local oddball.

Mad Dog checked the strange message on his answering machine again before he left the house. It was a woman's voice and it sounded hauntingly familiar. She wasn't a wrong number. She'd used his name.

"I'm sorry to call so early, Mad Dog, but I wanted to catch you before you got out of the house. I'm coming to Buffalo Springs this afternoon. I plan to attend the Buffalo Springs Day celebration and...

"I'm saying this all wrong, but this *is* important. I'd like to talk to you. I'll...I'll call you later, or I'll see you at the celebration. That is, if you want to see *me*..."

She'd sighed, then broken the connection without saying goodbye. Or mentioning who she was. He should know. The voice was so familiar—and so beyond his ability to put a name or face to it.

Well, if whoever it was that wanted to see him planned to be at Buffalo Springs Day—the annual celebration of the town's long-lost glory and class/family reunions, all rolled into one—then he was most likely to discover who she was if he drove to Buffalo Springs. Things wouldn't get started until the potluck at noon. Then there'd be the parade: half a dozen convertibles bearing local politicians and pretty girls and the latest Buffalo Springs High Homecoming Queen, a dozen duded up horseback riders, two clowns—one the rodeo version, the other, a woman who couldn't decide whether she was a mime or the circus variety, a juggler, an Uncle Sam on stilts, and the high school marching band. The evening would be topped off by a banquet and dance at the school gym. Big doings for a small community.

Mad Dog thought he might drop by the courthouse as soon as he got to town. Stick his head in the sheriff's office. Mrs. Kraus should be at her post behind the reception desk by the time he got there. There wasn't much that went on in Buffalo Springs that Mrs. Kraus didn't know about.

The sun formed a brilliant orb just above the eastern horizon, glowing with the promise of a perfect day. Mad Dog and Hailey let themselves out the back door and wove through the tulips and irises his mother had planted outside her kitchen. They bloomed in their full glory, thanks to a warm spring accompanied by ample rain. The county's wheat crop looked similarly promising, which meant the price for a bushel would be absurdly low.

For years, Mad Dog had cemented his role as local oddball by being the only person in the county to own a Saab. No more. Even Swedish engineers hadn't been able to build a product capable of surviving the confluence of two hundred thousand miles and Mad Dog's lead foot. The result, a catastrophic example of metal fatigue, brought in repair estimates so far beyond the vehicle's worth that his considerable sentimental attachment waned. He'd replaced it. It was time, he'd thought, to show the community how age was mellowing his peculiar streak and that he could blend into the local vehicular environment of pickups, sedans, hatchbacks, and SUVs.

Mad Dog pulled the garage door open. The garage seemed bigger than it used to. Fortunately, the bright-red Mini Cooper with the British flag emblazoned on its roof was roomier on the inside than its squat, boxy exterior made it appear. Hailey liked the rear seat. The lack of foot room back there didn't trouble her. Mad Dog ushered her in, folded himself behind the wheel, opened the windows so Hailey could satisfy her wind-in-the-face addiction, and let the supercharged engine whisk him out of the driveway and onto the road. He found his way to the blacktop by pulling his John Deere cap low enough to shade his eyes. It failed to screen a pickup with a flat tire which blocked most of the intersection. The driver, standing in the only vacant spot Mad Dog might have used to pass, madly waved him down.

Hailey seemed to realize this would be a temporary stop. She checked out the guy and the truck, then turned around three times and settled herself to wait. Mad Dog stepped out to see what aid he could offer.

"Thanks for stopping." The guy was young and handsome and clean cut by modern standards. His earring and nasal stud made it unlikely he was a Kansan, as did his lack of twang. "We've got a flat. I'm a total nerd at mechanical stuff. Like, I can't even find the spare."

His passenger was doing a better job. She was crouched and peering under the rear bumper. "It's here," she announced. "Is the jack under here too?"

"That'd probably be somewhere in the cab," Mad Dog told them.

"Only Jack I know about is my passenger," the kid said with an embarrassed shrug. "And I'm Chad."

Mad Dog introduced himself and offered to look for the jack. There weren't many able-bodied Kansans who would leave a tourist with a flat stuck by the side of the road. Getting two people in the Mini with him and Hailey wouldn't be easy because most people got nervous about crowding a wolf. Maybe he could change the tire for them without getting too dirty.

He started toward the cab as the girl stood up behind the bumper and began brushing dirt off her jeans. Mad Dog glanced at her and lost his ability to move or speak or even reason a little. The girl was saying something, only he couldn't work out what it was.

"Janie!" he croaked, suddenly knowing whose voice had been on his answering machine. "Janie Jorgenson."

It had been more than forty years since the two of them were voted most perfect couple by their classmates at Buffalo Springs High—football hero and head cheerleader, best athlete and best student. Jesus, how could she still look so good. She had hardly changed at all. Still had that gorgeous blond hair, that elfin face that hinted you were in for fun and trouble. He hadn't seen her since she gave him back his ring—threw it back, actually, on that summer night in 1962. He wanted to open his arms and see if she would come into them.

She just stood there and looked perplexed.

"I'm Jack," she said, "or Jackie. Janie Jorgenson is my grandmother."

The sheriff was slick with sweat. A small, fatuous smile hung on his face, unrecognized and not easily removed.

Judy sighed, deep and satisfied. She bent and kissed his bruised lips, gently this time, rolled off, and went across the room to the window, backlit by the rising sun.

It was hard to believe she was midway between forty and fifty. He knew he saw her through a lover's eyes, but he also knew she really was still spectacular. It didn't matter whether it took hard work and careful diet these days, instead of youth and luck. Judy could turn heads in any crowd.

"Wow!" the sheriff breathed. He almost tacked on a "What brought that on?" but he wasn't sure he wanted this wild and lusty moment to end just yet. He knew his wife well enough to understand asking why was not the thing to do.

Not that they didn't make love anymore. They did, and pretty regularly. Perhaps too regularly, as the years and their schedules increasingly forced their intimacies into whatever time slots were open. But they didn't make love like this, not usually. The sheriff couldn't remember the last time he'd hit the trifecta. Hell, even doubles had become rare. This had been like when they were first married and desire and availability had suddenly been evenly matched. He had wakened from a sound sleep to gentle but insistent caresses. Then once was not enough, nor was twice. They couldn't get enough of each other. He sighed and wondered whether he would have the strength to get through his day…and how he might lure her back for more.

"God I love you, Englishman," she said. Judy was one of the few people who got away with calling him Englishman. He had the misfortune of having a brother whose nickname, as high school football hero, had been Mad Dog. Once you had a Mad Dog, and a last name like English, you naturally became Englishman.

Their school days were long past, and their nicknames might have vanished as well, except that Mad Dog had taken their mother's claim to be a half-breed Cheyenne seriously enough to commit himself to that culture, and to legally adopt the alias. Now, everyone in Benteen County knew Mad Dog and

Englishman, but only a select few called Mad Dog's little brother anything other than Sheriff English to his face.

He realized, suddenly, that Judy was standing in an open window and presenting the neighbors with a viewing opportunity more likely on certain streets in Amsterdam than Buffalo Springs. If anyone saw her, they might complain to the school board. Not many people in Benteen County, Kansas, would think the Vice Principal of Buffalo Springs High should be offering sex education visual aids to anyone passing down Cherry Street this morning. The sheriff thought about telling her, but he was enjoying his view of her delightful bottom too much, and he didn't have the energy to spare. Not while there was a chance she might come back to their bed again.

"I want to go to Paris," Judy said.

The sheriff smiled. "Why would anyone want to go to Texas?" he teased.

She swung around, closing her hands into fists and planting them on the hips with which she might now be mooning their neighbors. The view from this side was even better, he decided, though it was plain she wasn't thinking about jumping his bones anymore.

"I'm not kidding, Englishman."

He knew she wasn't. She'd wanted to go to Paris—the one in France—for as long as he could remember.

"You promised you'd take me."

That was also true. Though he'd convinced himself that the fulfillment of that promise could be put off until their girls were on their own and he and Judy had achieved those golden years that would mark their retirement.

"Well…"

"A well is a hole in the ground," Judy said. "As I'm constantly telling my students who'd like to find one to hide in because they can't give me the answer I want."

"This isn't a good time. I mean, what with our relations with the French over Iraq."

"And terrorist threats, and we can't really afford it, and I'll bet you can come up with at least a hundred other reasons. You always have. I'm starting to think you always will. That's why I went online this morning and made reservations. Sometimes you can get astounding deals at the last minute. I did. We fly out of Wichita this afternoon."

The sheriff sat up in bed. He was relieved to see that the nearest neighbor's windows were tightly closed and the blinds secured. He was less relieved by what he saw in Judy's eyes.

"Say what?"

She stalked across the room to the dresser and picked up a couple of sheets of paper—computer printout. "Here they are, Wichita to Atlanta to Paris. I've got us booked into a little hotel for a couple of nights while we get a feel for the city."

"Judy, I can't just walk away from my job." He was going to tell her that she couldn't either, only he realized it was the end of May. Classes at Buffalo Springs High were over. She'd finished grading all her tests and papers. No one would put up much of a fuss if she didn't show for graduation.

"Why not? You haven't taken a real day off in years. It's not like we're in the middle of a crime wave. Nothing serious has happened in Benteen County in more than two years.

"I mean, really, Englishman. Why not? The girls are in college. They're old enough to take care of themselves and they're headed for summer school. You've finally got competent help. You said this Deputy Parker is the real thing—the first legitimate law enforcement officer you've ever had. Put Parker in charge. Things won't fall apart in two weeks. Please, Englishman. This is important to me."

The sheriff felt like he'd been trapped in a room to which all the exits were sealed. He really didn't want to go to Paris, of all places. Well, actually, he didn't want to go anywhere. He was one of those people for whom the favorite part of travel was coming home. But he had promised, and he did love Judy. There wasn't really anything going on in Benteen County just now. Except the sound of their phone ringing.

Maybe that would be a good excuse. He picked it up and it was.

Mrs. Kraus stepped out of Bertha's Café into the most beautiful morning she could imagine. It was time for her to clock in behind the reception desk over at the sheriff's office in the courthouse, but not before she took a moment to appreciate the glory of this rare and perfect spring day. Weather in Benteen County tended to extremes of heat and cold, punctuated by storms that seemed like the personal wrath of God, but in between…like just now, this morning. She took a breath and knew why she lived here, and would never dream of living anywhere else.

The rising sun turned the streets of Buffalo Springs into swaths of gold. They gleamed, resembling the fabled pavement for which Coronado had once come searching. Or maybe not, since the sun was also highlighting verdant clumps of Bermuda that pushed through cracks in the pavement, and a profusion of wildflowers that most folks would call weeds, blooming in Veterans Memorial Park across the street.

Mrs. Kraus was pleasantly bloated after a Bertha's breakfast special. She would have been drowsy if she hadn't accompanied it with several cups of Bertha's coffee, strong enough, it had been rumored, to dissolve an occasional spoon. The combination of cholesterol and caffeine induced a heightened awareness in her, an almost drugged state of well-being and alertness. She was acutely conscious of meadowlarks flirting in the park and the overwhelmingly bawdy perfume with which spring's flowers tantalized the gentle breeze. A honey bee buzzed her, briefly considered whether her flowered smock was sluttish enough for a stop, then rushed to the welcoming embrace of a clump of sunflowers between the sidewalk and the curb.

Fecund, that's what the morning was. Fecund wasn't a word Mrs. Kraus had found much use for in recent years, especially not since her beloved Floyd had passed on. But *fecund*, she realized, was the only appropriate description for this soft spring morning. Kansas, it seemed, was in the mood to procreate.

She stepped across the street and strolled toward the county courthouse. From a block away, and in this spectacular lighting, it looked like something out of a picture postcard. Up close, she knew, the building and the government it housed were in serious need of repair.

She passed a pair of young Mexican men trying to start the county's mower so they could wade into those weeds across the street from the church. She wondered if they were illegals. Surely not, if they were working for the county—though some of the supervisors were cheap enough to hire off the books and pay below minimum wage. Then she stopped worrying about it because the men were peeling off their shirts and their lean, bronze bodies rippled with youthful muscle. Firm butts did nice things for their blue jeans, too.

Mrs. Kraus mentally slapped herself upside the head. Fecund, she decided, might not be putting it strongly enough. She glanced at her cheap Chinese wristwatch—8:09—and lengthened her stride, heading for the courthouse's front doors. For the first time she could remember, she was going to be late for work.

The doors weren't locked. They were warped too badly for the bolt to match the hole in which it was supposed to seat. Besides, they didn't guard anything of value, other than official records stored in the building. And there was nearly always someone in the sheriff's office to keep an eye on things. Usually, that would be her, working the phones and radios and holding down the reception desk.

Locked or not, she had trouble getting the doors open. Then she noticed why. Someone had jammed a short piece of pipe so that it was stuck against the base of the doors. It was so obvious and out of place that she couldn't imagine why she hadn't noticed before. Odd, she thought, that someone would block the entry. Kids, maybe. She didn't know. She kicked at the thing so she could go relieve Deputy Wynn and start earning her less than satisfactory hourly wage.

The pipe was really jammed in there. She had to kick the thing half a dozen times before it popped loose and began to roll down the steps and onto the walk that sloped to the street and the park beyond. She pulled the door open and started to go inside. The pipe rolled off the edge of the walk and disappeared into the ditch that drained the courthouse lawn. Then part of the ditch disappeared, along with a chunk of sidewalk, some of which rained down around her. What she'd been kicking the hell out of, Mrs. Kraus realized, had been a pipe bomb.

It wasn't hard for the sheriff to locate the murder scene. There were close to a dozen vehicles lined up on either side of the road. A little crowd of people clustered along the bridge and hung out near the edge of a strip of bright yellow crime scene tape. He hadn't expected so many people, but the tape was a bigger surprise. The department hadn't supplied it. Every time the sheriff tried to get things like that included in his budget, the supervisors turned him down.

The sheriff parked his truck behind the county coroner's beige Buick station wagon and let himself out. A couple of rubberneckers came to greet him, asking questions he couldn't have answered yet even if he had wanted to. He told them so, politely, then ducked under the tape and followed the path down through a profusion of sunflowers and other blooming weeds to the sandbar at the edge of the creek.

"Yours?" the sheriff asked as Deputy Parker came to meet him. Parker had a body that was made for a uniform. She was tall, broad shouldered, trim hipped. The sheriff found himself wondering if the woman's legs might not be as perfectly pleated as the crease in her slacks.

"Mine?"

"The tape," the sheriff said, gesturing to the yellow line that ran from the corner of the bridge to a pair of nearby trees before circling off to disappear in the verdant underbrush.

"Yes, sir. Sorry. Hope that's all right. I picked some up when I was over in Wichita."

The sheriff tried to remember the last time one of his deputies had dipped into their meager pay to supplement the department's resources out of their own pockets. Unable to do so, he asked, "What've you got?"

"No more, really, than I told you on the phone." She flipped open a notebook. "Victim is one Michael 'Spotted Elk' Ramsey, age sixteen."

"One of the people in that PBS Cheyenne-village thing they're filming here?"

"Right." She gestured, "The encampment is just a few hundred yards over in the pasture. We've got a positive ID from the victim's parents. Sorry. I'm afraid the crime scene was pretty well trampled by the time I got here. The girl the vic was with naturally went back to the camp for help, then pretty much everybody there tried to give it. They pulled the arrow out. Did CPR, wandered all through the brush down here, even searched along the edge of the road for the shooter. Generally made a mess of things."

"But he *is* dead?"

"Oh yeah. Stone cold. Doctor Jones is having a look at him now. And I had Deputy Wynn herd everybody back to the encampment. Wynn's taking statements, but you'll probably want to talk to them again yourself."

She was right there. Deputy Wynn was an example of just how hard it normally was to fill law enforcement positions in Benteen County. He was a foul-up whose regular misadventures had christened him Wynn Some, Lose Some. Deputy Wynn wouldn't have passed muster for the county's force but for the fact that his father was Chairman of the Board of Supervisors. The kid's tendency to offset regular screw-ups with occasional acts approaching the heroic helped a little too.

"Nobody else was available?" The sheriff was virtually sure nobody was. He did the scheduling, and it was tough to keep even one officer on duty twenty-four/seven.

"No, sir. That's what Wynn tells me, and I haven't been able to reach anybody at the office. It's just turned eight. Mrs. Kraus isn't in yet."

The sheriff rolled his eyes, but not before turning his head so Parker couldn't see. Wynn had been assigned to the office and told not to leave it for anything until Mrs. Kraus came. With Wynn out and Mrs. Kraus not yet on duty, there would be nobody to field calls at the sheriff's office. Armed robbers could be knocking over the Texaco or the Dillons. A latter day Dillinger could be blasting his way into the Farmers & Merchants Bank. Terrorists could be invading the town and taking hostages. There would be no way for the sheriff to know, not unless someone happened to contact Judy and she called his cell phone. Well, there was nothing he could do about that now.

"You got a feel for what happened?"

She shrugged, but she snapped it off as if she'd already prepared her testimony for cross examination. "Kid's naked. Girl was, too, when she got back to the village. Out for a predawn quickie, I suppose. She says some guy with a dog jogged by, then the arrow came from their direction. Be a hell of a shot, and there doesn't seem to be any motive, but she's convinced he's the one who did it."

The sheriff nodded. "She have any idea who the runner was?"

"Well, sir…" She paused for a minute. "When I asked for descriptions, the girl said the dog looked like a wolf. And the guy had a shaved head. I guess you know who that would be?"

The sheriff did. That would be his brother, Mad Dog.

Mrs. Kraus didn't believe in cell phones. She did believe in her Glock 19. She pulled it from her purse before the echo of the blast began to fade. No terrorists appeared, ready to charge the courthouse doors and seize the building, or give her the opportunity to defend it at the cost of their lives. In fact, no one else seemed to have noticed. Even the Mexican laborers were going about their business, apparently unaware that the seat of government for Benteen County had just been attacked. Their lawn mower had roared to life at the same moment as the bomb detonated, and they were concentrating, now, on a thick stand of weeds at the edge of Oak Street.

Mrs. Kraus marched down the walk and examined the crater. It wasn't large, nor was there much of a hole in the edge of the concrete where the walk bridged a drain pipe that allowed water to flow freely in the direction of Calf Creek. Still, the damage was sufficient to engage Mrs. Kraus' imagination. The manner in which the thing might have vaporized her legs, had it gone off moments earlier, was clearly etched in her mind.

She entered the courthouse, Glock preceding her. Either no one was about or they were remarkably hard of hearing.

Wynn was supposed to be manning the radio and the phones in the sheriff's office. She wasn't surprised to find him missing. In her experience, Deputy Wynn more often botched his duties than fulfilled them.

She headed straight for her desk. The sheriff needed to know about this immediately. She stopped well short of her goal when she realized another piece of pipe was standing on the counter. After one heart-stopping moment in which she was sure she'd found a second bomb, she realized this was only a perfectly normal, and hollow, piece of one-inch galvanized pipe. She could tell because someone had stuffed a piece of rolled up paper inside and it protruded for several inches from either end.

Mrs. Kraus double checked the rest of the office for additional bombs, foreign objects, or foreign invaders, before she bent and extracted the paper from the pipe. She kept the Glock firmly in one hand as she did so. She used a clothespin to grab the note. She kept a few in her desk drawer for the stacks of paperwork that were too big for paper clips. She didn't want to contaminate evidence. Benteen County didn't have forensic experts, but they might be able to lift fingerprints.

It was an unremarkable eight-and-one-half-by-eleven sheet of paper, suitable for typing, copying, or computer printout.

She couldn't see any watermarks, just the text that covered the top third of the page.

> government buildings are legitimate targets in a war. our device was timed to minimize collateral damage, but, should deaths occur, we are prepared to accept them, as has your nation. while the united states occupies the sovereign territory of iraq—in the name of democracy but for purposes of imperialism and to possess oil resources—we shall counterstrike at the heartland of our enemy. this is the first. those to follow shall escalate.
>
> prepare to experience your own shock and awe. fear us. we are the holy **J**udgment against **I**nfidels, **H**eresy **A**nd global **D**omination.

Even Mrs. Kraus was quick to note that the only capitalized letters contained in the message spelled *JIHAD*.

◇◇◇

"He's over here," Doc said, waving toward a path above the creek.

Doctor Jones was Benteen County Coroner. He was nearing retirement age, though few would guess it. Most days. More and more, however, the sheriff had observed that the years weighed on Doc when he had to preside over rites of passage involving violent deaths of the young. Not that Benteen County had many of those, and virtually none of a criminal nature. But it had accidents—too much booze and too many horsepower, too little attention paid to sharp and powerful farm machinery, too much certainty that the gun wasn't loaded. Occasionally, too much despair.

"You okay, Englishman?" Doc asked, indicating Doc wasn't the only one the worse for wear this morning. "Things all right at home?" The sheriff was glad his dark complexion disguised the flush he felt wash across his face.

"Just the usual," he grossly exaggerated.

Doc didn't press it. "Your crime scene's been stomped all to hell and gone, but when I heard you were on the way I decided I'd leave him where he died until you got a look."

The sheriff nodded. He and Deputy Parker followed as Doc led the way up from the creek and into the trees and foliage that hugged its banks. The body lay in a muddy clearing beneath a thick cottonwood. It was under a plastic sheet that Doc bent and pulled aside. The soil was rust-colored, softened and tinted by a considerable quantity of blood. The boy was pale from the loss.

This clearing was more apparent than real. A trail of sorts passed through here, but had been widened by the frenzied footprints of those who crowded around and tried to save this boy.

The corpse lay on its back, naked. In death, it seemed too young and innocent to have been enjoying vigorous sex when it died.

"What can you tell me, Doc?"

Doc sighed and tugged on one of his big, protruding ears for a moment. He pulled a notebook out of his pocket, but he didn't bother to refer to it.

"Boy's sixteen, a perfectly normal adolescent male. Evidence of recent sexual activity. Got a wound in his back just below his left shoulder blade. An arrow, I'm told. I'll know more when I get him back to Klausen's Funeral Parlor for an autopsy, but I don't think we're gonna find any surprises. From what they tell me, they pulled the arrow out and didn't get the tip. I expect it's still in there, and it perforated the heart or one of the main arteries. Kid probably died in seconds. If not, they sure worked that point around in him while they were doing CPR. I may have a hell of a time figuring out what got damaged first. Fellow who did the CPR, he's a trained med-tech for the PBS people. Says he couldn't find a pulse when he got here. Still, didn't think he had any choice but to try. Looks to me like all he managed was to pump a lot of blood out of the wound and into the ground."

The sheriff grunted in agreement.

"When you're through, you and Parker can help me load him in a body bag and tote him to my Buick."

"I can't think of anything he can tell me," the sheriff said. "Let's get him ready to go." He turned to Deputy Parker. "Where's the arrow?"

It was in a plastic bag at the base of the cottonwood. It didn't look at all like what the sheriff had expected. "This come from a museum?" he frowned. "Shit! Don't tell me. It's Cheyenne, right?"

Parker nodded. "That's what the one legitimate Cheyenne who's here says. The man took one look and pointed at those four grooves that circle the shaft and the turkey feathers it's fletched with and said it was the kind his tribe used to make."

"One more reason to talk to my brother," the sheriff observed.

"Maybe," Parker said, "but don't forget, this PBS thing is supposed to recreate an 1860s Cheyenne village. All the participants have been issued bows and quivers."

"Like this one?" The sheriff's cell phone went off and he answered and almost missed her response beneath the frantic voice of Mrs. Kraus.

"No," Parker said. "That old man—the real Cheyenne—he told us none of the others are authentic."

Deputy Wynn was questioning suspects. It wasn't going quite the way he'd pictured it. Part of the problem was that everybody was a suspect, and thus, not to be let out of his sight. And part of it was that questioning required a level of individual privacy you couldn't achieve while guarding the whole bunch.

It didn't help that he wasn't sure where some of them had gone. He hadn't even been able to get an accurate count, but he was sure there'd been more witnesses as he herded them back from the crime site at Deputy Parker's suggestion.

He hadn't been enthusiastic about that at first. Then she'd offered to begin the investigation while he stayed behind and kept anyone else from disturbing evidence until Doc Jones and

Englishman got there. Wynn had been quick to see which was the interesting job and jump on it.

Wynn decided right off not to take them back to the fake Indian encampment. Tents didn't appeal to him. They brought back unpleasant memories of his Boy Scout days—frogs and insects in his sleeping bag and, once, most of a can of pressurized whipped cream.

What did he have? Maybe twenty, maybe more. Four families of "Indians," the people attempting to recreate the lifestyle of the Cheyenne, numbered more than a dozen all by themselves. Being around the "Indians" made him feel awkward. First, they were all clothed in funny robes and dresses. Most of the men wore embarrassing breechcloths and leggings and not much else. And the Ramseys, the parents of the naked kid lying in the mud down by the creek, were demanding to know what happened and what was going to be done about it. Craving reassurance that everything would be all right, including the hideous truth. Hell, their kid was dead. Things were definitely not going to be all right. Wynn was relieved when some of the film crew and a couple of women from the other families led them away to console them elsewhere. Well, he would get around to suspecting the immediate family later, when they weren't so obviously upset.

Part of the film crew wasn't at the site. He'd gotten that from the producer, a big man with prematurely graying hair who seemed more concerned about what the death was going to do to his schedule than the grief visited upon the Ramseys. The rest, another dozen or so, went about putting together coffee and food for everyone. They had the disturbing habit of disappearing into the cluster of big recreational vehicles that made up their offices and living quarters. He couldn't keep track of them, but, by setting up his investigation under an awning attached to one of those vehicles, he kept a clear view of the road into the pasture. He contented himself with being sure no one was making a break for it in the variety of cars and trucks associated with the project.

Wynn was pretty confident that Daphne Alights on the Cloud wasn't the killer. Maybe she'd been at the scene, but she was obviously an innocent bystander. Wynn let his glance travel over the remarkable curves hardly disguised by the shorts and halter she'd put on after reporting the death. He was not the sort who would normally try to picture what things looked like while a murder happened, but he couldn't stop thinking about Daphne in the altogether. That, of course, was one of the reasons she couldn't be guilty. Where would she hide the murder weapon?

It was his job, he reminded himself, to recreate the crime scene in his mind. Unfortunately, he had a hard time putting the deceased in the image that resulted.

He was leaning toward the old Cheyenne guy, Mr. Stone, as the best candidate for an appointment with the state's executioner. Bud Stone was part of the village, though participating in a different capacity. The other families were descendants of Native Americans. But none of them had been living in their original culture in their day-to-day lives. They were from the outside world. That was the gimmick for this TV program. Get a bunch of modern Indians who had never lived like Indians, take them out in the middle of the Great Plains, and see how well they mastered a lifestyle that had been gone for nearly a hundred and fifty years. Not too well, from what he'd heard. That reassured him somehow.

Old man Stone and a couple of his kin were staying in the encampment with the rest of the Indians, only they were the real thing. The guy was a living, breathing Cheyenne. Of course, he didn't normally reside in a tent either, but he knew his culture and could tell them how his ancestors had lived. The old man was there to help see that this was done authentically—to guide the rest of the participants and make sure nothing sacred got mocked.

Since the kid was killed by a real Cheyenne arrow and the old man was the only person there who even seemed to know what one looked like, Wynn figured he was also the only one who might have made it. From which, his deductive powers led straight to a conclusion. Elementary, the old bastard was guilty. He even had a motive. The kids were out there fooling around, something real Cheyenne folks would have frowned on, or so Stone had said.

Wynn had a strategy for tricking confessions out of killers. He tried it now. "That why you killed him?" he asked Stone.

The old man was standing at the edge of the awning's shade, staring off across the flat pasture at a distant line of Osage orange trees.

"Didn't," the old man said, not bothering to turn and look Wynn in the eye—one more reason for suspicion, in the deputy's mind.

"Who else could have made that arrow?" Let's see the coot answer that one, he thought.

"Good question," the old man nodded. "You should find out."

The guy was going to be tougher to break than Wynn had expected. "Where were you when the kid was killed?"

"Visiting my grandfather," the old man said. "It was a good visit. I did not like to come back."

Just how many real Cheyenne were here? And if this old guy was with his grandfather, the grandfather must be a truly ancient character.

"And he can confirm that?" Wynn prepared to jot the information in his notebook.

"Yes." The old man turned at last to face the deputy. He had features that belonged on an old nickel, scarred and weathered.

"Where can I find him?"

"Where I left him."

This was getting annoying. "And that would be?"

"Beyond the Milky Way," the Cheyenne said. He wasn't smiling and neither was Wynn. "My grandfather, you see, he was murdered by Custer and his men on the Washita. In 1868. Guess he was more like a great-great-grandfather, as you reckon it."

Wynn's jaw dropped, ready for fly trapping.

"I'll go have some coffee now," the Indian said, "while you confirm my alibi."

"How?"

Old man Stone paused and finally looked Wynn straight in the eyes. He raised his right hand. "How yourself," he said, and turned and walked away.

Judy was packed and ready to leave in less than an hour. She filled a suitcase for Englishman too, though she didn't think he'd be going with her. She took their luggage downstairs to the living room and set everything by the door. She put Englishman's passport on the end table beside his bag. Her own went into her fanny pack along with her billfold and checkbook and flight confirmations. She wasn't letting any of that out of her possession in the hours before her departure.

She had put on jeans and a purple K-State tee shirt. The outfit she would wear on the plane was laid out up on the bed, along with Englishman's single pair of dress slacks, his best shirt, and his only presentable sports coat. Changing wouldn't take long.

Judy let herself out the door and was overwhelmed by a blend of rich aromas thick enough to cut and sweet enough to cause weight gain. The flower beds she'd spent years establishing in their otherwise dull yard were going insane this spring.

She wheeled her bicycle off the porch, down the walk, and out the front gate. She closed it behind her without thinking, even though they had reluctantly said farewell to the dog it was meant to contain months ago. Tears came as she realized what she'd done, along with a fresh tightening in her chest. She mounted the bike and pumped off, angry about letting her emotions surface so easily. She was going to be tough, she'd promised herself. This wasn't a good start.

She was getting used to doing without their station wagon most of the time. Things were tight with two daughters in their first year of college. They'd kept tuition to a minimum by sending the girls to the junior college in Hutchinson, but the combined incomes of a rural sheriff and the local school vice principal weren't enough to run a third car. Englishman used the departmental black and white when he could so she would have access to his truck, but that was mostly when he was the only officer on duty. They had decided the girls needed her Taurus more than she did, not only to get to and from Hutch, but to get around in such a big city. There were at least 40,000 people in Hutchinson. Buffalo Springs High was only a couple of blocks from the English household. Hell, the whole municipality was within a mile of where their house stood near the east edge of town. Bicycling and walking were useful tools for a middle-aged woman working hard to continue looking younger than her driver's license claimed.

She could have taken the station wagon this morning. She'd heard the girls come in late last night. Like most teenagers, they were heavy sleepers—thank goodness. They probably wouldn't be up before she got back. But she would leave the car for them in case they needed it. Frankly, on a morning as beautiful as this, Judy preferred the bike.

There weren't many places to go, other than visiting, in Buffalo Springs. Most of the old downtown was boarded up, or occupied by second-hand merchants disguising themselves as antique stores. Turning west on Main took Judy past three of the city's most prosperous businesses, the Bisonte Bar, Klausen's Funeral Parlor, and Dillons grocery store. The other three economic success stories, Bertha's Café, the Buffalo Burger Drive In, and the Texaco, were all visible and no more than a couple of blocks from her route.

It wasn't until she pulled up in front of the Farmers & Merchants Bank that she realized it was far too early for them to be open. She'd been awake since four. She felt like it should be almost noon. The rest of the county continued to run on central daylight savings time and it was only a few minutes after eight. She had two hours to wait. Even a few carefully chosen, magic words didn't change that.

The bank wasn't as impressive as it used to be. The old location, an ornate two-story sandstone, had been abandoned as too expensive to repair a decade ago. The new one stood in a former parking lot a couple of blocks south of Main. Manufactured was what they called these prefab buildings now. It was just a fancy trailer as far as Judy was concerned. She walked over and gave the front door a swift kick. It vibrated alarmingly, but the hours printed on the glass remained the same.

Patience. She needed a little patience. It wasn't her strong suit.

Millie's beauty parlor was a couple of doors down, and, according to the sign in the front door, was open. Judy hadn't had her hair done in ages. Suddenly, it felt like a good idea. Something to do instead of pedaling home and twiddling her thumbs, or, worse, snacking her way through the interval at the deli in Dillons or with one of Bertha's sinful cinnamon rolls.

"Judy English!" Millie was obviously surprised to see her. Millie was sitting in one of her styling chairs—actually a barber's chair since that had been her establishment's former function. She still had the mirrors on both walls that let you stare right past infinity to the end of the universe, though now they were festooned with plastic vines and garlands of fake flowers. Millie put the chair back in an upright position and stepped down onto the old-fashioned checkerboard tiles. "What can I do for you?" she asked, folding a magazine and putting it on the counter behind her.

"Blond," Judy said, "and short." She pointed at the rack that, in former days, would have held sports and hunting, and maybe even girly magazines. They were all girly magazines now, though in a different way. "Like that," she said, indicating a cover where a minor movie star with platinum hair smiled beneath her pixie cut.

Millie raised her eyebrows and stared at the thick auburn curls that, even pulled back and held by a clip, hung below Judy's shoulders. "You're kidding," Millie said.

Judy's request surprised even herself. She'd thought she could use a professional trim, a little touching up to make the sprinkles of gray disappear, maybe even a manicure—whatever it took until the bank opened. But suddenly she knew that wasn't enough. She wanted to be somebody else. She wanted to be someone who would hop on an international flight at a moment's notice, not a middle-aged, central Kansas mother and educator who hadn't been outside the state in years. This hairdo defined her look as an adult in Buffalo Springs. That's not who she was anymore. Just now, she needed to look anything other than Kansan.

"Very short and very blond," Judy said.

"Lord, honey. Why would you want to cut off all that gorgeous hair?"

"I'm going to France," Judy said, as if that explained it.

That seemed to shock Millie even more. "France? After the way they've turned on us?"

There were American flags hanging on either side of the entry to Millie's beauty parlor. There were lots of flags waving in politically conservative Benteen County these days. But more than a few hung beside anti-war slogans and peace signs. There were many fundamentalist Christians here, delighted that any Middle Eastern war seemed to put them closer to the end times they expected and the rapture that would be their salvation. Lots of just plain conservatives could be counted, too, who thought anyone saying anything opposed to the government in a time of war should be shot as a traitor. But this was central Kansas. There were also plenty of pacifist Christians. And isolationists. Even a few liberals.

"We haven't been trading shots with them, just verbal barbs," Judy said. "Besides, I'm not going there to make a statement. I've wanted to see Paris all my life. It may not be the politically correct time, but, thanks to that, prices are finally where I can afford them. If I don't go now, I never will."

"They do say it's a beautiful city," Millie conceded, offering Judy the chair she'd been occupying as well as a flowered cloak to protect her clothes from clippings. Business probably wasn't good enough to let patriotism stand between her and the price of a haircut and a bleach job.

"Englishman going with you?"

"I hope so," Judy said.

"You'd go on your own without him?" Millie paused in her selection of shears and chemicals.

"Yeah," Judy declared, unable to hide her anger. "And if he doesn't come, I may not be back."

"You're right, of course," the sheriff told Deputy Parker as Doc's Buick, in its role as county mortuary transport (or meat wagon), disappeared in its own dust on the way to Buffalo Springs.

"I'm not the one who should question Mad Dog. If he's been out running around these back roads, taking pot shots into the bushes with a homemade bow and arrow, he's got to be held responsible, even if he had no idea anyone was down by the stream. I can handle that, but folks will think I've been too soft on him. Since I know my brother would never hurt anyone on purpose, I probably would be."

"But you want me to start with this pipe bomb Mrs. Kraus found at the courthouse?"

"Yeah. I need a quick heads up to tell me how serious that is. I mean, are we dealing with some kids' prank, or might there be a legitimate terrorist in Benteen County?"

The sheriff ran a hand over his chin and realized he'd neglected to shave this morning. He wouldn't worry about it. He and Mad Dog were part Cheyenne. Mad Dog took that part a lot more seriously, but it was the sheriff who had inherited the high cheekbones, the dark complexion, and the relative lack of facial hair. It was likely to be evening before anyone noticed his second day shadow…and by evening, he was supposed to be on a plane to Paris.

He ushered Parker to the county's black and white, a high-performance Chevy that was old enough to vote. The last of the curious onlookers had packed up and driven off after the body left. All that remained were the black and white, the sheriff's pickup, and Deputy Wynn's Lexus. Daddy had paid for the Lexus.

"Wynn's probably confused enough witnesses by now. I'll send him along to the courthouse. You can put him on temporary guard duty, if you think there's any need, or send him home to rest before his next shift. I'll take a whack at this film crew and our celebrities. See if I get a hint of behind-the-scenes problems that might have something to do with the shooting."

Parker slid behind the wheel.

"Update me as you go, Deputy. If Buffalo Springs is safe and Mad Dog's not clearly guilty, I need you back out here as soon as possible."

Parker dipped her chin in a crisp affirmative. "We could use outside help if there's anything to this bomb."

The sheriff agreed. "If we can get any." He knew his own budgetary problems were echoed in law enforcement agencies throughout the state. Parker nodded again, more doubtful this time. She wasn't used to the reality of rural Kansas policing yet.

Parker created her own dust cloud and the sheriff headed back toward the creek. Deputy Wynn was climbing up the path beside the bridge to meet him, followed by a spectacularly built young woman wearing tight shorts and a tighter halter. Pretty face too, the sheriff thought, but vacuous.

"I know who done it," Wynn proclaimed, breathing hard, from excitement or from the effort of walking back to the bridge.

"Mad Dog?" The sheriff's question took the wind out of Wynn's sails.

"How'd you know?"

The sheriff shrugged. How hard was it? Bald jogger out running with a wolf-like dog. They were less than two miles from Mad Dog's place and he ran with Hailey almost every morning. Add to that Mad Dog's commitment to all things Cheyenne and you had narrowed the list of suspects.

"Well, big thing is we got a witness who can identify him. Sorry, Sheriff, I know he's your brother, but Daphne here says she saw him clear as day. Can pick him out of a lineup, no problem."

The sheriff thought that was probably true, unless they came up with a group of similarly large men who also shaved their heads. It didn't matter, though. He was already convinced the jogger was Mad Dog.

"That true, Miss?"

The girl seemed to expect to be the focus of masculine attention. The sheriff watched her blossom as she got it.

"That's right. I saw super clear. The moonlight was like real bright."

"Describe him for me, please." The sheriff pulled out his notebook.

"Big guy," she said. "Several inches more than six feet, I'd say. Bulked up. Big dog, long legs, like a wolf."

"Hair?"

"That was what made the guy unforgettable," she said. "He didn't have any. I mean, he wasn't just some baldy. There was no hair on his head at all."

Mad Dog, sure enough. "How was he dressed?"

"Just running shorts and a sweatband," she said. "No shirt, that's how I could tell he was so buff."

"He carrying the bow and arrows, or were they strapped across his back?"

"Oh wow!" she said, looking suddenly puzzled. "You're right. He wasn't carrying anything."

Wynn looked disappointed.

"Then somebody else shot Michael."

"I'm still thinking about it." The Chairman of the Benteen County Board of Supervisors frowned at the flier Jud Haines had thrust between him and the platter of scrambled eggs, hash browns, and sausage Bertha had just delivered to his table by the window overlooking Veterans Memorial Park. Chairman Wynn would prefer to concentrate on breakfast, but Jud Haines was a supervisor, an up-and-comer in a big hurry—maybe in a big hurry to take over as chairman.

"I tell you, Mr. Chairman," Haines enthused, "opportunity knocks, we gotta answer. This is the biggest thing to hit Benteen County since wheat."

The chairman folded the flier and slipped it into the inside pocket of his sports coat. "Why don't we talk about this at the office," he suggested, pointedly reaching for the ketchup. He liked it on practically everything.

"I'll be there," Haines said. "But you think about this. We're talking jobs for everybody who wants them. Lord knows, Benteen County hasn't got many of those just now. Especially good paying jobs."

The chairman looked wistfully at his breakfast. "Yeah," he agreed, "good jobs, for a while. Then most of them will go away."

"But not all." Jud Haines was a natural politician. He was good-looking, well-groomed, and well-dressed, at least by Buffalo Springs standards. With his artfully rumpled shock of blond hair and his winning smile, he had the look of the all-American boy every mother wanted her son to grow into, or the All-American man every girl in search of a mate hoped to hook. Chairman Wynn recognized the type. Jud Haines was himself, a couple of decades and a lot of energy back. But Haines was also a contradiction. He was a college graduate who had moved *to* Benteen County, not from it. Haines had had his fingers in every scheme for a quick buck that had wandered through the county since he arrived. And, surprisingly, he'd made just enough of them pay off to fund a successful run for the board of supervisors. Now, he'd hooked his star to this latest scheme, though so had lots of others, the chairman among them. Maybe Haines was right. Maybe there were fortunes to be made in wind power.

"Even a few good jobs that stay here would be a big improvement. But after construction, when most of the jobs go away, plenty of benefits remain. For those smart enough to invest in this, it's gonna be a money tree. I mean, big, big returns on every dollar."

The chairman noticed a lot of people in Bertha's were eaves-dropping. Some of them had already bought in. Most of the rest were probably thinking about it—if they had anything to invest. The average household income in Benteen County was just under $20,000 a year, rising that high only because the top ten percent were so far above everyone else—America in microcosm, with less of a middle class.

"The way we're writing this up," Haines continued, "a per-centage of our profits will flow into the community for improve-ments in perpetuity. We're talking street lights, sidewalks, street maintenance, replacing washed-out bridges. Hell, even a new courthouse. And this thing's sure to draw tourists, but we got to get those last few sections of land tied up. Got to put pressure on Ed Jacques and Mad Dog and the Eismingers. Show them the light. Help them get rich while they help the rest of us do the same."

Bertha elbowed past, carrying a couple of platters of bacon and pancakes, refilling coffee cups in her wake. The chairman knew his breakfast was rapidly cooling.

"All right, give me fifteen minutes and we'll talk. See about getting this on our agenda."

"Thank you, Mr. Chairman." Haines prevented Wynn from picking up his fork by reaching out and grabbing his hand and pumping it like he expected to draw water. "God bless you, sir. You won't be sorry. It's for the community." Haines' voice was rising as he finally let go and headed for the door. "Everyone in Benteen County is gonna sing your praises, sir, cause everybody in this community is gonna profit from the Benteen County Energy Cooperative Wind Farm."

He got to the door. Opened it, turned back for the exit line the chairman had been sure he would deliver. Haines grinned and smiled at Bertha's customers. "Got wind?" he called to them. Then he was gone.

Chairman Wynn studied the congealing grease on his plate. He picked up his fork and tasted it. Not bad. And given the copious use of onions and garlic in Bertha's breakfasts, wind was something her customers could count on before the day was over.

Mrs. Kraus was on the lookout for small dark men with thick eyebrows, five o'clock shadows, and box cutters—or maybe pipe bombs. What she got instead was Mad Dog.

Good Lord, what was he doing with war paint streaked across his face? Could the county's born-again Cheyenne actually have shot that boy?

"Morning, Mrs. Kraus," Mad Dog greeted her. He was flushed with excitement, and as he got closer she could see it wasn't war paint after all, it was grease. The war paint Mad Dog used was flavored body paint that came from a sex shop in Wichita—she knew because she'd picked some up there herself a time or two. Yeah, grease, and a little dust maybe.

"What, that new car of yours break down on you already? You look like you've been exploring your engine from the inside."

He brushed at the cheek that was still clean. The grease on his hand left a new streak that almost matched the other side.

"Sorry," he said. "I helped some folks fix a flat tire on my way to town. I was in a hurry to see you, so I haven't stopped by a mirror yet."

"What do you want to see me about?" Considering what the morning had brought, and Mad Dog's possible involvement in some of it, she wasn't sure she wanted to be the person on his agenda. She glanced down to check the open drawer of her desk and make sure her Glock was right where she'd put it.

"Well," he said. "I got this phone message. Somebody coming to town and wanting to talk to me, and I didn't know who it was until I stopped to help fix that tire. Did you know Janie Jorgenson has a granddaughter and she's in Benteen County?"

Mrs. Kraus breathed a little easier. Janie Jorgenson. That explained the state Mad Dog was in. He and Janie had been quite the item back when they were in high school. Most people thought Mad Dog had never gotten over her. After all, he hadn't married. Never even dated seriously since, not that there were many women in the county willing to share a house with a wolf, or go on vision quests and perform other heathen rites.

"Yeah," Mrs. Kraus admitted. "Seems like I heard that."

"It was Janie who called. Said she wanted to see me. That it was important. And then it turns out her granddaughter is working on this PBS project they're filming just down the road from me. You know what this is about?"

Mrs. Kraus made herself look wise. "I might," she said. "But Janie could be here any minute. You should go over to the restroom and clean up a bit. Then come back to the office and I'll tell you what I can."

"Coming here? She's coming here?" Mad Dog looked flustered again.

"Yes, and she wants to talk to you something awful," Mrs. Kraus said. It was a different she—Deputy Parker, not Janie Jorgenson—that Mrs. Kraus knew was heading his way. Still… Mrs. Kraus had heard Janie was expected in town today, and that she had been asking whether Mad Dog was still around. Maybe Janie was divorced or widowed or wondering if she might find a spark with her first true love all these years later. Maybe she just wanted to spit in his face one more time. But Deputy Parker was coming to investigate a pipe bomb and a killing. Mrs. Kraus thought it would be helpful if Mad Dog stuck around and made himself available for questioning.

"Maybe she'll let me apologize," Mad Dog said. "Maybe I can try to explain." He was backing across the sheriff's office toward the door, wiping at his face with his hands again and smearing the grease around even worse.

"Only how do you apologize for murder?"

And then Mad Dog was gone down the hall and Mrs. Kraus had the Glock out because his last words had just registered.

❖❖❖

The sheriff parked his Chevy behind a Dodge pickup that was being unloaded by a crowd of young workers.

"They part of the PBS crew?" he asked Daphne as they got out of his truck.

"Yeah. Most of them are college students doing this for course credit. You need me for anything else?"

"Not now, but I may have more questions after I talk to the others. Where will you be?"

The college kids pulled a tarp off the load in the Dodge's bed. The sheriff was surprised to see a stuffed buffalo in there. Daphne was more interested in one of the workers, a blond guy who had peeled off his shirt and revealed washboard abs.

"I'm gonna see if I can use somebody's computer," she said. "Check my email, maybe watch some music videos. I mean, it's been like a week."

The sheriff didn't ask for further clarification. He was sure any of the young men who crowded this camp would be able to tell him where Daphne was if he needed her again.

The sheriff turned back to the Dodge. "A stuffed buffalo, huh?"

The man he addressed was older, but not old, hair dark but graying dramatically and prematurely. The sheriff guessed he wasn't a student.

"Wow! You must be another example of local law enforcement, with powers of deduction like that."

The sheriff was wearing jeans and boots and a cotton shirt, as well as his Stetson. His badge was pinned over his heart. Wise guy, he thought. He was still upset about what had happened with Judy this morning. He briefly considered inviting the man to visit the Benteen County jail until his attorney, wherever he might be, maneuvered through local legal channels and forced him to be charged or released. Too bad he didn't work that way. Besides, the guy had obviously had to deal with Wynn Some.

The sheriff decided to give him a second chance. "It doesn't take deductive powers so much as getting enough votes every four years. I'm Sheriff English. Who are you and what's the buffalo for?"

"Sorry, I'm having a bad day." The man had the good sense to seem faintly embarrassed. "I'm Bradley Davis, Brad, director of this mini-series turned major disaster. I've filmed all over the globe—including in the middle of civil wars—and never lost a cast or crew member until now. Then one of your deputies spent the morning asking everyone here, including me, why we killed the kid."

"Good help is hard to find on our budget. What's with the buffalo?"

"Uhh, target practice, actually."

"Bows and arrows?"

"Yeah." The man brushed some dirt from his cargo pants and adjusted his polo shirt. "That's probably not a good thing to admit right now, is it? But look, you know what we're trying to do out here, right?"

"Pretend I don't."

"You get PBS?"

"With a satellite dish," the sheriff said. "Or cable, if you can afford to pay them to run you a hook-up. Most people have one or the other. Not much else to do here after dark, unless you're young and in love."

"Have you seen our program *Manor House*? It ran just a few weeks ago. Or *Prairie House* last year?"

The sheriff nodded. "I saw *Prairie House*, and some of that last *Upstairs, Downstairs* thing."

Davis bobbed his head. "Then you know the concept. This is just like those programs. We take modern people, give them some basic training, then set them down in a historical lifestyle to see how they manage. It's high-brow reality TV. *Survivor* for people who wouldn't be caught dead watching *Survivor*.

"We're stretching things further with this one. Taking people back to the 1860s, sticking them into the daily routine of the people who shared these prairies with our ancestors."

"Cheyenne Indians, in this case."

"Exactly! And we thought it would be fun to find actual Native Americans, people who trace their ancestry to the way of life we're trying to recreate. Only finding westernized Native Americans willing to try the old ways didn't turn out to be easy."

Considering his brother's obsession with that very thing, the sheriff would have guessed otherwise.

"You were planning to have them shoot a stuffed buffalo full of holes?"

"It's a moth-eaten old exhibit from a small-town museum that went out of business. Turned out to be cheaper than the wheeled one our prop department would have built. And it's not like our would-be Cheyenne are showing much aptitude for archery."

"Somebody has. Maybe your subjects would do better if you supplied them with authentic hand-made bows and arrows like the real Cheyenne carried."

"I planned to. I sent some staff down to Oklahoma to pick up half a dozen bows and sixty arrows."

"Don't tell me," the sheriff said. "You mean the real things, legitimate Cheyenne stuff like the one that ended up killing that boy? I heard you didn't have anything like that."

"We didn't until yesterday. And no one knew. I was going to make it a surprise. I locked it all up in storage last night."

"But it's not all there now, is it?"

"Well…" Davis wasn't happy admitting it. "I checked after we came back to camp this morning. Most of it's still there."

"Except one bow and arrow?"

"Right," the director said. "Just one bow. But ten arrows are missing. Nine now."

Mad Dog knew where the janitor kept his cleaning supplies. By the time he came out of the courthouse restroom he was relatively free of dirt and grime. The knees of his jeans would probably never be presentable again, and his shirt sleeve bore a fresh swoosh a Nike representative might have claimed as trademark infringement. Otherwise, he sparkled from toe to shaven crown. His grin slipped when he realized the woman waiting for him in the hallway was not Janie Jorgenson.

"How far you run this morning, Mad Dog?" Deputy Parker looked up from the burst piece of water pipe she was examining and examined him instead.

"Six miles," he said, always pleased to be able to discuss running with a fellow enthusiast. "Woke up and couldn't get back to sleep and decided to run over by that mock Cheyenne village in Lancaster's pasture. How about you, Deputy?"

"Haven't run yet," she said. "Maybe after my shift. You see anything interesting over at *This Old Tepee?*"

"Sun wasn't up yet. Nobody about. But that ring of lodges looked pretty impressive in the moonlight. Sent a chill up the back of my neck. You know, they've got a real Cheyenne shaman over there. They promised they'd introduce me to him after they wrap things up if I let them do some filming in my buffalo herd."

"A buffalo hunt?"

"Hey, no way. I'm raising breeding stock, not hamburger."

"I heard they were going to stage a buffalo hunt, bows and arrows, the whole works." She stopped turning the pipe over in her hands and he noticed, for the first time, that she was wearing a pair of surgical gloves, as if she didn't want to contaminate a piece of evidence. "What's…"

She didn't let him finish the question. "Ever do any bow and arrow hunting, Mad Dog?"

"No. I don't hunt," then Mad Dog choked back a half laugh. "Well, not since I was a kid. Bunch of us decided to get a buck during archery season when I was in high school. One of the guys scooted into the back seat where we'd tossed our equipment and impaled himself on an arrow. By the time we got him to the hospital over in Hutchinson, and the doctors and nurses stopped laughing at his predicament and were able to do something about it, there wasn't enough daylight left. After that, none of us could bend a bow without busting a gut."

"How about Cheyenne bows and arrows? Haven't you ever been curious what shooting one of those would be like?"

"Sure," Mad Dog said. "You know where I can find one?" He'd love to savor the feel of a real Cheyenne bow, test its pull, see whether he was a natural archer the way he sometimes thought he was a natural shaman. Except that he didn't think Parker could find him one. Besides, he was curious why she kept fooling with that piece of pipe and treating it like it could be some sort of critical evidence.

"Actually," she said, "I do."

It felt more like stepping inside a luxury suite at a resort hotel instead of into a glorified Greyhound. There was a door to the driver's compartment, closed at the moment. It appeared to be made of carved mahogany and was flanked by papered walls on which hung a pair of original oils. Modern in style, they resisted the sheriff's efforts to determine whether they were erotic nudes, as he first thought, or, on second glance, whether they were even human.

Brad Davis led the way between a plush sofa and a pair of easy chairs across carpet thick and green enough to mow. He was followed by the sheriff and a young man who, but for costume, was so athletic and sun bronzed he might have stepped right off the set of *Baywatch*. Davis had introduced him as his associate producer, Sean, and the man who'd provided such heroic efforts in trying to get Michael Ramsey's heart restarted that morning.

"I hope you don't think PBS is paying for accommodations like this," Davis said as they exited the living room and entered the kitchenette. There were two ovens, in case you needed a multi-course dinner. "But it is a benefit of working for PBS. We have some wealthy and generous benefactors. The use of this RV was donated to us for the duration of our filming here. And as director, well, I got first choice."

Just past the kitchenette was a hall that ran along the starboard side of the vehicle, off which a number of equally ornate doors led to what might include a master bath, or even a formal dining room. Davis stopped at the second one and pulled out a set of keys.

"Closet," he said, before selecting the key he wanted. He turned to his associate. "Sean, you took them from the guy who picked up the bows and arrows and brought them in last night, right?"

"Must have been about nine," the man said. "I brought them here and we locked them in this closet."

Davis opened the door. It was a walk-in closet with cedar walls that perfumed the air, further evidence that the director of *This Old Tepee* was living in very different circumstances than the subjects of his program. The garments within, though, including plenty of furs, appeared to belong in the encampment instead of the RV.

"Space is at a real premium," Sean explained. "So Mr. Davis let us appropriate this as a spare wardrobe. Since we aren't going to have our subjects actually go out and kill anything to make their own clothing, we've got at least one back-up costume for everyone. One of the ladies has already discovered you can't launder a leather dress the way you would fabric."

A stack of bows lay on a shelf across from the furs and leathers. Several bundles of arrows were layered on the shelf just above. Below stood an assortment of moccasins. Shoe shelves, the sheriff guessed, with nearly enough space to have satisfied Imelda Marcos.

"This is where we left them," Sean said.

"Yeah," Davis agreed. "They don't look disturbed. I might never have noticed any were missing unless we needed all six bows."

The sheriff counted. There were only five. "Then one of the arrows ended up in Michael Ramsey's back and you came to check?"

"Right," Davis said. "Just got to it a few minutes before you drove in. I was trying to decide what I should do about it. Frankly, your deputy didn't seem like the guy I'd admit something like that to, not unless I'd already contacted my attorney."

The sheriff had to concede that Davis' judgment was sound. Wynn Some, Lose Some had known Mad Dog all his life, yet he'd been ready to lock up the sheriff's brother a few minutes ago without a second thought.

"The closet was still locked when you checked?"

"Uhh, actually, no."

"You sure you locked it?"

Davis shrugged. "I was, now I'm not. But I locked it before I left again. Didn't want any more of these to go missing."

The sheriff sighed. "Kind of like locking the barn door after your horse has been stolen," he observed—a favorite Benteen County expression, even if it had been decades since a horse had gone missing here.

"No, he locked it," Sean said. "I remember. Because of the Sharps…"

Davis' assistant's voice trailed off and he pointed at a spot by the door next to where a buffalo hide robe hung inside a plastic drycleaner's bag.

"What?" the sheriff was puzzled. There didn't seem to be anything there.

"It's gone!" Davis' voice was outraged.

"What's gone?" The sheriff felt half a step behind the world. Maybe three times had been too much of a good thing.

"A Sharps fifty-caliber buffalo gun," Davis said. "And a box of ammunition. It was right there by the door. Fuck your horse and barn door. That gun's an antique and worth a fortune. Sucker'll bowl over an ox at close to a mile."

It wouldn't do a human being much good either, the sheriff thought. Especially if it was now in the hands of the person who had the bow and arrows.

"Mad Dog's not guilty," Wynn Some said as he came clomping down the hall from the back door that led to the parking lot behind the courthouse. Most people who had business here parked there, though the streets, except where they were crowded with Bertha's customers, offered plenty of options.

"What?" Parker and Mad Dog chorused.

"You sure?" Parker demanded.

Mad Dog, more seriously confused, asked, "Not guilty of what?" His question was ignored, since, not guilty, he was no longer of much interest to either deputy.

"Got us a witness," Wynn Some told Parker. "Daphne, the girl who was at the scene when the crime was perpetrated. She says Mad Dog was there, too, but not armed. He was only wearing running shorts and obviously not packing a bow and arrow."

"Did somebody get shot with an arrow?" Mad Dog wanted in.

"You're absolutely sure of this?" Parker asked Wynn.

"Course. Englishman sent me back to help you investigate the pipe bomb, or do it myself so you can head back out to the Indian camp and help him. Call him if you don't believe me."

Mad Dog could see from Parker's eyes that she intended to do just that. Double checking anything Wynn said was a good idea…then the rest of what Wynn had said registered. "Pipe bomb?"

"We should still question him," Wynn continued, as if Mad Dog weren't standing right there. "If Daphne saw him only moments before the shooting, he may know something." He turned on Mad Dog like a terrier suddenly discovering the stranger in his house didn't intend to feed him. "How about it, Mad Dog? What did you see?"

Mad Dog was still stuck on what he'd suddenly realized Deputy Parker had been examining. "Is that a pipe bomb?"

"It's been a busy morning," Parker confessed. "What about it, Mad Dog? Did you notice anything unusual when you ran by the PBS site this morning?"

"Was there a bombing out there or something? What should I have noticed?"

Parker told him about Michael Spotted Elk. Wynn tried to help, but mostly he just described Daphne. Mad Dog gathered she must be quite a dish.

He chewed his lower lip and thought about it.

"Well, there were a couple of things. I was pretty sure there was somebody ahead of me on the road as I ran by Lancaster's pasture. He was far enough away I never actually spotted him in the moonlight and he didn't have any lights on. By the time I got to the bridge over Catfish Creek, I thought he was gone. Or she. And I didn't see or hear those kids.

"The other peculiar thing was that Hailey knocked me down just after we passed the bridge. That's the only time she's ever done that on one of our runs. Then a motorcycle blasted out of the brush just ahead of us."

"Damn," Wynn exclaimed. "I'll bet the biker was the killer and Hailey saved you from getting hit by that arrow. That wolf is smart enough to be human."

Smarter, in Mad Dog's opinion. Certainly smarter than Wynn, who had just leaped to yet another in a string of ill-considered conclusions. Of course, leap often enough and sooner or later you might get one right. Mad Dog had thought he heard something whoosh by, but the pain of the road burn had erased that memory until now.

"You saying I might have been the target?" Wynn and Parker turned and looked at him with fresh appraisal in their eyes, making it clear neither had considered the point until he'd been foolish enough to suggest it.

"It *was* a Cheyenne arrow," Parker said. "Aside from those pretend Indians in that pasture, how many Cheyenne live in this county?"

She had a point. Mad Dog knew there were people he annoyed, what with his vociferous opinions on local and national issues. International too, since he'd been ranting against America's new foreign policy adventure, the conquest of Iraq. But no one was angry enough to want to attack him. At least he didn't think so. Still, it made him wonder—and it reminded him Hailey was out back in the Mini. If somebody wanted to hurt him, they might be willing to do it through her.

"Be right back." He startled the deputies by sprinting down the hall to the back door.

The Cooper sat there with its windows open, empty. "Hailey," he shouted. A mockingbird made indecent suggestions from a nearby elm. A gentle breeze rippled through its leaves and ruffled flowerbeds in the back yards behind the courthouse. Hailey didn't respond. Mad Dog stepped back into the hall as the pair of deputies arrived behind him, Wynn with his pistol drawn, apparently worried that Mad Dog was attempting to escape.

"I was just looking for Hailey," Mad Dog explained. Something thumped against the door as he closed it. "Maybe that's her now." He opened the door again but the lot behind the courthouse remained empty of wolves or people. There was another thump, however, as he again pulled it closed.

Deputy Parker pushed by him. "Let me look," she told him, hand on her own sidearm. When she got like that, Mad Dog knew there was no point in arguing.

She inched the door open and peered around its edge. Mad Dog watched her check out the parking lot, then scan the environment beyond. When she was satisfied, she slipped her head out and took a look at the outside face of the door. She pulled her head back and looked at him with wide eyes and a puzzled expression. Mad Dog brushed past, and checked out the back of the door for himself, before she grabbed his belt and yanked him back in.

There were two arrows embedded in the door's hardwood surface. Cheyenne arrows. Apparently, Mad Dog decided, he was the target.

What Judy had in mind was sort of a Meg Ryan look. Like she'd seen in that movie on the dish the other night, the one where Meg went off to Paris chasing her old flame and fell in love for real. Judy wanted to take her old flame to Paris and fall in love with him all over again. And look young and cute and perky in the process.

Instead, she looked like an extreme version of the girl who did bit parts on *Xena* and *Buffy the Vampire Slayer*, and played the title role in *Cleopatra 2525*. The look might be okay for one of her daughters, if either had dared it, but Judy didn't think your average forty-five-year-old could carry it off. She was stuck with it, though, so she would try. But she didn't leave Millie much of a tip for making her look more campy than cute, even if the cut was pretty much what she'd asked for.

But for a pickup truck coming from the direction of the grain elevator, the street outside Millie's was deserted. No surprise there. The streets were nearly always deserted in Buffalo Springs.

There were a couple of cars in the lot behind the Farmers & Merchants. People were at work over there now. She glanced at her watch and found she still had five minutes until they were due to open. But people didn't stand on ceremony much in Buffalo Springs. She jaywalked across the street and went up and peered through the glass door. A teller glanced at her, then pointedly looked away. The pickup went by behind Judy and someone wolf whistled. She turned to see who was making fun of her. The only person nearby was a farmer in the pickup. She knew him slightly, too slightly for such teasing familiarity. He had slowed way down and was leaning out the window.

"Want to go for a ride, honey?" He was fifty-something, and so was his wife. He had three grandchildren that Judy knew of, maybe more by now.

"Sure, Fred," Judy called. "Let's you and me go get Pauline and do just that." Pauline was his wife of more than thirty years. Fred's jaw dropped and he pulled his head back inside the truck and accelerated hard toward Main.

That was weird, Judy thought. She went up and tapped on the front door of the bank and the teller looked at her and glared. Judy pointed at her watch and shrugged her shoulders. The teller waved at the clock on the wall behind her. It was still three minutes short of ten. There would be no favors done for Judy English this morning.

Judy leaned against the wall and tapped her fingers impatiently against its surface. There was a night deposit box just next to her. The flap over its slot wasn't fully closed. Curious, she thought. She reached over and lifted it and found that someone had tried to stuff a thick envelope in the opening. It hadn't fit, maybe because it was wrapped in duct tape that outlined several odd shapes inside. She reached over and picked it up and wondered what it contained—rolls of coins maybe?

Mrs. Kraus, over at the courthouse and freshly aware of the danger of finding strange things in unusual places, could have made a better guess.

Judy and the sheriff had two eighteen-year-old daughters, one by the normal method, the other by adoption. Both were named Heather. They might not be confused by their shared name, but others were, occasionally even their parents, who could easily distinguish one from the other. Most folks couldn't do that. Though their blood tie was distant, their height, coloring, and features were enough alike to make strangers think they were twins.

Two Heathers in one house should have been enough to prompt a name change. But giving up a name neither had especially liked, until the prospect of doing without it arose, proved an unsatisfactory option. So, Heather Lane had kept her last name. It worked as far as formal listings, like school, were concerned, to distinguish her from Heather English. But it didn't work for people dealing with both of them at the same time. That's where their nicknames, One of Two and Two of Two, came in.

Heather English was a major Trekkie. For as long as she could remember, she had followed the adventures of the *Star Trek* crews who boldly went where no one had gone before. When the character Seven of Nine appeared on *Star Trek Voyager* about the same time a second Heather came into her life, the answer to their name problem became immediately clear. It didn't hurt that Seven of Nine was sexy and dangerous, qualities both Heathers secretly craved. Heather English became One of Two, or One, for short. She got to be One because she was the first Heather in the English household and the person who came up with the solution. Two hadn't objected. She was glad to have a place to live and people who wanted her to live with them.

"Anybody else up?" One asked, still rubbing the sleep out of her eyes. Like most teens, they were heavy sleepers when they had the chance. This morning, on their last weekend at home between spring semester and summer school, it had saved them from discovering that sex, especially three times before breakfast, wasn't something exclusively reserved for their generation.

Her sister, Two, was picking out her wardrobe for the day—a western shirt, silver and turquoise jewelry, and a pair of tight jeans to tuck in her boots. There was a guy who would be home from KU this weekend whom Heather knew Two would enjoy pleasing with her selections—or teasing, depending on her mood.

"You kidding?" Two asked, glancing at the clock. "When was the last time Judy slept until ten?" She called their parents Judy and Englishman. One was still in the habit of using Mom and Dad. "And Englishman was going in early for Buffalo Springs Day. I'm sure he's been at work for hours."

"I don't think Mom's home," One observed. She was gathering her own outfit. Having grown up a country girl, she was less comfortable looking the part. She went with shorts and sneakers and one of those bare midriff blouses that were so popular with the guys. She wasn't dressing for anyone special, but lots of boys she'd dated, or wanted to date, would be home for the celebration.

"Mom would have roused us at least an hour ago." She padded across the carpet to the hall door, opened it, and did what teenagers usually do when they want something. "Mom?" she shouted. The house remained quiet.

She went down the hall. Two followed right behind her, both girls carrying their clothes instead of wearing them. They slept in super-sized tee shirts, One's bearing a Blue Dragon logo, Two's advertising a seed company. "Anybody home?" One called.

Nobody was.

"I wonder if Mom left us breakfast." Judy had done so regularly while they were in high school and had continued the habit when they came home from college for weekends and holidays. As far as Judy was concerned, they were still kids—too young for most of the things they wanted to do. Heather and her sister had become passionate advocates of their independence, except when it came to preparing meals.

One started down the stairs toward the living room. Two left her clothing in a pile beside the banister across from the bathroom and followed. Squirming into tight jeans was best dealt with after breakfast.

"What this?" One had just spotted the suitcases by the door.

"Looks like someone's going on a trip," Two said. "You suppose it's us?"

She joined her sister and examined the unfamiliar luggage. Their parents hadn't been anywhere requiring suitcases in years. "Jeez," Two said. "I know they fight and Judy threatens to kick him out from time to time, but I never thought she'd kick him out far enough to need this."

"Ohmygod!" One said, looking at the passport. "I didn't even know Dad had one of these. He hasn't been out of the country since he was in Vietnam."

"I'll bet Judy's been making him renew it," Two said. "You know how much she wants to travel."

"But why would he be going now?"

Two shook her head. "And more important, why wouldn't someone have told us?"

Why stick a deposit inside a big duct-taped envelope? Then, when it didn't fit into the slot to the deposit box, leave it there so anyone who came along could swipe it? Judy didn't get much time to puzzle over these questions. The lock on the front door to the bank clicked behind her.

It was a glorious day outside, middle seventies, light breeze, popcorn clouds drifting across a sky almost as blue as Englishman's eyes. Inside, it was cold and dry. They were running the air conditioning, filtering out all those spring scents, sanitizing it. Inside, she decided, it smelled like money.

The teller took her time getting back to her window after unlocking the door. She was paying more attention to a piece of paper she was reading than to Judy.

Judy knew the teller, though not well. The woman's daughter had been a problem student and Judy had been forced to call the teller and her husband in on several occasions in search of help or clues. The clues were obvious. Denial appeared to have been a dominant gene in both parents.

Judy couldn't remember her name at the moment and it didn't matter. The woman must have remembered her, though, and decided, in this minor role reversal in which she was in charge, to make Judy pay for those visits to the vice principal's office. She forced Judy to stand and wait in front of her counter for a few extra moments as she reread that sheet of paper over and over again.

"Here," Judy finally said. When the woman looked up, Judy handed her the duct-taped envelope. If this was someone's deposit, she needed to pass it along for proper handling. "Do you know what this is?"

The woman's eyes got big. Maybe some elderly farmer who had spent too many years inhaling insecticides and herbicides preferred to make his deposits this way. Silly, because the result looked like something illegal—a packet of drugs, or even a letter bomb. Only this was Buffalo Springs. There were plenty of screwballs here, but none of them screwy enough to stuff drugs or a bomb in the bank's night deposit. She felt sure of that because Mad Dog was her brother-in-law. She didn't have to look far for an example.

"What do you want?" The teller wasn't even pretending to be polite. Okay, Judy already had plenty of things to be testy about this morning. She was ready to give as good as she got.

"Money, of course."

"Of course," the woman agreed. She opened her cash drawer and began pulling out a stack of bills.

"I only want hundreds," Judy told her. "Fifty of them."

"Yes," the woman said. She reached into another compartment and pulled out a stack of hundred dollar bills and handed it to Judy without counting them. "Here, take them and go."

Judy wasn't sure there was $5000 there. She picked up the stack and began counting. There was more than $5000. She stopped when she got to fifty and pushed the rest back. "Mistake like that could ruin your day," Judy told her. Rude was one thing, incompetent, something else. "Let me speak to the manager."

There was a little hall behind the tellers' counter off which several offices opened.

"Yes, I'll go get Mr. Brown for you," the woman said, and practically ran into it.

Judy waited. She had worked way too hard to put that money away. Then this rude bitch wasn't even capable of counting it accurately. Come to think of it, she hadn't asked Judy to sign a withdrawal slip or provided a receipt for the transaction. The woman disappeared through a door at the end of the hall and slammed it behind her.

Judy was steaming by now. And the woman hadn't taken the duct-taped envelope either. It was just sitting there, on the counter, along with a couple of stacks of bills. Judy didn't want to cost the woman her job, but there was simply no excuse for behavior like this. She stood and drummed her fingers on the counter top and waited for Mr. Brown. And waited. And waited some more.

After a couple of minutes, she'd had it. She would tell Englishman about this. Get him to take care of it. Or Deputy Parker, maybe, since she didn't want Englishman investigating more weird behavior today. She leaned over the counter and stuffed the extra cash into the open teller's drawer. She wasn't sure whether she got the bills in the right slots, but at least they would be out of sight if someone else wandered in while the teller's window was unattended. She dropped the envelope in there too. If it was full of cash, it shouldn't be left lying about.

She slammed the drawer closed, stuffed her fifty one-hundred-dollar bills into her fanny pack, paused to glare up at the little camera that recorded every transaction in the Benteen County Farmers & Merchants Bank, and stomped out.

The street was, surprise, empty. She got on her bike and started burning off her anger in an effort to calm down enough for her next errand. She was half a block short of Main when the bank did an imitation of Mount St. Helens. She almost crashed getting the bike stopped and turning around to see what had exploded. Clouds of smoke belched from the bank and filled the sky with something that looked like dry leaves, rectangular dry leaves—the greenback variety.

The sheriff thought Bud Stone looked like he belonged in one of those lodges in that circle out on the prairie. The man had the cheekbones for it, and the complexion. His skin was weathered and wrinkled, but every wrinkle had probably been earned mastering an environment just like this one. His dark eyes seemed to see through the trucks and trailers and RVs, through the artificial windrows and fence lines beyond, even past the occasional distant elevator right back to a short-grass prairie filled with the great herds—a place he and those lodges belonged.

Stone had changed into blue jeans and a light cotton shirt with a western cut in a bright floral pattern. His boots had pointed toes, but no fancy stitching. He wore a baseball cap with an embroidered patch that read LUCKY STAR CASINO, and his gray braids hung neatly over both shoulders. He sat in a picnic chair under an awning beside one of the RVs and sipped a cup of coffee. The sheriff took the chair next to him.

"Mr. Stone," the sheriff said. "My deputy tells me you have a rotten alibi or a twisted sense of humor."

"Don't have much of either. Do I need them?"

Stone hadn't turned to look at him. He just continued to stare across the pasture into infinity. Or maybe he was trying to avoid looking at the stuffed buffalo, now leaning casually against the side of a semi trailer a few feet away.

"Alibis are always handy when there's been a murder. But you're hardly alone if you don't have one. Not many here do. As for a sense of humor, seems to me it'd be hard to survive without one."

The sheriff tried a smile on the old man and got no response. "So, Deputy Wynn says you were with one of your grandfathers when Michael Ramsey died?"

"Yes."

The sheriff waited, letting the silence lengthen. He was in a hurry, but he sensed that his time constraints didn't mean a thing to Stone.

"That's what I told that deputy. He didn't understand how that could be, since my grandfather died more than a century ago."

"In a dream," the sheriff said. He remembered how Mad Dog would put it. "Your spirit left your body and traveled to be with him?"

The old man finally turned and looked at the sheriff. "You aren't like your deputy. Are you a person?"

Through Mad Dog, the sheriff knew Cheyenne believed only those who had existed as the original people when the world began could be people again. People had spirits. They were recognizable by their deeds. The spirits of people were reborn, over and over. The rest of the world's teeming population weren't people, they were just meat. It wasn't a world view he was completely comfortable with, whether he qualified as a person or not.

"Yeah, I'm a person. So's my deputy," the sheriff said. "Just not a very alert one. I'm not always alert either, but now and then I hear what someone tells me. And, if you mean am I *Tsistsistas*, then the answer is barely."

"Ahh," Stone said, something coming to life in the depths of his eyes. "You are the Mad Dog's Englishman."

Normally, the sheriff would have explained his dislike for that nickname, and asked the old man not to use it. But, somehow, on this man's lips it sounded more like a compliment. "You know about my brother and me?"

"I have heard that there are men here who may be distant relatives. One of them might wish to serve the spirit world. That is part of the reason I came. My people, we decided, if PBS was going to do this, one of us needed to see that they did it…" He paused for a moment, looking for the right word. "…with respect," he continued, having, the sheriff thought, found exactly the one he wanted.

"Your brother has come to Oklahoma to try to make contact with me, or one of the other old men. I am afraid we avoided him. There are many who seek wisdom for the wrong reasons. They are not people. Among the *Tsistsistas*, some are willing to sell our secrets, even when they don't really know them. The ones who do that, they are not people either. We encounter real people in search of truths so seldom. In your brother's case, we may have been wrong. Or so my grandfather tells me."

"Mad Dog will be delighted to speak with you. And I'd love to be there to listen. But right now, I've got a murder to investigate."

The old man nodded. "I see. You have *not* chosen to serve the spirit world. At least not yet."

The sheriff allowed himself a self-conscious laugh. "My brother has had some astounding insights. He's told me things that turned out to be accurate, and there's no rational way to explain how he could know them. But he's the natural-born shaman in our family, not me. Philosophically, I'm…Well, I don't know what I am. Undecided, I suppose. But I'm sheriff of this county and we have a dead body. What I'm serving right now is the law. And what I need are answers. Who wanted to kill Michael Ramsey? And why?"

"Before you find answers, sometimes you must first ask the right questions."

The sheriff shook his head. This was like talking to Mad Dog when he was doing his Zen Cheyenne thing.

Bud Stone smiled at the sheriff's confusion. Maybe he had a sense of humor after all.

"I do not think anyone wanted to kill Michael Ramsey," Stone said. "That is what my grandfather was explaining before I was called back to this time and place."

Despite the source, the concept was uncomfortably similar to the one the sheriff had already begun to consider. Mad Dog had been the target. Michael Ramsey was just in the wrong place at the wrong time. The sheriff opened his mouth to ask Bud Stone if "Who might want to kill Mad Dog?" was the right question when his cell phone chirped.

"English," he said into the receiver.

And just like that, the question changed.

Why would a terrorist pick on Buffalo Springs?

"Two words," Jud Haines said. "Eminent domain."

Chairman Wynn pushed his chair back from his desk and shook his head. "Hold on now," he said. Those two words could lose him the next election.

"Damn right, hold on," Supervisor Finfrock said. He leaned forward until he was on the edge of his seat, a worn leather sofa beneath the chairman's windows. "Folks vote Republican in Benteen County, not because they're conservative, though they are. It's more because they're libertarians, even if they don't know it. We go and seize somebody's land, even Mad Dog's, there'll be new faces on the board after the next election and they won't be ours."

"Yeah," the chairman agreed. "Take Mad Dog's land today, what's to keep you from coming after mine next? That's what they'll think."

"We're talking a special case here," Haines argued, pacing in front of the chairman's desk and swiping his blond mop out of his eyes. "I mean, let's face it. Mad Dog's the only one stand-ing in the way of this wind farm. He's the reason the other two land owners haven't agreed to sell yet. They're sure we'll never get Mad Dog's land. Without it, our land isn't contiguous and we got no wind farm."

"Wind blows the same damn speed everywhere in this county," Finfrock said. Craig Finfrock was a short, muscular man with a flat nose he claimed was the result of an undistinguished boxing career. He owned the Bisonte Bar and Buffalo Springs' only liquor store. This might be Carrie Nation country, but decades after she wielded her ax it remained a profitable business. The chairman had watched it make Finfrock a wealthy man.

"Look here, Finfrock," Jud Haines said. "Where else in this county are you going to find ten sections that line up east to west and aren't already controlled by one or two families? I mean, think about it. We don't put this together, somebody else will. One of those corporate farmers gets to thinking on this before we get the contract signed, they can go around us. Hook themselves up with Windreapers, or one of them other firms, and put this thing in themselves. Then, those of us who've invested in the Benteen Energy Coop can kiss our front money goodbye."

"Persuasive argument," Finfrock admitted. He was one of the larger investors. "But I still don't like this. Surely Mad Dog can be persuaded. I mean, he's a damn conservationist, right?"

"A conservationist? With oil wells on his property?" Haines scoffed. "Give me a break. And you've heard him criticize the president and the war in Iraq. I mean, I wouldn't be surprised if Mad Dog was involved with OPEC or one of them other Communist fronts."

The chairman leaned forward and rubbed his chin. The tone of this conversation troubled him. "Mad Dog is a lot of things," he said, "pain in the ass being one of them, but he's no Communist."

"Islamisist, then," Haines countered. "Pretty much the same thing. Didn't you tell me Mad Dog claimed to be a Negro once? Spent time advocating Black power?"

"Yes, but…" The chairman had to admit it was so. Then Mad Dog had traded Black power for Rastafarianism, then the new-age crystal thing. And, of course, there was his hippie period and the grape boycott and…

"There you go," Haines asserted. "Black power—Black Muslim, most likely. And this Cheyenne thing. Hell, it's probably a sham. He might be planning to strike at his neighbors with a suicide bomb or some such, now that our beloved U S of A is involved in a holy crusade against satanic Islam. I'll bet we could seize his land through the Patriot Act."

Chairman Wynn had heard enough. Mad Dog might be a nut case, but he owed his own life to that nut. Probably his son's as well. He wasn't going to allow a quest for profit on a wind farm to turn into a witch hunt. He opened his mouth to protest, but the door opened first and his son stuck his uniformed body through it and smiled.

"You guys seen Mad Dog?" Wynn Junior asked.

The supervisors shook their heads.

"I was supposed to keep him here for Deputy Parker," Junior continued, "only he seems to have slipped off. Oh, and did you hear about the pipe bomb here at the courthouse?"

Jaws dropped. Before anybody could respond, the windows rattled with the sound of an explosion.

"Lord," the younger Wynn declared. "You don't suppose that could be another one?"

Slipping away from Wynn Some hadn't been hard, though Mad Dog's initial attempt to follow Deputy Parker through the back door was blocked.

"No siree Bob," Deputy Wynn had told him. "Parker said to keep you here and that's what I aim to do."

Mad Dog knew Wynn well enough not to argue. But he intended to make sure Hailey was all right. "Okay, then," Mad Dog said. "I'll go wait in the office with Mrs. Kraus while you keep Parker's back covered."

Wynn had squared his shoulders and looked proud about securing Parker's back. He'd continued to look proud clear to where Mad Dog exited the hall and could no longer see or be seen.

The front doors were just across the foyer. After that, it was only a matter of ducking around the outside of the building. Mad Dog got there in time to see Parker work her way along a hedge between the houses in back of the courthouse. Since she was doing so behind a raised pistol, Mad Dog decided not to come up behind her and provoke an unpleasant surprise. Instead, he trotted through a rose garden at the south end of the back yard of one of those houses, hopped a fence that let him out on Oak Street, and proceeded west toward the corner.

A row of catalpa trees lined the block ahead. Pale blossoms turned their thick foliage a ghostly shade of green and left the street in deep shadow. The north side of the street, past Monroe, was a green-gold wheat field, out of which a small figure ran, pell-mell, to where a motorcycle waited. The figure vaulted aboard, gunned the engine, then did a block-long wheelie, closely pursued. If the biker's torn pant leg was any indication, Hailey had crossed his path while he was up to no good.

Mad Dog whistled for her. She didn't come and it didn't surprise him. Even when she wasn't busy protecting him from bad guys, or evil squirrels and rabbits, she didn't obey commands and only occasionally met requests. She was his friend and partner, not his pet.

Mad Dog couldn't imagine what was going on. Apparently, someone had been shot by an arrow on Catfish Creek this morning. It had happened at the same time he was jogging by and Deputy Parker, whose opinion was not to be taken as lightly as Deputy Wynn's, thought Mad Dog might have been the intended target. The manifest absurdity of that had to be weighed against the evidence of the two arrows he'd seen protruding from the back door to the courthouse. A motorcyclist had been present on both occasions. There didn't seem much doubt the arrows at the courthouse had been meant for him, especially if Hailey was in full pursuit of the archer. The figure that had hopped on the Japanese crotch rocket had something slung over his shoulder. It could have been a bow.

Hailey wouldn't catch the motorcycle. Not unless she realized it had to turn south where Oak ended two blocks down at Van Buren. If she cut across a few yards, leapt a fence or two, and if the biker had to slow for traffic on Main, she just might catch him at the intersection. If she did, Mad Dog's money was on Hailey. But, he didn't want her hurt. In Buffalo Springs, there was always the chance of a farmer happening along with guns in the rack in his pickup's back window. None of them was apt to stop and ask whether Mad Dog's wolf-hybrid had good reason to be attacking a motorcycle rider. Most figured it was only a matter of time till she began killing their livestock or raiding their hen houses anyway.

Mad Dog considered going back for the Mini, then abandoned the idea. He could get there faster taking his own shortcut through lawns, gardens, and alleys down to Main.

Hailey did cut south before the motorcycle negotiated the corner. She was so smart it scared him sometimes.

Mad Dog ducked beneath catalpas, dodged a row of evergreens, and listened hard to the note of the bike's exhaust. He was waiting for the dramatic change in pitch that might indicate Hailey's interception had succeeded.

Mad Dog knew the quickest way through this neighborhood. He'd spent a lot of time here, back in the days when he was courting Janie Jorgenson. She'd lived just half a block north of Main on Jackson. He slid around familiar evergreens, bigger now, vaulted a fence he didn't recall at all, discovered a new hole in the hedge that bordered the alley, and hit Jackson just short of Main. From the sound of it, his arrival there coincided with the moment the motorcycle cleared Main and Van Buren. To his surprise, the biker turned east, his direction. Mad Dog put on a burst, but the corner was just too far. The bike blasted past just as a silver-haired tundra wolf cleared a thick row of peonies in front of him. A middle-aged woman scuttled out of the flowerbed on hands and knees, frantically backing away from Hailey. Mad Dog lost his balance trying not to run over her, and, for the second time that day, went down hard on his left knee and the heels of his hands.

He was calling on a different god than the one he favored when Hailey came back to apologize by slathering his face with kisses. He turned to the woman then.

"Are you all right?" he asked. Hailey had transferred her tongue and attention to the woman's face and she was trying to brush herself off and avoid the wettest of Hailey's acts of contrition.

"Yes," she said. "Nothing bruised but my pride, I think. And I apologize about the flowerbed. I thought you'd set your dog on me, though I see now that she isn't so much angry as affectionate."

The woman looked familiar. Not surprising, since, sooner or later, locals could hardly avoid encounters at the limited venues available for shopping or socializing. He didn't understand about the flowerbed, though. She seemed to think it was his.

"About the flowers…" he began.

"I'm terribly, terribly sorry," she said. "I didn't mean to hurt your peonies. It's just that I think my mother planted those and they're so healthy and so beautiful. I didn't think I'd do them much harm if I dug up a bit of root to try to start a bush at home."

Hailey was back, checking out Mad Dog's injuries. His jeans had a fresh, blood-stained hole in one knee. A wound on the heel of his hand was seeping again as well. He was a mess, and suddenly very conscious of it because he knew who she was.

The house where the row of peonies stood on the edge of the street was the one in which Janie Jorgenson had lived. The woman he and Hailey had bowled over looked familiar because she was the spitting image of Janie's mother, the woman who'd tried to persuade her daughter she could do a lot better than Harvey Edward "Mad Dog" Maddox.

"Janie?" he said, throwing an arm around Hailey's shoulder because he had a sudden, desperate need to hold on to something. "Janie Jorgenson? Is that really you?"

God, she was old. Still pretty, but no longer the adolescent cheerleader he'd fallen in love with. Was he so changed as well?

"Do I know you?" she said. Apparently he was.

He looked at her face more closely. There were lines there. And more flesh and it sagged a little, but underneath all that was a face he knew. Not her mother's after all. Hell, she must be almost twenty years older than her mother had been. And so was he. Her eyes, though, they were the proof. They still sparkled, even at this moment of uncertainty and embarrassment—intelligent, laughing, irreverent, and home to a soul seeking something he'd been unable to provide.

"I don't know," he said, and shook his head. He could still hear the archer on the motorcycle heading east on the blacktop as they sat in the middle of the street, safe, for the moment, in Buffalo Springs where nothing exciting ever happened.

There were no cars behind Janie on Main Street, or south on Jackson all the way down to the railroad track. Just some girl, with platinum-blond punk hair, riding a bicycle.

Janie squinted a little. "No," she said. "Mad Dog?"

And then the street south of Main disappeared in a cloud of smoke and a roar like thunder.

"Keep him here," Deputy Parker had said. Then she'd left Mad Dog and Wynn Some. She drew her SIG-Sauer as she went out the door. She stayed low and surveyed the environment for threats and targets. She couldn't see any, nor did more arrows come from the vicinity of the hedge that lined the north end of the lot behind the courthouse. Judging from the angle at which the arrows stuck out of the back door, that seemed their likely source.

The SIG was hers. She had put a lot of rounds through it on a variety of target ranges and she trusted it—far more than the worn .38 Smith & Wesson Sheriff English had offered with the job.

Parker was accustomed to a more urban environment. She was used to checking rooftops and garbage bins rather than neatly trimmed hedges.

Her first dash took her to the rear of Mad Dog's new Mini Cooper. He'd parked near the back door, almost perfectly broadside to the hedge. She used the car's body as a shield and the low roof for a firing platform. Nothing. No movement near the house behind the parking lot or along that thick hedge, other than the gentle teasing of leaves by a breeze that smelled better than her most expensive perfume.

There was another arrow in the Mini Cooper. It lay in the driver's seat, apparently having ricocheted after glancing off the dash. There was a tuft of hair near it, and a little blood. Mad Dog's wolf had apparently been a target too. No wonder she wasn't faithfully waiting for him in the car.

Parker's next sprint was across thirty yards of empty lot to the nearest corner of the hedge. It was the kind of run that made her sweat, and not because she was working muscles hard or because summer was on the way. It was feeling that target on her chest, the one that had been painted there since that day in Tucson.

She'd been working Glenn Campbell's greatest hits. That's what motorcycle cops on the radar beat called a favorite spot on Glenn Street, a couple of blocks east of the intersection with Campbell Avenue. Traffic tended to bunch up and get frustrated about the time it reached Glenn. Angry drivers look for shortcuts, so Glenn got more than its share of people exceeding the thirty-mile-per-hour limit.

She had pulled the old Chevrolet pickup over at a spot where one of Tucson's many washes disappeared beneath the street. The truck's tag was bent and muddy and illegible, matching the rest of the vehicle. She called in her position and a description, stepped off her bike, checked that her gun was free, and advanced to the driver's window with the usual license and registration line.

The driver had pale blue eyes and a crooked smile. That was all she noticed before she caught sight of the battered woman bound in duct tape on the passenger's side floorboards. Even that hardly managed to register before he raised a pistol from his lap and pointed it squarely between her breasts. A year later, crossing a dusty Kansas parking lot, she still felt phantom echoes of the

.45 slug that slammed into her vest, broke a couple of ribs, and knocked her on her backside, right out in the middle of Glenn. She remembered him adjusting his aim, raising the pistol to point at her face for the second shot. Maybe the UPS truck that missed clipping her by inches distracted him. He missed, but she didn't. She blew his face off, never realizing there had been a UPS truck until she read witness reports afterward.

The man in the pickup was dead. She'd known that before she got up off the street. Brain matter and bone and blood spoiled the truck's headliner. It was the first time Parker had fired a shot at a person. It was hard enough, dealing with the result, even if he had tried to kill her twice, but not nearly as hard as what she found in the truck.

The woman on the floorboards was struggling madly against the tape that bound her. When she saw Parker, she met her eyes with desperate intensity. "Mmmm," she was saying. The duct tape wrapped around her mouth kept her from saying anything more plainly. But her eyes spoke. They flashed from Parker's eyes to the belt of her freshly dead captor, then back again. "Mmmm," she said. Parker looked where the woman's eyes demanded and thought she understood.

There was a switch on his belt. And wires. Bomb! That's what Parker decided the woman was trying to say. The man's hand, the one that hadn't been holding the .45, was resting on the switch, but just barely. As she watched, Parker saw it begin to slip away. She reached through the window and grabbed his hand and the switch and made sure neither moved. The captive's eyes rolled with what Parker thought was relief, but it was clear the woman was still terrified. She made the "Mmmm" sound again and Parker decided it was a dead man's switch, the wires leading to a bomb under his jacket.

She got the man's body out of the cab without letting his hand leave the switch. He was a big man, but that didn't matter, not with the adrenaline pumping and the woman's terror feeding Parker's own. She dragged him to the edge of the arroyo. It was almost six feet down to where the pipe went under Glenn.

There were concrete walls around the pipe that would contain the explosion, direct it away from the street. Parker wrestled him to the edge, trailing blood from his ruined skull.

His captive had managed to wiggle up into the passenger's seat to where she could look out the window. As Parker maneuvered his body so that it would fall without taking her with it, she looked back. The woman's eyes darted from Parker to the inside of the truck, like some trapped wild thing desperately seeking an escape.

Here's your freedom, Parker thought, and let go. His coat brushed the barricade that kept cars out of the wash. It pulled away from the place the wires went and Parker saw, even as she was diving for the street, that they weren't connected to a bomb. It was a radio transmitter.

And then he disappeared over the edge and there was a muffled crump from inside the truck. When Parker went to look, blood was everywhere—and broken glass and smoke and flame and a captive who'd been literally blown in two. The bomb had been under the duct tape that bound the woman, not on the man who couldn't let her live without him.

Both sides of the hedge behind the Benteen County courthouse were clear. There was no one at the corner of either of the houses whose yards it divided. No one hid in the thick vegetation. There was blood on the grass, though. Hailey's? Parker chose the corner of the house on the south and sprinted again. Had Hailey come after the archer? Even wounded?

A two-cycle motor whined to life just as she got to the building. She heard it scream its way through a couple of gears before she got her head around the corner behind her SIG. It was a motorcycle, painted an anonymous black and without a plate. The rider was bent low, an uncertain outline impossible to describe. The only thing that stood out was that he had something slung across his shoulder. A bow, maybe. And he, or she, had a torn pant leg, probably thanks to the pursuing wolf that followed the motorcycle as hard as she could go.

Parker grabbed her radio to set up an intercept, only there was no one out there to do it. Deputy Wynn was in the court-house. Sheriff English was miles away, interviewing people at this morning's crime scene. The rest of the deputies were off duty and inconveniently distant. A murder suspect might get away unless a very determined wolf managed to run down a high performance motorcycle.

She jammed the radio back in her belt and the SIG in its holster, disgusted, and turned to trot back to the courthouse. She was in the middle of the parking lot when she heard the explosion. It reminded her of the sheriff's request that she determine whether a pipe bomber might be dangerous. The smoke that began clearing the tree tops south of her made her think the answer was affirmative.

It sounded like a sonic boom, maybe one of those Air Force fly boys on his way to McConnell over in Wichita, playing loose with the sound barrier. No matter what it sounded like, Mrs. Kraus knew what it was—another bomb.

Her suspicions were confirmed in moments. They'd upgraded to two phone lines into the sheriff's department a couple of years back. Both began to ring simultaneously.

"The bank just blew up," someone told her. She didn't even manage to ask whether anyone was injured before the guy hung up without identifying himself.

Line two was more helpful. It was the manager of the Farmers & Merchants. "We've been blown up," Mr. Brown told her. "And robbed." Line one began ringing again but Mrs. Kraus decided to let it go. This one promised to have the information Englishman and his deputies were going to need.

"Anyone hurt?" That was the first thing to ask. Did she need to find Doc Jones or see if any of the other doctors who some-times spent a day at the local clinic were in town? Get some help headed to the bank? Did she need to call an ambulance and emergency rescue crews? They'd have to come from outside the county so the sooner she got them on the way the better.

"One of the tellers has a paper cut, and I bruised my shoulder on the door jamb when we were trying to evacuate the building. Other than that, we're fine. What we really need, though, is for Englishman and his crew to get down here and secure the street. Mrs. Kraus, there's cash money blowing down Jackson. We need help picking it up before it commences to disappear into people's pockets. And we need that terrorist found right now."

"Terrorist?" Somehow it didn't come as much of a shock to Mrs. Kraus. Not after her experience this morning. "You got a note?"

"How'd you know that?"

"I don't just set over here in the courthouse and paint my nails," she told him. "I been in law enforcement for…" She didn't care to tell him how long it had actually been. She'd been gradually rinsing the gray away with that Egyptian Formula stuff she'd bought at Millie's beauty shop and she was convinced many folks had begun to doubt she could have lived and worked in Buffalo Springs as long as she actually had. Those were doubts she preferred to encourage.

"Never mind," she continued. "Tell me what you know. Just the facts." She hadn't taken many reports of serious crimes. Benteen County seldom gave her practice, but she'd seen Joe Friday on *Dragnet* often enough to have an opinion about how it should be done.

"Was that a bomb?" Chairman Wynn wanted to know, bursting through the door from the foyer and into the sheriff's office. Supervisors Finfrock and Haines followed hard on his heels. Deputy Wynn tagged along and was equally helpful. "Aren't you going to get that other line?"

Mrs. Kraus ignored them. She was taking notes so fast she wasn't sure she would be able to read them later, not that she was likely to forget what Brown was telling her.

"There was a blond woman at the door when we opened this morning. Real short hair. Mean looking, my teller said. Said she didn't want to open, only it was time and we've never been robbed before."

"Yes," Mrs. Kraus scrawled away.

"Yes? It was a bomb?" Finfrock's voice rose.

Line one stopped ringing and Wynn Some scowled at her. "You never answered that," he accused. "It might of been important."

"We think she was an Ay-Rab in disguise. My teller, Lucy, found her note on the floor where she'd slipped it under the door. Read it after she let that woman in and just before she got handed the bomb. Then the robber demanded money. Hundreds. Probably part of a plan to copy them and use counterfeit bills and ruin our nation's economy and destroy the western world."

"A note?" Mrs. Kraus asked. "Do you have it?"

"What do I need a note for?" Wynn Some wanted to know. "Oh, and have you seen Mad Dog?"

"What's going on, Mrs. Kraus?" This time it was the chairman himself asking. It didn't matter. Mrs. Kraus had tuned out everyone but the man on the other end of the phone line.

"Yeah. I got it right here," Brown said. "It says: 'We now target your financial institutions. Capitalism cannot exist without banks. As you target the economy of Iraq, we target the Farmers & Merchants of Buffalo Springs. You seized Iraq's oil fields. Now we will control yours. Shut them down at once. Close your service stations. No petroleum products are to be sold in Benteen County or our next strike will deliver more than mere shock and awe. Fear us and obey.'"

His voice paused and Mrs. Kraus took that to mean he'd finished the note. "That all?" she demanded. "Isn't it signed by somebody who's claiming responsibility?"

"Say, you do know your stuff," the manager conceded. "There's the name of some terrorist front at the bottom of the page."

"What is it?"

"I was gonna get to it," Brown grumbled. "Let's see, here it is. 'We are a brotherhood laboring to quench America's evil designs and aggressions.'"

"And none of your note is capitalized," Mrs. Kraus said. Line one was ringing again. She continued to ignore it. "Except for a few words at the end. What are the capital letters, Mr. Brown? Read them to me."

"Wow," Brown told her. "I never knew you were such a professional. You're right again, though. There are a few capitalized letters down there. I just figured whoever wrote it, they must be uneducated heathens and that's why they only capitalized a few letters at random, but Jesus. You're right. Those capital letters, they spell al Qaeda."

"My God!" the supervisors chorused as they saw Mrs. Kraus add the dreaded name to her notes. Wynn Some hadn't been paying attention. He'd finally decided to make himself useful and answer line one himself.

"Hey," he said. "You won't believe this. Somebody blew up the bank."

Judy sat on her bike in the middle of Jackson Street and told herself things like that didn't happen in Benteen County.

The Farmers & Merchants had already stopped burning. Dust and greenbacks were beginning to settle, some carried toward her on today's gentle version of the constant winds that swept the Plains looking for a mountain range or a hill, or even an occasional prairie dog mound, to slow them down.

A crowd was gathering in the street. Maybe a dozen people—all the merchants and shoppers who'd been in nearby buildings on this business day. There wasn't a lot of business in Buffalo Springs anymore, so it wasn't much of a crowd.

"Anyone killed?" someone called.

"No. Not even hurt to speak of. We all got out in time." That was the teller's voice, the one who'd waited on her…and apparently taken her for a bank robber. What had been in that note the woman picked up off the floor as she unlocked the front door? Judy didn't like the possibilities.

Damn it to hell. All she wanted to do was get herself aboard a Paris-bound jet, and drag her husband, a reluctant traveler under any circumstances, along with her. She thought she'd nearly had him. Their unusually passionate morning, and a healthy dose of guilt, seemed to have weakened him. Then he got that phone call. A body out where they were filming *This Old Tepee*. And now this, a bombing, in which she might have played an unintentional role. Lord, she really would play hell getting Englishman on that plane now.

And might play hell getting herself on it, if she were identified as the bomber. She opened her fanny pack and pulled out the crumpled baseball cap she kept in there with the seldom fulfilled intention of screening the sun from freckling her nose. She set it atop her newly blond skull—not much of a disguise, but all she had.

No one was hurt. She didn't know a thing about that envelope, except that it had been stuffed under the flap that covered the night deposit drop instead of inside the building, where she'd delivered it. Out there, it probably wouldn't have done nearly as much damage. Not unless someone was walking past when it went off.

This didn't seem like the moment to explain that to people. She would tell Englishman later. Maybe when they were over the Atlantic and he couldn't turn around and go back to save the county from this latest crime wave.

Some of the crowd was headed her way, running around, trying to pick up the cash that was blowing down the street like autumn leaves. One of them might have noticed the blond bomber leaving the scene of the crime on a bicycle. It might not be much of a leap to put that together with the recently baseball-capped bicyclist watching from where the bomber had gone. Judy got her feet on the pedals and aimed herself into the gap between a couple of buildings where there had once been a blacksmith's shop. Now it was just a vacant lot filled with grass and blooming weeds and a bit of debris that included plastic bags and crumpled newspaper and a few federal reserve notes.

That Murphy guy had been on to something when he postulated his law. Nothing ever happened in Benteen County. There hadn't ever been a murder here until six years ago, or not one that'd been public knowledge until Mad Dog's wolf started finding human skeletal remains in that blizzard a couple of years back. Let one little murder happen and it seemed like everything else started going to hell in a handbasket.

How was she going to get Englishman on that plane? She shook her head and stuck to the back streets as she pedaled home. She didn't want anyone to recognize her just now. Not until she decided how to handle her involvement, and who, if anyone, needed to know.

Now Englishman was really going to dig in. Unless she was lucky and the murderer had been standing over the body on Catfish Creek, ready to sign a confession, Englishman would be neck deep in that investigation. On top of that, he was about to get mixed up in the hunt for a blond bombsheller cum bank robber, with whom he'd had gratuitous sex that very morning—then, when she'd explained, after the person who left the bomb in the deposit box to begin with. He wasn't going to want to leave town until both the murder and the bombing were solved. He didn't want to leave in the first place. She was going to have to be very persuasive. The whole bag of tricks—threats, tears, love, lies. Whatever it took. Judy was going to Paris today, and if there was any way possible, she was dragging Englishman with her.

Just what the sheriff needed, the kind of emergency that forced him to abandon a murder investigation well before he had a suspect. Mrs. Kraus was clear, though. The bank had been robbed and blown up. There was no longer any question of whether they should take the pipe bomb seriously. They were damn lucky no one had been hurt yet. The bomber's notes seemed to indicate this hadn't been just about the money, not with more explosions threatened.

On top of that, Mrs. Kraus told him, someone had been taking archery practice at Mad Dog when he tried to leave the courthouse a few minutes ago. Then that someone hopped on a motorcycle and sped away before anyone could pursue him. And now Mad Dog had gone missing again. If the sheriff's brother knew who was after him, he hadn't shared the knowledge before skipping out on the ever-less-than-vigilant Deputy Wynn.

"Okay," the sheriff said to Mrs. Kraus. "I'm on my way. See if you can call in any more deputies. Send Parker to the bank to secure the scene and start interviewing witnesses. Have Wynn knock on doors out back of the courthouse, then through the neighborhood down to Main. Ask if anyone saw our archer or his motorcycle and recognized him, or noticed something that'll help us identify him. Maybe the supervisors can volunteer to help him. I'll be there in ten minutes."

Mrs. Kraus acknowledged his instructions and he hung up the cell phone and clipped it on his belt, just behind his .38 Smith & Wesson Police Special. He was faster drawing the cell phone these days.

The sheriff turned toward his truck and was surprised to discover his passenger's seat was occupied. Bud Stone sat there, impassive, staring across the peeling paint on the Chevy's hood toward the circle of tepees in the Lancasters' pasture.

"Look," the sheriff told him. "I've got an emergency in town."

"My daughter and granddaughter are packing. They will load our car and come to town to pick me up. We're going home to Oklahoma. The boy's death, it spoils what I hoped to do here."

"I'm not sure I can let you leave while I'm still investigating this."

"That's one reason I will ride with you. I can answer any questions you have. Then, when the women come, you will have no more need for me."

"Oh, hell," the sheriff said. "What I don't have time to do is sit here and argue. Belt yourself in. This will be a quick trip."

The old man seemed completely unaffected by the sheriff's wild exit from the pasture.

"And I hope to be able to find your brother. Talk with him a little before we leave." His voice came out a bit uneven, but it was only because of the way the truck was bouncing down a dirt road that hadn't been maintained well enough to encourage speed.

"I'd like to find him myself," the sheriff said. "Well, we're headed the right direction. He was in town, last anybody saw him, and his car's still there."

Stone nodded, as if he'd known Mad Dog was there all along. The sheriff caught it out of the corner of his eye. He was too busy watching for potholes and soft sand to spare a glance.

"I do not know your brother," the old man said, "so I have no opinion whether someone might want to kill him. But I have come to know the people with whom I was encamped. Michael was a confused boy. I say boy rather than man because that is what I mean. He was younger than his years, though he did not think so. People might want to use him, because he could be used, but he did not stand for anything, did not have anything that could not be taken from him."

The sheriff narrowly missed a chicken that picked a bad time to explore the eternal question of why it should cross the road.

"You already told me you don't think he was the target."

"I do not know who the target was. There are those who might want to hurt Michael to keep Daphne from him, but they would not need to kill him. She would not have stayed with him. There is not a man here she would not go with. Even me. She will collect men for a while, until she collects the wrong one."

"You think the girl might have been the target?" The sheriff put the truck in a power slide that took them around the first corner leading to the nearest blacktop.

"She does not stand for anything either, but she has something men want. Some men want it exclusively. She would not accept that."

"Interesting," the sheriff said, more confused than enlightened, "but we're pretty sure that arrow was meant for my brother. He was nearly hit. And from where the bowman stood, it would have been hard to see those kids by the creek. Michael getting shot…I'm almost certain it was just a case of being in the wrong place at the wrong time taken to its extreme."

The old man shook his head. "None of us, I think, were anywhere other than where we had to be."

The truck dropped into a low spot, a dusky stretch where a domed loft of cottonwoods meandered along the road while following another shallow creek. The red and blue lights on the sheriff's front bumper lit the shadows as the truck rattled the bridge at the bottom, then spat gravel climbing back to the flatlands above.

"You really should talk to my brother," the sheriff said. And then he got busy because a motorcycle had appeared out of nowhere, dropping down from the far end of the shady corridor even faster than they rose to meet it. The sheriff's antilock brakes didn't matter much on sand and washboard gravel. Two-wheeled vehicles were even less capable of panic stops. The sheriff tried to hug his ditch, only there wasn't really one to hug, just blooming weeds and clumps of saplings before he would begin testing the Chevy's bumper against immense tree trunks.

In retrospect, the sheriff didn't see how it was possible, but he not only missed the cottonwoods, he missed the motorcycle. The motorcycle careened by, inches from his door, before losing momentum and balance and toppling over as it crossed the bridge. If the rider had still been aboard, he would have impacted the sheriff's driver's side mirror as he went by.

"What happened to him?" the sheriff said, trying to check everywhere at once. His truck had stopped crossways in the road, enfolded by a cloud of dust.

"Over there," Stone said. The sheriff looked where the Cheyenne's eyes pointed. A tangle of bloody rags lay at the base of one of the cottonwoods. It no longer resembled clothing. Nor did what was inside it resemble a human being.

"Oh God, I've killed somebody out for an innocent ride."

"More his fault than yours," Stone observed, "and not so innocent, I think." He nodded a few yards back up the road to where a broken pile of sticks and feathers lay bound together by a piece of cord.

"That was a Cheyenne bow and he had it slung across his shoulder."

"You haven't changed," Mad Dog said. She had, of course. She'd changed so much that he hadn't recognized her, and then his first thought was of her mother. But, when he said it now, he was being absolutely honest. He'd looked into her eyes and found her there. This fifty-seven-year-old woman sitting in the street beside him had miraculously shed more than forty years in an instant. Knowing her, he would never again see her as anything but young and vivacious and stunningly beautiful, just as she'd been when they were teenagers exploring the uncharted territories of lust and romance.

She shook her head and smiled and he recognized the smile and adored it, just as he always had.

"You still say the most outrageous things, and almost make me believe them. But even with that moonstruck look in your eyes, that's too much. I'm four decades older, thirty pounds heavier, and look about as much like the head cheerleader of the Buffalo Springs Bisons as you do." Her eyes twinkled. "But thank you for lying about it anyway."

"No, really…" Mad Dog began, but he didn't know how to explain it.

"I won't be quite so generous, Mad Dog, but I will say the years have been kind to you. And I'd go on with more of that lovely chit-chat, except I believe a building just blew up down the street. Don't you think we should go see if anyone needs help?"

Fallout was beginning to drift across Main Street. It consisted of a bit of smoke, a lot of dust, an assortment of paper, and a couple of twenty dollar bills. Mad Dog got up and collected them. They were crisp and new and clean, until he touched them. He had blood on his hand. He had forgotten he was hurt again. He wiped his hands on his Levis.

"Looks like it might have been the Farmers & Merchants," he said. One of his hands was reasonably clean. No blood anyway. He offered it to Janie. "I'll go check it out with you as long as you promise not to run out on me again. Not before we have a chance to talk."

"Maybe one of the things we should talk about," she said, taking his hand and climbing back to her feet, "is who ran out on whom."

Mad Dog looked surprised. "Me? I'm still here. I live in the same house I did when you left. And I tried hard to find out where you'd gone…at least for a while."

"Oh sure. I left and you didn't. And I knew you tried to find me. You always were a bit of a stalker. But who left the relationship? That's what I mean."

Mad Dog grabbed a stray five dollar bill and the two of them crossed Main and headed south on Jackson. They could hear people calling each other, marveling that no one had been hurt.

"Stalker?"

"Sure. Don't you remember that time I went on a date with Fred Hendershot and you trailed us all the way to the Cinerama in Wichita and back?"

Mad Dog looked sheepish. "I was only…"

"Or when we had the fight and I thought we broke up and you decided not to call me for a few days to teach me a lesson. Then Stan Bowser asked me to go roller skating and you came and kidnapped me right out of the rink."

"I thought I was doing what John Wayne would do. Or Bogart. You and I were only kids and I…Well, I suppose you're right. Your mother never forgave me for that one."

"She was your confirmed enemy long before that. She knew you wanted in her little girl's pants, and were making significant progress toward getting there. Actually, I've never been quite sure whether that kidnapping was a terrible male-chauvinist act of dominance, or the most romantic thing that ever happened to me. But they'd call you a stalker these days, or worse, and my mother would get a restraining order and maybe put you in jail."

Mad Dog laughed as he reached down and rumpled Hailey's ears. She was sticking unusually close to him, a little jealous maybe. "It seemed like the thing to do at the time," he said. "But it sure caused a commotion in Buffalo Springs that summer."

He bent and plucked a couple of ones from a clump of Bermuda that was making good use of a crack in the pavement. The bills came up bloody, like the twenties. His hand had stopped bleeding. He started checking his arm for a wound.

"Oh dear," Janie said, interrupting their reminiscences and his self examination, focusing his train of thought, quite thoroughly, elsewhere. "You're not bleeding. It's your dog."

Chaos. Deputy Parker didn't like chaos. It reminded her of that bleak day in Tucson.

She parked the Benteen County black and white in front of the bank and stepped out into a street filled with citizens who wanted to tell her what had happened, and didn't really know.

Someone handed her a shoe box and told her, "I think we've found most of it." It was one of the Heathers, the sheriff's daughters. Parker never could tell which was which. Not that it mattered, since she only had to remember one name. "But you'll want to count it."

What she didn't like about the Heathers was the way they seemed to think their father's employees were incapable of making competent decisions without direction. Of course, considering the rest of Englishman's deputies, they were right.

"Thanks, Heather," she said. "Have you counted it?"

"Sure. $4,878. Mr. Brown, the manager, said they only had ten thousand out of the vault and the robber said she wanted exactly five, all in hundreds. They had seven thousand in hundreds, the rest in smaller bills. We've found all but one of the hundreds. Mr. Brown thinks we're only missing that and a twenty and two ones. We've got people looking."

Parker popped the lid and glanced inside. The box was filled with cash. Some of it looked singed, some crisp and new. At least one bill was blood soaked.

"Mad Dog found that one," the Heather said. "Hailey was hurt. You know, his wolf. He gave Heather the money, then took off to get Hailey's wound looked at."

Parker nodded. She wasn't done with Mad Dog, but she didn't have time to go looking for him now. She jotted the dollar amount Heather had given her on top of the box, along with the date and time, and the name, Heather English.

"Lane, actually," Heather corrected her. That would make this Heather number Two, the sheriff's adopted daughter. Parker made the correction, popped the trunk, and locked the box of money in the black and white. She took out her roll of crime-scene tape and began boxing off the front of the bank. The walls seemed faintly bowed out and the front door hung ajar. Its safety glass, checkered with cracks, lay on the steps and sidewalk.

"Were you a witness?"

"No," Heather Two said. "We were headed for the Buffalo Burger Drive In for breakfast when we heard the explosion. We came back to look, then got involved in picking up cash."

"I need to talk to witnesses."

Two understood. She nodded to where several people huddled, comforting each other, on the curb just down the block. "There's Mr. Brown and his tellers. I can finish stringing this tape if you want to talk to them."

That wasn't the way it was supposed to work, but Parker, with no other deputies available, could use the help. And the Heathers probably knew more about police procedures than anyone else she was likely to find.

"Good," Parker told her. "Just surround the building, or, if you can't, block the entrances and exits. Then, you and your sister can start sorting through this crowd for me. Find out who actually saw something and who's just here rubbernecking. Send the sightseers home."

"Sure," Heather agreed. The idea of helping seemed to appeal to her. And following reasonable instructions instead of delivering them didn't appear to be a problem either. Maybe, Parker reassured herself as she went to where the bank's employees clustered, the sheriff's daughters had helped handle crises like this before. Only this was Buffalo Springs, she remembered, where nothing ever happened. It was why she had taken a job here.

Mr. Brown was drawn to her uniform. He left the group and came to meet her. "I'm the manager," he told her, establishing his importance. "Have you caught her yet?"

"Were you a witness to the robbery, sir?" she countered. She'd discovered that men like Brown were used to bullying the sheriff's deputies, and they weren't used to deferring to women as authority figures, except maybe their mothers. Bullying right back was usually the best way to establish who was in charge.

"Uhh, well, no, but I know what happened and the bank is my responsibility."

"Good. Then you'll want to help me deal with this as efficiently as possible. Mrs. Kraus said you read her a note. Do you have it?"

He reached into the pocket of his sports coat. "That I do," he said, unfolding it.

She reached in a pocket of her own and removed a plastic bag. "Put it directly in here, please. Don't let it touch me." He recoiled a little, but he did what she asked. The good thing about combining a uniform with no-nonsense commands was that people generally did what you told them.

"Has anyone else touched this? Has it been anywhere other than in your pocket?"

"Lucy touched it. My teller. She was the one who picked it up in the first place, and let that woman in to rob us. But nobody else. She gave it to me and I've kept ahold of it since."

"Good," she said. "We'll probably need to get your fingerprints, and hers, and DNA samples. And I'll take that coat of yours now, too, if you don't mind."

Paper was notoriously bad about yielding fingerprints. As for the rest of it, they had no DNA test equipment and no one to analyze fibers from the letter or the jacket, but he seemed steadily less inclined to argue, and more convinced that the Benteen County Sheriff's Department knew what it was doing.

She glanced at the note through the plastic. It was just one of those freezer bags with the strip that changes color when it's properly sealed, but he didn't know that.

The note said what Mrs. Kraus had told her it would, and nothing more. She transferred it, and Brown's coat, to the trunk of the black and white beside the money. "That's all I need from you for now, Mr. Brown. Would you please send Lucy over to talk to me? Just Lucy. Thank you for your cooperation." And sign the traffic ticket and have a nice day.

Brown retreated and his teller replaced him. Parker opened the front door of the black and white for her. Lucy looked doubtful, like she thought maybe Parker was going to haul her to jail and charge her with aiding and abetting the crime.

"I thought you might like to sit somewhere other than on the curb for a few minutes," the deputy explained. "And we can have a little privacy."

Lucy nodded and sat and Parker closed the door and went around and slipped behind the wheel. She pulled out her notebook and pen.

"I've been thinking," Lucy said. "That face. I mean, right from the beginning I thought it seemed familiar. For a minute, I thought it might have been one of my daughter's teachers from back when she was in school here, but that's crazy. And so's this, I suppose, but I believe I know who it was."

"Really?" That would be a break. They could use one after two bombs, one murder, and another attempt.

"Yes," she said. "I didn't tell anyone because I was afraid they'd laugh at me."

"I understand," Parker said, not understanding at all but trying to cut to the important part. "Who was it?"

"Well, anybody can disguise their voice, right? And cut their hair real short. And bleach it blond."

"Yes?"

"I mean, it was the eyes, really. They were so intense."

"You recognized the eyes?"

"Right. I mean, it makes sense. An al Qaeda terrorist would want to be disguised. Speak in falsetto, cut your hair short and bleach it blond, get rid of the turban and the beard, and it could be him."

"Beard? Turban?"

"Don't you see? Our bank robber, I think he was Osama bin Laden."

Judy would not have been flattered to know the teller had confused her with Osama bin Laden. Though maybe there was something about the eyes…She might have thought so if she'd bothered to study them just then. She was too busy examining her platinum crew cut.

Judy had ridden a couple of blocks from the bank before she realized she couldn't let Englishman get bogged down searching for a blond bank robber. She checked her fanny pack for her cell phone, then remembered it was plugged in at home, getting charged so it would be ready when she left for Paris.

Home was where she wanted to go, but then she wanted the Heathers up and involved in their own plans before she broke the news about Paris. Considering Englishman's response, she thought later rather than sooner would be the best time to tell them about her sudden vacation plans. It was after ten, now. The girls had probably left the house, but they were teenagers and might lounge about on a morning without school. She didn't want them overhearing her conversation with their father, especially if it didn't go well. And Judy could see how it might not go well, since she still expected him to be with her on that Paris flight, in spite of a murder and the bomb in the Farmers & Merchants. Paris was a must. She didn't care how many things he needed to deal with.

That was why she detoured to the courthouse. She'd hoped Englishman might be back from the murder site. Maybe she could explain, and make him understand, face to face in his office, especially if Mrs. Kraus could be persuaded to take a coffee break and give them some privacy.

But, once through the front door, she'd realized how dramatically different she looked, and that Englishman's deputies might be watching for someone who fitted her description. Wynn Some had been known to shoot first and ask questions later, so she'd ducked into the restroom instead of the sheriff's office. She peered into the mirror at what she increasingly thought of as an ultimate bad-hair choice. She couldn't let anyone see her like this. Not before she explained to Englishman.

She rummaged through her fanny pack again. She kept a bandana in there, one of Englishman's. He never used it. She'd appropriated it as something colorful to tie up her hair. There was nothing to tie up anymore, but she found she could wrap the cloth around her head and bunch it to cover the blond. With the cap back in place, it looked like she was hiding her hair instead of no longer in possession of it.

The ruse seemed to work on Mrs. Kraus. "Hi, Judy," the little woman with the Marianne Faithful rasp said. "Englishman's not here. I just got off the line with him. He might be awhile. Seems he just killed a prime suspect in that bow-and-arrow murder this morning."

"Oh good," Judy responded, causing Mrs. Kraus to raise a shocked eyebrow. "Not that somebody's dead," Judy clarified. "Just that one crime may be solved. He's leaving on vacation today. Did he tell you?"

The second eyebrow followed. "Vacation?" Pole axed would be a good way to describe her reaction. "While a terrorist runs around bombing Buffalo Springs?"

"That's what I wanted to talk to him about. Could I maybe borrow one of your phones? I could cover the office while you run get yourself something over at Bertha's if you want."

"This might not be a good time," Mrs. Kraus said. "Englishman's got his hands full with that new body just now, and I've got to stay here to direct the citywide search that's going on."

"Oh." So much for that plan. Judy smiled and started backing toward the door. "Well, when you talk to him again, just tell him I was kind of a witness at the bank and he should call me as soon as he can."

"Might not be soon," Mrs. Kraus said. One of her phones rang and she turned to answer it.

Coming here had been a really bad idea and Judy punished herself with a quick smack to the forehead, inadvertently knocking her cap and bandanna to the floor of the foyer. She bent and picked them up and sprinted for the front door, restoring her disguise as she went to retrieve her bicycle.

She was quick, but not quick enough to prevent Mrs. Kraus from turning to see that Judy had disappeared, but the blond terrorist who'd hit the bank was darting past her door. Judy would have been impressed at how fast two bombs, and Mrs. Kraus' panic, resulted in the evacuation of the courthouse.

The sheriff began by checking for a pulse. Since the motorcyclist's skull was about half the size it had been before encountering the tree trunk, he wasn't surprised when he didn't find one. No point in trying CPR. Not on a rib cage that had been smashed to a pulp filled with jagged bone fragments.

After a quick call to Mrs. Kraus to let her know why he would be delayed, he pulled out his digital camera and recorded the scene, the skid marks, the motorcycle, and the position of the body before he moved it more than his preliminary examination had required. He considered asking Doc to come pick up another one, then decided there wasn't time. Not with a bomber running around Buffalo Springs, assaulting the courthouse and now robbing the city's only financial institution. He had to get to town and quick.

He removed a pair of surgical gloves and some plastic bags from the truck. Traffic accidents were the most common form of violent death in Benteen County. He had handled too many.

"Mr. Stone. I hate to ask, but I need a witness. Would you step out of the truck and watch while I examine the body."

The old man opened the door and walked across the road. The sheriff gently peeled the crumpled form off the cottonwood's trunk. Some of its teeth and a piece of cheekbone remained behind, imbedded in the bark until the sheriff removed and bagged them.

There would be no recognizing this face. Its features now conformed to the shape of the tree trunk, no longer remotely human. You should have worn a helmet, he thought, instead of that stocking cap, now stained with blood and brain matter like the curly blond locks that protruded from underneath.

The sheriff straightened the body on the grass at the edge of the road. It wasn't hard to do. It bent easily, too easily, and in places humans did not normally bend.

"I'm going to go through his pockets," the sheriff told Bud Stone. "That's what I want you to witness. Especially if I find anything of value, or something that might be incriminating."

He opened one of the plastic bags and set it beside the corpse. The remains of the bow were already in a larger bag. No arrows though. Either the man had fired the last of them or he'd lost them before encountering the sheriff…and a cottonwood, and eternity.

The sheriff got down on hands and knees on the opposite side of the body from where Stone stood and began going through pockets. He was glad for the gloves. There was a lot of blood and occasional bits of tissue that didn't belong on this side of skin. There was also nothing in any of the pockets. No change, no billfold, no driver's license. And the corpse wore no watch or any other jewelry. The sheriff was surprised. He had assumed this was someone local. If so, why bother removing things by which you could be identified, since one look at your face was normally all it would take? Too bad there was no longer a face.

"Nothing," he said. Stone nodded. And there hadn't been anything on the motorcycle either, including license plates. Could this guy be an outside professional? Or somehow related to their terrorist?

The only way to identify him might be through Doc Jones. Doc could take fingerprints—the sheriff had examined the man's hands and been relieved to see that there were normal looking ridges and swirls there. After everything else, he'd half expected to find them etched off or surgically removed. Or Doc might get what he needed for identification purposes from the teeth.

The sheriff took his evidence bags back to the truck and stored them. He emerged with a larger bag—a fancier version of what he'd seen too many buddies put into during his brief stint in Vietnam.

The man wasn't big and the sheriff managed to roll him into the body bag without much difficulty. Lifting him into the truck bed might be another matter. The sheriff didn't want to add post-mortem injuries by manhandling the corpse.

"Can you give me a hand with him?" the sheriff asked Stone.

"Sure," the old man said. The sheriff thought he detected some reluctance.

"Look, if you'd rather not…"

"No. It's all right," Stone said. "Do you have some sage?"

"Sage?" The sheriff didn't get it.

"Never mind. Shall I take his feet?"

The sheriff told him that would be great. They maneuvered their awkward package into the back of the pickup and placed it there, as gently as possible. Then the sheriff went back to move the motorcycle out of the road. It would have to wait.

When he turned back, Bud Stone was moving his arms from over his head, crossing them, and touching the ground. The man had crouched with his eyes closed, speaking words in a language the sheriff didn't understand.

"Are you all right, Mr. Stone?" he asked, when the Cheyenne finished.

"I am now," Stone said. "I purified myself, but sage would have helped."

"Uhh, right," the sheriff said, climbing behind the wheel.

Stone joined him in the cab. "You should do the same, you know."

The sheriff wondered if that might not be true.

◇ ◇ ◇

"Damn it, Mad Dog. I'm a medical doctor, not a veterinarian," Doc Jones said, rising from behind his desk in the coroner's office. "Excuse my language, ma'am." He directed that at Janie Jorgenson, who crowded into the little room behind Mad Dog and Hailey.

"I've heard worse." She smiled and offered her hand. "I'm Jane, Jane Jorgenson, Dr. Jones. Mad Dog tells me you're the best doctor in the state. I get the impression second best wouldn't be good enough for Hailey."

Doc smiled, straightening his perpetual scowl. "Pleased to meet you, Ms. Jorgenson. I shouldn't be surprised by this visit. Mad Dog has kindly let me tend to Hailey a time or two before, though he doesn't trust me to diagnose his own ills."

"I don't have any," Mad Dog said. He gestured toward Hailey's blood-soaked coat. "Can't you please…"

Doc knelt and examined Hailey's matted fur. He was gentle and she trusted him enough to put up with it. "What's happened to you?" he crooned, putting on the bedside manner he assumed for children, wolves, and similarly dangerous creatures.

"An arrow, I think," Mad Dog explained.

"Arrow?" Doc's brows furrowed and the scowl came back full force. "That's odd."

"Not really," Mad Dog explained. "That kid you've got down the hall. I think maybe I was the one that arrow was supposed to hit. At least, somebody had a couple of shots at me when I was over at the courthouse a few minutes ago. Hailey didn't take kindly to it. She chased him, got her teeth in his pant leg, I think. I'm guessing he shot her as well."

Doc was thorough. "There's a slash through one ear," he said. "It's a clean wound and it doesn't look like she's hurt anywhere else. Ears, they bleed a lot."

"Can you help her, Doc?" Mad Dog pleaded.

"I don't think so," Doc replied. Mad Dog blanched and Doc hurried to explain. "This looks worse than it is. I can knock her out and stitch it up, but we'd probably have to stick her in one of those cone collars to keep her from scratching the stitches right out. I don't think you want to put her through that, Mad Dog. She's nearly quit bleeding already and she's leaving it alone. We'll just apply a little antiseptic and let her get on with life with a notch in her ear. It'll bother you more than it does her. And it'll bother both of you less than turning her into a conehead for a couple of weeks. Those things are bad enough for dogs. Impossible for wolves, I expect."

"Right," Mad Dog agreed. "I can't see putting her in one of those things, but what about the blood she's lost?"

"She's got plenty left," Doc reassured him. "Just make sure she gets to drink all the water she wants, and maybe feed her a little extra protein the next few days. She'll be fine, long as you keep yourselves away from this mad archer. Why on earth would someone want to shoot you, Mad Dog?"

"I can't think of a single reason."

Janie cleared her throat. "Well I sure can," she told them.

"This is a waste of time," Supervisor Haines said. Deputy Wynn was inclined to agree. They had canvassed all the houses behind the courthouse and north of Main. All they'd found were a few people who'd heard a motorcycle leaving the area in a hurry. None of them had seen it. A couple had seen Mad Dog cutting through the neighborhood. One had seen Deputy Parker.

"We should be over at the Farmers & Merchants, where the action is," Finfrock said. Wynn Some agreed again, but his daddy didn't.

"No such thing," the chairman protested. "This had to be done and there aren't enough deputies for an emergency like this. Those of us without law enforcement skills, we've got to lend a hand now and then."

"Hey, I got law enforcement skills," Wynn Some complained.

His father glanced at him and continued. "Like I said. Besides, what could we do at the bank? I'm sure Deputy Parker has things under control. We'd just be in her way. Anyway, that's over. What we gotta do now is figure out how to stop this terrorist's next attack."

"Wouldn't hurt to go to the bank, though," Finfrock said. They had finished knocking on doors and were at the corner of Main and Van Buren, only about four blocks from the crime scene. "Folks like to know their supervisors care what's happened to them and their money."

"I'm with Finfrock," Haines said, "only let's take a minute and walk down to the Texaco. A motorcycle runs on gas. Maybe the guy stopped to fill up before he started turning the back of the courthouse into a pin cushion."

"Makes sense," the chairman said.

"And we could get us a soda," Wynn Some agreed, suddenly enthusiastic again. All that door to door effort had worked up a thirst.

The Texaco and the Buffalo Burger Drive In dominated the corner at Harrison and Main. The intersection was Buffalo Springs' busiest, since both streets were part of the Kansas State Highway system. Unlike other streets in town, these continued well beyond the municipal boundaries, and stayed paved. Both blacktops stretched straight and flat toward the edge of the world, or so it seemed from where a four-way stop and blinking red lights marked it.

The Texaco was the only place within twenty miles that was open twenty-four/seven. With people coming to town early because of Buffalo Springs Day, there were a couple of cars drawn up at the pumps and several more in the parking lot. A mechanic was finishing an oil change in the attached garage—all that remained after a shiny new food mart and self-serve gas pumps had replaced the original station.

"I'm thinking I want a root beer," Deputy Wynn told the supervisors.

"Iced tea would be good," Finfrock said.

They threaded their way around the cars by the pumps, exchanged greetings with the customers, and made their way toward the entrance. Wynn Some had his hand on the door when Haines' voice stopped them all in their tracks.

"Holy shit," he said. "Here's another one."

Wynn Some knew what he meant.

"Where?" his daddy asked.

"Right here, leaning against this pump." The pump in question was attached by a hose to a Ford F-250. The pump's digital display was flashing an ever increasing dollar and gallon total. A bomb and gas vapors didn't sound like a good combination to Deputy Wynn. He knew what he had to do.

"Run for your lives," he shouted, pushing through the door to the food mart and the cashier's counter. The customers all turned and looked at him, but nobody ran—he was blocking the exit. Back out toward the bomb and pumps wasn't where the deputy had intended to go, but he needed to move. He turned and considered his choices. He didn't get time. Jud Haines bent and picked the thing up.

"Don't touch it," the deputy's father shouted, too late.

Haines took two steps toward the intersection. Like an outfielder trying to pick off a batter with plans to stretch a single into extra bases, he put everything into his throw. The lot across the highway was empty but for high weeds and a drainage ditch that fed into nearby Calf Creek. Wynn Some didn't hear the splash when the bomb landed, but he did see the geyser of mud and grass and water that erupted the moment it exploded. Little chunks of slime and mulch plastered the window of the Texaco.

"Jesus," Finfrock said, grabbing hold of a customer as if he would have otherwise been forced to sit right down on the concrete. "If you hadn't grabbed that just then…"

"There wouldn't be a Texaco anymore," Wynn's daddy continued. "And we'd all be dead."

It was a concept that penetrated even Wynn Some's imagination. He stumbled out of the Texaco's doorway and left his breakfast in the nearest waste bin.

◇◇◇

Deputy Parker could tell the Heathers were getting a kick out of this. Adults who, all their lives, had treated them like little kids—ignored them or done pat-on-the-head, isn't-she-cute stuff—were suddenly listening to and obeying them. They were Englishman's daughters. Somebody had to take charge. Parker was the power behind their thrones, but she'd been interviewing witnesses, none of whom had proved of much value yet. That left the Heathers to handle crowd control.

"What a kick," she heard one Heather tell the other. "I just sent our old chemistry teacher home and told him it was because he didn't know anything."

So far, only two people had actually seen the bomber: the teller, who was convinced it had been Osama bin Laden in drag, and the farmer who'd driven by just minutes before the blast.

"I sure didn't see no Osama," he said. The figure he'd seen was some hot young babe decked out in come-fuck-me clothes, though that wasn't how he phrased it. "Tight-ass jeans and a clingy tee shirt," he said. He hadn't recognized her, but she'd known him well enough to shout an insult that named his wife. Or so he claimed.

"Anybody left?" Deputy Parker asked a Heather. The deputy was through with the farmer whose recollection was of an under-dressed Jezebel instead of a cross-dressed zealot.

"Just Millie. She runs the beauty parlor down the block. She didn't see the bank robber, but she says Mom was in this morning and planning to go to the bank. Millie thinks Mom might have seen something, since she left the beauty shop just before the blast."

Parker shook her head. "Doesn't seem likely, does it? If your mother were a witness, she'd have stuck around, or been in touch with your father right away. Still, I suppose I better talk to this Millie person. Where is she?"

Heather English looked around. Thanks to the girls' efficiency, there was no longer a crowd concealing Millie. "There she is," Heather said, pointing across the street at the beauty parlor.

Millie was standing, looking at her place of business from just beyond the curb. Her body language indicated she was seeing it in a different light than before. She looked cowed, overwhelmed, as if she'd suddenly realized this ugly converted barbershop was not the key to the beachfront retirement which she'd planned.

"Excuse me," Heather called. "Deputy Parker is ready for you now." Millie took a couple of steps toward them, but she was backing up, paying no attention to Heather's summons.

Parker considered calling out herself, but she was reluctant to address the woman by her first name and she didn't know Millie's last. The sign over the front door just said MILLIE'S PAVILION OF BEAUTY. Under that, the pale outline of one of the barbershop's former offerings could be made out through the fading paint—FLATTOPS, OUR SPECIALTY.

"Uhh, Millie, the deputy wants you."

Millie finally turned. There was such a look of horror in her eyes that Parker immediately put her hand on the butt of her weapon and half crouched.

"Help," Millie squeaked. "There's another one, right in my front door."

Heather took a step into the street, angling for a better look. That was where she ran into Parker's arm.

"Get back," Parker said, voice strained. "Get everyone off the street and under cover. Do it now."

There really wasn't anyone other than the Heathers in need of doing what Parker asked. The people from the Farmers & Merchants hid behind cars and buildings. The other business owners from the neighborhood were similarly hunkered down.

"Come on," the other Heather urged. The sheriff's daughter let her sister drag her behind the black and white. Parker shifted her attention to Millie's entry. Something stood on the concrete next to a screen door that kept out flies, but not this morning's glorious spring breeze.

Parker edged to Millie's side. Millie was pointing. "You see it?"

"Looks like an ordinary paper bag," Parker said. It did. A plain brown paper bag, about the size that would hold a double-cheese buffalo burger and an order of freedom fries from the nearby drive in.

"It buzzed at me," Millie said.

"Get across the street, Ma'am," Parker said. "Get behind something. Let me check this out."

Millie did, but not before leaving a plea in the Deputy's ear. "Please," she said. "I'm not insured."

Parker advanced on the sack. She was sweating profusely now, her heart pounding so hard it felt like it might tear through her Kevlar vest. She wanted to run, she wanted to hide. Hell, she thought she had—all the way to a rural county in Kansas where nothing ever happened. Halfway across the country from where an afternoon in Tucson stole her nerve.

On the Buffalo Springs sidewalk, it was all Parker could do to make herself approach the bag. She took each step with exaggerated care. The slightest disturbance might be enough to set the thing off. She had been foolish enough to look at what that bomb had done in Tucson. Afterward, she'd filled out paperwork, and when she was through, filled out one more sheet—her resignation.

It was deathly still on the street. Even the wind seemed to hold its breath. Parker was in mid-step when the bag buzzed again. She closed her eyes, balanced precariously on one foot for a moment, then opened them to reassure herself she wasn't dead yet.

The buzzing stopped. Parker gently set her foot down and bent over the bag and tried to peer inside. "Fucking A," she said, and reached out and stretched the opening wider. She never used profanity, but she said it again. She lowered her face to within inches of the bag's mouth.

The explosion rattled windows up and down the street. Deputy Parker fell back on her butt and grabbed her heart and the contents of the bag went flying. But the explosion had come from elsewhere, maybe over toward the Texaco.

Parker was slow getting up. She stooped and picked up the thing that had been in the bag and went back across the street. She held out the object she'd retrieved for everyone to see. Parker's face was tight and pinched with anger. So was her voice.

"When I find the joker who stuck this pager in a bag and left it on vibrate…"

She didn't have to complete the sentence. Whatever Parker did to the perpetrator, her witnesses would have suggested worse.

"**G**ood," Doc said, looking up from his desk as the sheriff knocked on the door and stuck his head in. "I was about to call you with the autopsy results."

"Can we get a bulk discount?" the sheriff asked, holding the door open. "Come help me find a gurney so you can start on our latest victim."

"This another casualty of your mad archer?" Doc led the way down the antiseptic white hall in the back of Klausen's Funeral Parlor where they took deliveries. The Benteen County Coroner's office opened off that corridor. "Who is it?" He pulled a wheeled gurney out of the mortuary lab and trailed the sheriff toward the back door.

"That's what I'm hoping you'll tell me. He came off a motorcycle at speed and ended up face first against a tree. No helmet. Now, no face. He wasn't carrying any ID. I don't need you to tell me how or when this one died, just who he was."

"So, a vehicular mortality, not another crime victim?" Doc pushed the back door open, maneuvered the cart down the ramp, and followed the sheriff to the parking lot.

"Doc, I think this is our archer. He had a bow with him. Someone riding a motorcycle took a couple of shots at Mad Dog over at the courthouse a little while before this guy ran into the tree."

"Yeah," Doc said. "I heard about that. Hailey had a notch taken out of her ear and Mad Dog brought her over here for veterinary repairs."

The sheriff dropped the rear gate on his pickup, climbed in, and hauled the body bag back to where he and Doc could ease it onto the gurney. "Mad Dog was here? When? Do you know where he went? Every time stuff like this happens and I need to find him, he disappears on me." The sheriff stopped and looked around. "And, damn it, I seem to have lost another Cheyenne. I had a live passenger with me when I got here, now he's gone too."

"I don't know where Mad Dog went," Doc admitted. "They just left a few minutes ago. He and an attractive woman. Not young, but still a knockout. She seemed to know why your archer was after Mad Dog, but she wanted to talk about it in private."

They pushed the body back toward Klausen's. The back entrance was surrounded by lush flower beds containing a profusion of spring blossoms. Klausen's gardener was a wizard, but the sheriff always felt there was something vaguely inappropriate about this floral opulence—like scented toilet paper. The guy in the body bag had no use for the ornamentation. Those who accompanied the bodies that came through this door were in the death business. They didn't need artificial cheer either.

A bumblebee staggered out of a hollyhock and went looking for another romance. The sheriff shrugged. Mother Nature didn't care. Life, death—two sides of the same coin.

"The woman with Mad Dog. You know who she was?"

"She introduced herself," Doc said. "Jane, I think. And some Swedish last name. Hell, I can't remember already, but she had the most beautiful eyes."

"What's this, Doc. Are you smitten?"

"Must be this weather," Doc said. "Or a reaction to all the tragedies I'm forced to be around."

They pushed the body down the long sterile hallway. There was something appropriate about the transition, the sheriff thought. This corridor fit his view of what purgatory should be like. And the next door they opened would do for hell. The funerary lab was antiseptically clean and mostly white, but there were stainless-steel tables designed to drain bodily fluids, and embalming machines trailing tubes and needles. Doc's collection of autopsy tools, freshly washed after their recent duty, lay on a drain board beside an industrial sink.

"Let's have a look," Doc said as soon as they transferred the body from its bag onto one of the steel tables. He pulled a smock on over his clothing and stuck his hands in a pair of gloves before he stuck them into the ruined face. "I see what you mean."

The sheriff felt like turning away. He knew the disaster that had been a face too well. It was likely to turn up in his nightmares for weeks to come.

"The missing teeth and facial bones, what I could find anyway, they're in that plastic bag I put on the gurney."

"Another young one," Doc commented. "Wisdom teeth were just coming in and hardly any wear on the teeth that are left."

The sheriff needed to check on Parker's investigation at the bank, but he also had to know who this guy was. Since Mrs. Kraus hadn't called back after he told her he was bringing Doc a body, he figured the bank was under Deputy Parker's competent control.

"I checked all his pockets," the sheriff said. "You want to do a quick external exam before I have to leave and you open him up? See if there are any scars or moles or other identifying marks that might help you recognize our murderer?"

"Sure," Doc said. "Only that reminds me. I'm not sure he is a murderer."

"Oh, I know. We've got no proof he's the one who shot Michael Ramsey at Catfish Creek. But how many bikers are running around Benteen County with traditional Cheyenne bows?"

"No," Doc paused midway in his effort to cut off a pant leg and turned to look at the sheriff. "Ramsey. He didn't die from that arrow. Not immediately. I think he passed out from shock. The girl went for help and left his face in the mud and he couldn't breathe. The arrow didn't pierce his heart while he was alive."

"Jesus. You saying he suffocated?"

Doc shrugged, the corners of his mouth drooping even more than usual.

"What are the chances?" the sheriff wondered. He remembered what Bud Stone had said. The old man hadn't thought anyone wanted to kill the boy. Apparently, no one actually had, though a jury might have been convinced to hold the archer responsible.

The sheriff was considering how to come to terms with this philosophical conundrum when his cell phone rang. Only his office, his deputies, and his family had its number. Judy and the Heathers were forbidden to use it except for emergencies. That was why he was so surprised to hear Judy's voice. "Englishman," she said, "it's almost eleven-thirty. Our flight leaves at four-forty. It takes a couple of hours to drive to Wichita and they want you checked in at least two hours early because of all the extra security. That means we need to leave here around noon."

"Judy, I can't…"

"You can," she said. "Whether you will or not, that's up to you. Your bags are packed. All you need to do is get home in time to change into what you want to wear on the plane. If you aren't here, I'm going anyway."

"I've got two bodies, a terrorist, a bank robbery…"

She interrupted him again. "The bank robbery, that was me," she said. "It's a long story, a comedy of errors, really. You'll laugh."

He wasn't laughing yet. "You?"

"I went there to make a withdrawal, Englishman. Five thousand dollars—spending money for Paris. I thought that envelope was somebody else's deposit. I mean, it was all wrapped up with tape and someone had tried to stuff it in the night deposit box and…"

"In the deposit box?" The sheriff tried to process what she was telling him.

"I'll explain on the way to the airport," she said. "In the meantime, that's one less crime you have to solve. You may have bodies and bombs, but you don't have a bank robbery. So, hurry and wrap things up. I'll wait for you until noon. Then I'm outta here."

"Judy…" She didn't interrupt him this time. She hung up on him.

"How is Judy?" Doc asked, looking concerned.

The sheriff shook his head. He wasn't sure how to answer that just now. He started punching their home number into the key pad when the cell phone rang again.

"Don't hang up on me again," the sheriff commanded.

"Not to worry," Mrs. Kraus said, "but you ain't got time to chat right now. Somebody just blew up the Texaco."

"What can I getcha?" Mad Dog and Janie were adjusting to the darkness inside the Bisonte Bar. The bartender was one shadow among many. He leaned muscled shoulders over the polished mahogany surface and pointed and said, "Aw, Mad Dog. You know Mr. Finfrock don't want no pets comin' in here, much less your wolf. There's health regulations. 'Sides, she scares off some customers."

"She's a service wolf," Mad Dog responded. "Haven't you read the Americans with Disabilities Act? You can't deny me the right to bring her in here. I mean, you wouldn't keep out somebody's seeing-eye dog, would you?"

"Well, course not. Service wolf. See, you never told me that before. Service wolves are fine."

"I'd like a cup of coffee, black please," Janie said.

"Dr. Pepper for me," Mad Dog told him. "And a couple of hard boiled eggs and a bowl of water for Hailey."

"My pleasure," the bartender muttered. "Times are tough when nobody day drinks anymore."

Mad Dog led the ladies back to a booth in the corner, discovering along the way what the bartender was complaining about. They were the only customers. Well, it was only half past eleven on a Friday with a special event about to compete for business and wheat harvest looming. Still, Mad Dog was surprised the place was completely empty. He would have expected a couple of pool players and maybe a citizen who was desperate for some hair of the dog or a bartender's wisdom. But that was all he'd expected, and why he'd chosen the Bisonte. It was close and Janie had said she wanted to talk to him privately.

After they settled in the booth and got their order—Hailey was pleased with the eggs—Mad Dog asked for an explanation. "What's this all about? Why couldn't we talk in front of Doc?"

"You like him, don't you? You always were loyal to your friends."

"I like him and I'm loyal. What's that got to do with why you aren't surprised someone is trying to kill me?"

"There was a time I was mad enough to kill you myself."

"I'm really sorry about that," Mad Dog said. "I was just a kid, but that's no excuse. So were you. When we discovered you were pregnant…Well, I know better now. Abortion is unacceptable. I've been studying the Cheyenne Way. I've learned that every embryo has the potential to house a spirit from the moment of conception. I would never have been part of letting you get an abortion if I'd understood."

Janie's jaw dropped. "What? Have you become one of those pro-life nuts who run around and harass women and blow up abortion clinics?"

"No, no, you don't understand. I wouldn't interfere with another person's decision. I'd just try to tell them what they might be doing."

"Well, that's one you're going to have a tough time making me understand." She sat and steamed along with her coffee for a minute.

"You don't support infanticide," Mad Dog asked, "do you?"

She wasn't about to be pinned down. "I don't know, Mad Dog. In certain circumstances, maybe. Not as a general rule, I suppose."

He'd forgotten how much they used to fight over things. Stupid things, most of them, but big issues too, like politics and the war—another war then—and now, abortion.

"You remember I'm Cheyenne? That Mom was a half breed?" Janie nodded. "Well, the last few years I've begun to take my heritage seriously. I've read everything I can get my hands on. I

won't try to explain the whole Cheyenne belief system to you."
He saw her starting to color and added, "Not because you can't
understand it. It's just too much to get into when we're here to
talk about something else. But you need to know I'm serious
about it. It's my religion now. It's what I believe in, and one
of the things Cheyenne philosophy teaches is that our people
recycle. Not everyone in the world is a person. Most of them,
they don't have spirits. But every *person* has a spirit and has lived
before. After they die, they get to come back again, and that happens at the moment of conception. So, when you abort a fetus,
you could be killing a full blown person, not some microscopic
potential for life."

She reached out and put a hand on his. "I'm sorry," she said.
"I didn't mean to disparage your beliefs. I went off half cocked
there."

He recalled, too, how their fights had never bothered him
that much because of the way they made up afterward. A touch,
in those days, had regularly led to much more—in fact, in one
case, the very thing they were talking about.

"I wasn't mad because you let me get an abortion," she said.
"It was because you just gave me the money and then let me
go alone."

"I should have been there with you," he agreed. "I knew it
even then. Only I had a visit scheduled with a football recruiter
for the Wheat Shockers that day and I wasn't sure you wanted
me there." He paused and waved a hand at her. "No, that's not
right. I didn't know what you wanted. And I was scared. It was
easy to convince myself we needed me to get that scholarship
and you'd rather handle it on your own."

She laughed. "You were scared. I was terrified. And you know
what happened?"

"Did you try to get it done here in Benteen County?" She
nodded. "Then you went to my mother, didn't you?"

"You knew she did illegal abortions?"

"Not then. But I know now. Mom might have been Cheyenne,
but she didn't know anything about being Cheyenne. She grew

up without anyone to teach her. Otherwise, she never would have…Wait a minute. I thought she never let her clients know who she was. She made them wear a big hood the whole time. How'd you find out it was her?"

"Oh, Mad Dog. When she discovered who I was, she knew who the baby's father had to be. And she couldn't go through with it. Couldn't kill her baby's baby. She told me I should marry you and have the child and she'd help us with the bills and the babysitting."

Mad Dog shook his head in disbelief. "She never said a word to me. Never hinted. Why?"

"Probably, because she just made me more determined. I wasn't going to end up like my mom, stuck in some hick town with a kid to bring up on my own. I knew you were going to college on a football scholarship. I wanted an education too. I wanted to take on the world and get rich and maybe be president. And, you know, I got a lot closer than you might think. I knew I couldn't do those things and be responsible for a new life, no matter how much help your mother gave us. I told her, if she wouldn't do it, I'd go to Wichita. Find somebody there, or Kansas City, or St. Louis. Whatever it took. Your mom, she finally told me who to go to, and gave me the rest of the money it would take."

"I didn't know."

"And you didn't ask me. Remember that Friday night after I was supposed to have had it done. You never said a thing about it. Never touched me, either, like I was suddenly unclean. That's why, when I left, I didn't come back."

"So you had the abortion. Then you kept going, running from me?"

"No. I just ran, and then I had the baby. Talk about a justification for abortion, Mad Dog. Your son, he'll kill you in a heartbeat if he ever gets the chance."

Judy wouldn't answer the phone. Not her cell phone, either. The sheriff figured she wanted him to come home and talk to her in person about the bank. Then she'd try to persuade him not to leave again, except to catch the plane in Wichita.

He got an answer when he dialed a third number, though.

"Parker," his deputy said.

"You still at the bank?"

"Just leaving. Headed for the Texaco."

"I'm pulling out of Klausen's," the sheriff said. "I'll be right behind you." He flipped the switch and activated his light bar and siren. But not before he heard the black and white's wail echoing down Buffalo Springs' empty streets. He couldn't remember the last time two emergency vehicles had responded to anything in this peaceful little community.

There were no flames visible as he turned onto Main. No billowing cloud of smoke to indicate that Buffalo Springs might have lost one of its few successful businesses.

Five blocks didn't take long. He found the black and white, half in the Texaco, half still in the street. Its light bar strobed the crowd surrounding it, including Deputy Parker. The Chevy drew a crowd too, the moment he pulled in. People were shouting, too many and too confused for him to pick up more than "bomb" and "hero."

He shouldered the door open and fought his way out of the truck and into the miniature mob, reaching out to grab the first of its members who might know what had happened and be able to tell it accurately. Chairman Wynn was already trying to fill him in, but so were half a dozen others.

"Quiet!" the sheriff shouted. "One at a time. Mr. Chairman, what happened here?"

Parker elbowed her way over so she could hear too. She'd obviously been getting the same incomprehensible multitude of stories.

"Heroic! Magnificent! Saved dozens of lives, maybe more," Chairman Wynn said, so excited he was throwing his arms around as wildly as his praise. Kansans didn't do that, not in public for all the world to see. "I've never witnessed anything like it. I mean, Haines just reached down and picked that bomb up like a soldier in a foxhole grabbing an enemy grenade. He didn't stop to think about what could happen to him. He just snatched the thing and came up throwing. Hurled it clean across the highway toward that vacant lot. And just in time, too, 'cause that thing no sooner hit that ditch than it blew. Threw mud and grass and muck all the hell and gone." He spread his arms to display the muddy splotches on his slacks and short-sleeved shirt. "That bomb, it was right at the base of a working gas pump. Imagine…"

Chairman Wynn obviously had. So had the rest of the people who'd been there. Now Parker and the sheriff could as well.

"We might've lost half this town," Supervisor Finfrock said. He pointed toward where Jud Haines hung near the back of the crowd wearing an aw-shucks, tweren't-nothin' grin. "This boy deserves a medal. A statue, maybe."

"He's got my vote from now till eternity," a middle-aged farmer in coveralls and a feed company cap told them. "But for him, I'da been a dead man for sure. I was right next to that thing, filling my truck. I swear I never saw it till Jud picked it up. Been a snake, it'a bit me."

"I didn't think. I just acted," Haines explained. "But we got to do both now—think and act. This bomb was meant to kill people. Lots of people."

"Might have been the impact that set it off," the sheriff said. "The other explosions, bad as they were, seemed aimed to scare folks rather than hurt them."

"Not this time," Haines said. The crowd agreed with him.

"How can you be sure?" the sheriff asked.

"Because that's what the bomber says," Haines replied. He held up a sheet of paper. "Here's the note. Read it yourself."

"What's goin' on out there?" the bartender asked. "That's the second explosion I've heard, and now there's sirens." He didn't seem to expect an answer. He came around the bar and strolled over to the front door, pushed it open, and left Janie and Mad Dog and Hailey in complete privacy.

Mad Dog got a funny little smile on his face. "Me, a father. I've got a baby." His eyes went from unfocused and sentimental to intense, staring directly into her own. "You know, Janie, I always dreamed you and I would have kids."

"You don't have a baby," she said, exasperated. "He's all grown up—forty years old, middle-aged."

Mad Dog shook himself. "What's his name? What does he look like? Do you have pictures? Can I meet him? But you said he'd want to hurt me. Is that because of what I did to you?"

Janie twisted uncomfortably in her seat, making the vinyl complain. How did you explain forty missing years in a couple of sentences? She'd thought she knew how she wanted to do this, but now, face to face with those adoring eyes on her…

"You have a granddaughter, too, working for PBS. She's here in Benteen County this very minute."

"Jackie. She's mine? I met her," Mad Dog said. "This morning, on my way to town, there was a truck with a flat tire and this beautiful girl crawled out from under where she was looking for the spare and I thought she was you. And Jesus, now you're telling me she's my granddaughter?"

"You met Jackie? Oh dear, I should have come and told you all this sooner. I've always been afraid one or the other might want to investigate the place I ran away from. And that they might somehow discover you. Especially Sam."

"Sam? That's a great name."

"Samuel, actually. It was my father's name. You know he ran out on my mother and me, left her to bring up an illegitimate daughter in a community that never let either of us forget what we were. But I liked to pretend my father wasn't really like that. That he would come back and rescue us one day. So I named our son for him—another mistake." She paused for a moment, trying to think how to put it.

"Mad Dog, you said the Cheyenne don't believe everyone has a soul, a spirit. Did I get that right?"

Mad Dog nodded.

"Meat, you said. People without souls, they're just meat."

"Yes."

"Maybe it's because you're Cheyenne and I'm not. Maybe it's because one of us has some genetic flaw. Hell, I don't know. But what we got was an animal, not a person. I couldn't have found a better way to put it. Sam's meat. It's like he was born without a soul."

◇◇◇

The sheriff read it for himself.

you were warned and did not obey. you call civilian deaths collateral damage. what will you call these? shut down all oil and gas pipelines and filling stations in your county. if you do not, we will call these deaths the beginning.

we are the Original Sentinals of the lAws of MuhhAmed

The sheriff put it in a plastic envelope, then showed it to Deputies Parker and Wynn, and the other two supervisors.

"Is that how you spell Muhhamed?" Chairman Wynn wondered.

"It's one way," the sheriff said. "Where did you find this, Supervisor Haines?"

"Under the bomb."

"That doesn't make sense," Parker said. "If the bomb was supposed to go off in the Texaco, the message would have been destroyed along with the service station."

"Hey," Haines said, shaking his hair out of his eyes. "What do I know? Maybe it wasn't supposed to go off unless some idiot like me came along and tried to throw it a safe distance from the gas pumps. Whatever, we've got to do something. It was a bomb and I found it where there were gas fumes. That's a bad combination."

"He's right," the sheriff said. "Mr. Chairman, I think we've got to cancel Buffalo Springs Day."

"We can't do that." It was Finfrock, this time. "It's almost noon. People are already setting things up over at the Buffalo

Springs Non-Denominational Church. Folks will start arriving with their pot-luck dishes any time now."

"So," the sheriff countered, "if you wanted to place a bomb where it would do the most damage to the most people in this county today, where would you put it?"

Finfrock reluctantly agreed. "Okay, I'll grant you that, but what can we do? There's no way to get word out this late. People will show up anyway. And if we don't let them in, they'll just mill around outside. Maybe take their food over and eat it in the park."

"Say," the chairman mused. "That might be the answer. Move the celebration out of the building and into the park."

"Maybe," the sheriff conceded. "But you'll still have too many people in a concentrated space. There's nothing to keep our bomber from moving his bomb."

Chairman Wynn swung around in a quick circle, as if he expected someone to hold up a cue card with the answer on it. "Finfrock's right," he finally said. "It's too late to stop Buffalo Springs Day. We'll move it to the park, and get us more security. Can you bring in any other deputies?"

"It's possible," the sheriff said. "A couple of them were planning to attend the event, but I've had Mrs. Kraus trying to get hold of them since the bomb went off in the Farmers & Merchants. No luck so far."

"What about help from outside?" Finfrock wondered.

The sheriff nodded. "Yeah, I'm going to try that, but I wouldn't hold out too much hope."

"Come on. When we're under assault from al Qaeda?" Finfrock obviously didn't believe him.

"We'll see," the sheriff said. "Maybe those al Qaeda claims and the new Homeland Security Department will work in our favor. But none of the other jurisdictions I know have large enough budgets to cover their own problems right now, let alone ours."

"Now we're talking politics, Sheriff." Haines said, shaking his blond mop up and down with pleasure at coming to the rescue once again. "The Benteen County Board of Supervisors is all but straight Republican. I'll bet we can grease a few wheels out there, even up to the national level. I'll lay you odds we'll have federal investigators and maybe some National Guardsmen headed this way before lunch time. Only we got to get ahold of our other two supervisors right away. Then we can make those calls and address some other business associated with this crisis."

The crowd muttered its approval. The sheriff thought Haines was in for a rude awakening, but whatever, he needed to get back to his investigation. If the supervisor took on the responsibility of calling for outside help, it was one less thing he had to do. He didn't get to tell them that, though. His cell phone rang and he grabbed it. "English."

"Dad, what's going on?" It was Heather and she sounded concerned.

"A bomb at the Texaco," he said. He'd love to take the time to explain things to his daughter, but not in front of this crowd and not with so much needing his attention. "Nobody hurt, though. You needn't worry."

"We already know that," One said. "What we want to know is why there's a pile of luggage and your passport by the door? Are you going somewhere?"

Judy had packed for the trip and laid his passport out. Any last hopes he'd had of reasoning with his wife and talking her out of this drifted away on that news.

"No," he said. "We might have, but too many things have come up." That was true for him, but maybe not for Judy. Still, this wasn't the time to explain it to his daughters.

"When were you going to tell us?"

He was struggling with the answer when she spoke again. "Wait, here's Heather."

Two came on the line. Her voice was shaking.

"Englishman," she whispered in his ear. "I just found more bombs."

"Sometimes, it doesn't seem like any kid has a soul," Janie said. "I mean, I remember some awful things I did when I was little—feeding live bugs to spiders, taking red ants to black ant hills to watch them fight, and pushing Dale Miller in the Claytons' pond when we were six because I thought he was lying about not being able to swim." She smiled, remembering how hard it had been to get Dale back out. "You aren't surprised when kids get upset and maybe shed some tears because the butterfly they chased ends up crumpled and dead and not pretty and part of their game anymore. Sam wasn't like that. There was never any empathy in him—no connection with the creatures he injured.

"I denied it for a long time. The difference between boys and girls, I convinced myself. And he was so smart and clever. And manipulative. Sometimes he convinced me he hadn't really done what I'd just seen him do." She pushed herself back in the booth and Mad Dog followed her with his eyes.

"Then somebody gave him a pet bunny. Sam killed it. I should have made sure he could only get near it when he was supervised. I guess by then I already half expected him to hurt it. What surprised me was the way he did it. Slow, Mad Dog. He did it slow, not with some cold curiosity about what was inside that made it tick. He wanted to watch it suffer, see how much pain it could endure." There were tears on her cheeks now. "Did you know a rabbit can scream? I didn't until I heard it. That's when I caught him with the garden shears and a harmless little creature pumping out the last of its life's blood."

"I should have been there with you."

She rubbed a sleeve across her cheeks and shook her head. "No. It was my choice to bring him up on my own. I didn't want you there."

"I'm sorry," Mad Dog said. And this time, she noticed, he was smart enough not to say anything else.

"He couldn't charm me out of that one. Jesus! He'd documented what he was doing, filmed it with our eight millimeter movie camera. Oh God, it was so sick.

"From then on, he was constantly in treatment or in trouble. Then he was in institutions, as things got worse. Finally, I just couldn't keep him around anymore. He hurt kids in our neighborhood. I was afraid he might kill one of them, or maybe even me.

"Some good people tried hard to get through to him. I had lots of help, the best money could buy. I look back and I don't think there was anyone inside him to save. He really should have been aborted."

"No," Mad Dog protested.

"Oh yes," Janie said. "You see, eventually he did kill someone."

Mad Dog didn't say anything this time. Even the man with all the answers was finally out of them. So was she. But she wasn't through with her confession. The dark and empty bar seemed the ideal place for it.

"Sam went to prison. He was still a juvenile. What he'd done was bad enough for them to hold him longer than they would most kids. He got his GED while he was doing time, then a couple of college degrees. Got to be a member of the Aryan Brotherhood, too.

"He disappeared when he was paroled, but not before he left some poor girl pregnant, Jackie's mother. She was just a kid, so I took her in and supported her and finally raised Jackie myself. She's a troubled girl, but I think she'll turn out all right."

"What happened to our son?"

"I wasn't sorry to have him out of our lives, Jackie's and mine. I never heard of Sam again, not until a few months ago when I got a letter. It was from that White supremacist group in Oregon, the one that preaches about the mud peoples and how they're stealing the earth from God's chosen Aryans?"

Mad Dog nodded.

"I guess he'd applied for some position with them. Makes a mother so proud. They weren't prepared to accept him without some information about his genealogy.

"What I did was stupid, but he caused Jackie and me so much pain I wanted to hurt him back."

"So you told them about me," Mad Dog finished for her.

"I told them Sam's father was part Indian, part Black, and part Mexican. And I told them if they wanted to do a DNA check, they should contact a man named Mad Dog who lived in Buffalo Springs, Kansas."

"I'm all those things through one grandparent," Mad Dog said. "I don't suppose they'd care that the other three were lily white."

"He wrote me then. I won't tell you all the vile things he said. But he ended by warning me, if I wanted to stay alive, never to let anyone else find out about you. Some of what he said made me think he planned to make sure nobody could find out from you."

"So you think he'll come looking for me."

"Mad Dog, Jackie called me a couple of days ago. She said she'd seen her father. Your patricidal son is already here in Benteen County."

The Buffalo Springs Non-Denominational Church was on the south side of Veterans Memorial Park, about mid-way between the courthouse and Bertha's Café. It was a simple brick structure that looked more like a gymnasium from the outside than a church. And felt more like a gymnasium on the inside, the sheriff thought. Fundamentalist Christianity was supposed to be served up without formalities, but this place was so low-church that they used folding chairs and evaporative cooling. The only hint that you were in a place of worship came from the thick beams of the cross that hung on the back wall. Without pews, though, it made for a great place to house large public events. In the sheriff's experience, the congregation had always been too hard up to turn away anybody capable of paying to rent their space, including, once, an abortive attempt to start an atheists club.

The Heathers met the sheriff's pickup at the sidewalk. "We cleared everybody out of the building," One of Two told him. She was wearing too short shorts and exposing lots of skin at the midriff.

"When we said there was a bomb, they got out quick," Two added. "Word's out about the bank and the Texaco." The second Heather was more fully clothed, but her jeans were awfully tight. If they weren't his daughters, he wondered, would he still feel that way?

"And I need to investigate both of those," he said. He'd left Wynn Some standing guard over the muck-filled crater across from the Texaco. The sheriff had no training with explosives, other than what Uncle Sam provided before sending him to Southeast Asia. He would have preferred leaving Parker there to investigate it, but she was the only one with real law-enforce-ment-level training with volatile materials—mostly, she had told him, of the call-the-bomb-squad-and-don't-touch-it variety. Still, that made her the departmental expert.

"Where?"

"Back by the kitchen," his first daughter said as she led him toward the front door. "We promised we'd help set tables for the potluck. So we came over here after we knew the Texaco hadn't been destroyed. We wanted to talk to you and see what was going on down there, but a promise is a promise."

"The bombs are in a store room," the second Heather said, getting them back on topic. "They look like huge sticks of dyna-mite, all connected together with wires and stuff."

"Just tell Parker and me how to find it," the sheriff said as they reached the door. "You're staying out here. Keep everybody way back from the building."

"Aw, Dad," One complained.

"Jeez, Englishman," Two echoed. But they gave him careful directions, then headed back toward the sidewalk to enforce their father's edict.

"I wish I had a Kevlar vest to offer you," the sheriff told Parker as they made their way down the hall from the auditorium to the kitchen.

"I'm wearing one," she told him. "Doing that saved my life once. So I bought my own. I put it on as soon as things started getting wild this morning."

"Oh." The sheriff felt more vulnerable than he had a moment before.

"Don't worry," Parker told him, as they paused in front of the appropriate door. "If a bomb goes off while we're near it, I won't live any longer than you. They'll just find more of me to bury."

Suitably comforted, the sheriff put his hand on the door knob. "You ready for this?"

"No," she said, and he believed her, "but let's get it over with."

The sheriff pulled the door open. It was just like Two had described. Great round cylinders were mounted in rows on a wooden rack. Twelve of them, all connected by a series of multicolored wires.

Parker sighed and it didn't take the sheriff long to realize it was from relief. "I think I know what this is," she said, "and it's not bombs. Hang on a minute, while I get some light on it."

The sheriff reached for the switch by the door and didn't quite get his hand there before she stopped him with both of hers. "Let's not flip any switches until I'm sure," she said.

"Sorry." He felt embarrassed by his naiveté.

She must have sensed that because she offered an apology. "I'm probably being overly cautious, but after the morning we've had, why take chances?

"When I was in Tucson, they had this ritual. Every Fourth of July they set the little peak west of downtown on fire. Not on purpose, exactly. It's not much of a mountain, though it would draw a lot of interest if you set it down here in Kansas."

She edged into the closet and began tracing the wires, following them from tube to tube. "They called it Sentinel Peak in the old days, because they used to station people there to watch for raiding Apaches. Then some University of Arizona students whitewashed a bunch of rocks and piled them up into a huge letter 'A'. Now it's called A Mountain, and every Independence Day the city holds a fireworks show up there. If there aren't trees in the way, you can see it from nearly all over town."

She had been through most of the tubes without apparently finding anything to concern her. She might have skipped to the end but, like she'd said, it wasn't a day for shortcuts.

"That's what these are. Fireworks tubes. Probably a few aerial bombs, some star bursts, stuff like that. Smaller than I'm used to in Tucson, but they'd be impressive enough in Buffalo Springs. You hear anything about a fireworks display associated with today's celebration?"

"No," the sheriff said. "And I should have."

"That's the part that bothers me," she told him. "These things are dangerous enough. Set them off in here and we'd lose this building. Wouldn't do you and me any good either." She reached the last tube and there were no more wires. The fireworks weren't connected to anything that might set them off. "That's all these are. Fireworks, and nobody's rigged them into a bomb, so far anyway."

The sheriff pulled out his cell phone. He punched in numbers and it rang twice before he interrupted a meeting of the Benteen County Board of Supervisors.

"You forget to tell me about a fireworks display for tonight?" the sheriff asked the chairman.

All things considered, he didn't think "Oops" was a satisfactory answer.

"Sorry about the interruption," Chairman Wynn said. His voice echoed slightly in the courthouse's official meeting room. It had been designed for a county that would grow rather than shrink. The architect had expected more supervisors and an audience, and maybe some effort to maintain its former elegance. Today, with all five Benteen County Supervisors present, it simply felt empty and shabby—except for the massive oak table around which they sat.

"The sheriff just discovered our little surprise to climax this year's Buffalo Springs Day. In light of what he's been investigating, we probably should have let him in on the secret."

The rest of the board agreed.

"Think I suggested that from the beginning," Supervisor Fair said in an I-told-you-so tone. The chairman doubted whether Fair had really cared. As the only Democrat on the board, the man took it as his duty to oppose anything that might otherwise be unanimous.

"Point of order, Mr. Chairman." Supervisor Babcock was the only woman on the board. She was a little bit of a thing, but the vote you had to convince on any difficult question. She had a way of persuading others into a majority that reflected her views on nearly every issue. "While I appreciate getting brought up to date on these acts of terror, and agree that we must immediately contact federal and state officials to get Englishman some assistance, I don't understand the purpose of this special meeting of the board. Hell, boys, I got a casserole out in the car I need to deliver to the potluck. Besides, if this is anything other than an informational session, aren't we in danger of violating open meeting laws?"

The chairman knew hers was a valid concern, but it wasn't every day you found your community under assault by international terrorists. He didn't have to remind her of that. Supervisor Haines did it for him.

"I think we've got some latitude under the Patriot Act," he said, taking it to a level the chairman hadn't expected. "Not that there's much we can do about this terror threat other than make those calls for help. And we'll do that, just as soon as we finish here. But we got us another problem that can't wait on niceties and it's related to these bombs."

"I hardly think…" Chairman Wynn began.

"Nobody's thought," Haines interrupted, banging his fist on the table for emphasis. "That's the trouble. Think now and think wind. Think how much money we've raised and committed to the Benteen County Cooperative Wind Farm. It's more than a million dollars so far. All of us at this table are invested, heavily. We stand to make a handsome profit for ourselves and our friends, and provide tremendous benefits for the community—or we did before these terrorists hit."

"What's the one got to do with the other?" Fair interrupted.

"We've had to court Windreapers from the get go. You and I know the wind doesn't blow any harder here than it does in parts of Kansas miles closer to the energy grid. What we're selling Windreapers is a signed, sealed and delivered package. Ten uninterrupted miles for their turbines, a community that has taxed itself and pulled in a matching grant for economic development that, along with what we've raised, will build their infrastructure and a connection to the grid. And a county willing to give them every tax break and incentive under the sun."

"I still don't get you," Fair said, pausing to chew on the pencil he was making notes with.

"These terrorists are specifically attacking Benteen County's energy resources. What do you think Windreapers is gonna do when they hear that? Gentleman, and Ms. Babcock, Benteen County will be out of the wind farm business."

"Surely we'll catch this guy and…" Finfrock began.

"Oh come on," Haines said. "You really think Englishman and his deputies have a chance of catching a pro from al Qaeda? And who says there's just one? There could be a whole sleeper cell here. These bombings could go on for months, years even."

"So we're out of contention for a wind farm," Chairman Wynn summarized. "I guess we absorb our costs, shut down our little corporation, and return what we can to our investors. Build us an industrial park with our matching funds and hope someone's willing to use it."

"That's one option," Haines said, shaking his head and making his hair ripple like a field of ripe wheat in the wind. It was clear he thought it wasn't an acceptable option. "The other is to save this thing. I was on the phone with Windreapers Corporation just a few minutes ago. I told them about Buffalo Springs Day. I said it was important to us, for political reasons, to announce we'd signed a contract with them today—that our wind farm isn't just a dream, it's a commitment. I said, because of those special circumstances, we were willing to pay them a premium, today only. They could take it or leave it because, on Monday, we've agreed to meet with a team from their competitors. They didn't like it much, but I got them to name a figure—three million dollars—if it's in their hands before midnight."

"My God, that is a premium," the chairman said. "We'll have to pay out better than five million in order to buy the rest of the land and build our part of the infrastructure. Can we do that?"

"You bet we can," Haines affirmed, "with a solid deal. I move we vote to seize the three outstanding sections using eminent domain right now."

"That won't go over with voters," Finfrock said.

Haines brushed their objections aside with a wave of his hand and a glimpse at the alternative. "It'll go over better than letting this deal fall through, losing money for all who've invested. We'll pay premium prices for those properties. That'll ease the hurt. But we've got to do this right now. We've got to pay Windreapers today or kiss it all goodbye."

"How?" Finfrock asked. "We haven't got three million. What little we do have is in the Farmers & Merchants. You think they're gonna open back up after one robbery so we can make the kind of withdrawal they'll think is a second hit? And it's damn near noon on Friday, already. Other banks are gonna be closing."

"Those are problems," Haines admitted. "But this is the electronic age. With a few phone calls we can wire the money to any account Windreapers desires. All it takes is a little creative borrowing from county revenues and the retirement and salary accounts. We can pull this off."

"I don't know." Chairman Wynn felt like it was all coming too fast. He understood Haines was proposing they violate all kinds of statutes, but Benteen County was an economic disaster area. If this wind farm, or some other financial miracle, didn't happen, he might preside over Benteen's slide into insolvency in the next few years. No politician worth his salt was willing to do that.

"We put together the package, arrange to have the funds available, then I take a code number for those funds and your approval and go meet with Windreapers in Denver tonight, face to face. When I have the signed contract in my hand, I transfer the funds. I know we're cutting a lot of corners here, but you all understand what's going to become of this county if we let this get away."

They did. Not five minutes later, far more than an open meeting law had been violated by the Benteen County Board of Supervisors.

◇◇◇

The front door to the Bisonte opened and a young couple came in, followed by the hulking bartender. Mad Dog watched the pair slide onto one bench and snuggle in a dark corner as the bartender went to fill their orders.

"Looks like some kind of wreck down by the Texaco," the bartender told Mad Dog and Janie as he passed. "Some other excitement, too. Your brother's pickup went flying toward the courthouse a few minutes ago behind his lights and siren."

Mad Dog nodded. "Might be something to do with Buffalo Springs Day."

"That it could," the man admitted, then took his company elsewhere after both declined refills.

"Thanks for the warning about my son," Mad Dog said. "But why'd you deliver it in person? You could have just called."

Janie reached into her purse and pulled out an envelope. "There are some pictures of Sam in here. Nothing more recent than when he got out of jail. He's almost twenty years older now, but I though they might help you recognize him."

Mad Dog took a quick glimpse, then stuffed them in a pocket. "I know Buffalo Springs is only about three miles from the edge of the world, but even we get faxes these days. Hell, I'm on the Internet. You could have sent me an email and a jpeg."

She shrugged. "I thought maybe, if I was here, he might not be so likely to act. That maybe I could…"

"Aren't you afraid of him yourself? You said you felt like he was a threat to you when he was little. How will you being here help slow him down? Seems more likely he'd be inclined to do a little two-for-one shopping."

"I didn't want him to hurt you."

"Weren't you listening to the bartender? My little brother, you remember Englishman, he's the sheriff of Benteen County. If you checked to see if I was still here, you probably knew that too. So, be honest Janie, why'd you really come?"

She bit her upper lip for a moment and stared at her hands, then she looked up and met his eyes. "I don't know, Mad Dog. I thought that was why I came. But maybe I wanted an excuse to see you. To find out who you really are. You only lose your heart for the first time once. I guess I wondered whether you were the bastard I ran away from or the guy I loved too much to stay with."

"Oh," Mad Dog said. He wondered too. In a way, this was the answer he'd hoped for. In another, it was the one that scared him the most. He reached down to ruffle Hailey's fur and reassure them both, only she wasn't there.

He looked for her. She was trotting around from behind the bar toward their table. She had something in her mouth. It was metallic and kind of pineapple shaped. She set it on the floor by his feet. It looked just like he remembered from all those war movies. It looked like a hand grenade.

"You get me any help yet?" The sheriff was coming out of the narrow hall that led back to the jail as Chairman Wynn emerged from the more opulent corridor that housed Benteen County government.

"Help?" the chairman jumped and spun toward the sound of the sheriff's voice. "Uhh, no, not yet." He reached for his cell phone. "I'll get right on it. You catch somebody?" Obviously, the chairman had noticed what part of the building the sheriff was coming from.

"Just your fireworks. I locked them in a cell up on the second tier where nobody's even apt to notice them. I'll give them back to you tonight, if I think it's safe. I left Deputy Parker across the street to keep an eye on the potluck in the park. Ideal situation, one deputy providing security for several hundred people."

The sheriff glanced over the chairman's shoulder as a parade of cars, Haines, followed by Babcock, Fair, and Finfrock, pulled out of the driveway at the front of the courthouse and turned south toward downtown.

"You have a board meeting?"

"No," the chairman shook his head. "Not really. Just bringing everybody up to speed on this crisis."

"That required everybody coming here?"

It was quiet in the foyer. Almost quiet enough to hear the gears turn while Chairman Wynn considered how to frame his answer. The chairman was as skittish as a bull calf before a Rocky Mountain Oyster banquet. The sheriff had been around minor felons, and teenagers, long enough to know when he was talking to someone with a guilty conscience.

"What's up? The board into something I should know about?"

"Oh no," the chairman reassured him. "We talked about what emergency measures we might take. Considered martial law, thought about how we'd evacuate the county if we had to."

"Hey," the sheriff protested, "you just vetoed my suggestion to shut down Buffalo Springs Day. Now you're talking about abandoning the county. That's a big turnaround. You sure you don't know something I should?"

"Englishman, what if we had to seize property to insure our community's existence?"

"You tell me whose property to seize. If it'll stop this bomber from hurting somebody, I'll do it, and worry about the court order later. You got a name?"

"No. We don't know anything that hasn't come from you. It's just, well, some of the potential solutions troubled me a little. You know, does the end justify the means, that sort of thing. But thanks, talking to you has made me feel a lot better."

"Sure." And what the hell was that about, the sheriff asked himself as the chairman headed for the front doors. He wondered if he should pursue it further, but Mrs. Kraus stuck her head out of his office and refocused his thoughts.

"Wynn Junior's on the line," she rasped. "Says there's a foreigner over at the Texaco acting suspicious. Wonders what he should do about it."

"What's suspicious about the guy?" the sheriff asked.

She reached up and ran her fingers through her darkened locks. "I'm not sure I understood this right, but Wynn seemed to think it was peculiar. This guy, he was asking where he could find some sagebrush."

The bartender met Mad Dog at the cash register. "Hey," Mad Dog greeted him. "You by any chance missing a hand grenade?"

That's what it was, even on close inspection. Not some kids' toy—the real thing, complete with the curved metal safety lever you released when you threw it, and the pin that kept that lever from releasing. As far as Mad Dog could tell, this thing would go off if you pulled the pin, released the lever, and waited a few seconds.

The bartender's eyes got big. "Where'd you find that?"

"I didn't find it. Hailey did."

"Damn," the bartender said, looking from Mad Dog to where Janie stood just behind him, and then down at Hailey. "I've heard of dogs playing fetch, but a thing like this could turn the game right serious." He grinned but Mad Dog didn't grin back. Neither did Janie. She'd remained wordless since she saw what Hailey had brought them. Hailey's only indication of amusement was the wicked twinkle in her eyes.

"Never knew Mr. Finfrock to leave that room unlocked," the man told them. "Come on back and I'll show you, then we can put it away."

He went down to the end of the bar farthest from the entrance and pushed on the door that led into the back. It didn't open.

"Huh," he muttered. "Guess she musta brushed it and it closed behind her." Mad Dog didn't comment. Hailey had an almost supernatural way of appearing on the other side of locked doors and closed windows. Mad Dog had learned not to bother trying to keep her penned. Nothing ever held her.

The bartender turned the handle and held the door for them. Janie seemed reluctant, so Hailey led the way. They went by a kitchen that persuaded Mad Dog to pass on future opportunities to sample the Bisonte's happy hour snacks. Next was a walk-in refrigerator, then, at the end of the hall, another anonymous door. It was also closed, and, when the bartender tried the knob, proved locked as well. He gave Hailey a real funny look as he dug into his pocket and came out with a ring of keys.

"I don't know where she got it," Mad Dog told him. "I just saw her bring it from behind the bar."

It was just one of those push-the-button-on-the-doorknob locks.

"Musta been locked but not closed," the man said, trying to convince himself. The door opened onto what was obviously a man's office with dark wood paneling, leather upholstery, plush carpet, and some impressive artwork—not for its quality, but for the imagination that had gone into combining Barbie-proportioned women with equally improbable weaponry.

"Mr. Finfrock, he's a collector," the bartender explained.

Mad Dog guessed he didn't mean of fine art.

There was a third door behind the desk. At last, one that was neither locked nor closed. It was a heavy metal door, more like you would expect on a safe. The bartender pushed it further open and reached in and flipped on the lights.

It was like a museum in there. Weapons, far more outrageous than those in the paintings in the office, hung on the walls. Rows of them, carefully displayed with focused lighting. Everything, from pistols that would have made Dirty Harry envious, to full-fledged machine guns trailing belts of gleaming ammunition. And a row of grenades in a variety of styles, from which Hailey's trophy was obviously missing. Antiques too, including a rifle that didn't yet have its own space. It was obviously a prize, though, since it lay on a piece of crushed velvet atop a glass case filled with gleaming steel blades.

"That must be a new one," the bartender said. Mad Dog bent and bobbed his head over it, looking for the right focal length.

Janie finally managed to find her voice. "Is it legal to own guns like these?"

"Sure thing, ma'am," the bartender reassured her. "Read your Second Amendment."

Mad Dog finally found the spot where the lettering on the rifle came into focus. "Sharps," he whispered.

The bartender must have thought he was looking at the display inside the glass. "Course they're sharp," he said, "they're swords."

There was a row of high-dollar vehicles at the curb when Chairman Wynn added his Cadillac and stepped out beside the bright yellow strand of crime scene tape surrounding the Farmers & Merchants. The building didn't look like it had been bombed. It wasn't missing any large sections, nor was it bowed out along the seams like an over-inflated balloon. The only indications were the missing glass in doors and windows, and the piece of skylight that hung from the end of some stretched insulation off the edge of the roof.

The street was deserted. Even the three or four businesses still operating in the immediate vicinity had shut down for the kickoff of Buffalo Springs Day. The chairman could hear the band tuning up in the distance. It reminded him he was supposed to be climbing in the back of a convertible about now, along with the rest of the board. Well, he supposed, the parade might wait on them. The community's future wouldn't.

He ducked under the tape and crunched his way across the broken glass to the front doors and stuck his head inside. "You guys in there?"

The manager came out of a hallway behind the remains of the teller's counter. He had something in his hand that looked heavy enough for Schwartznegger to pump in case he wanted to bulk up a little.

"That you, Mr. Chairman?"

"Sweet Jesus, Brown. Don't point that thing at me. What is it, anyway, a hand gun or an artillery piece?"

Brown let the weight of it pull the barrel back down toward the floor. "It's a fifty caliber Smith & Wesson," he said. "Most powerful hand gun you can buy. Just ask Supervisor Finfrock."

Supervisors Finfrock and Haines had followed Brown into the hall.

"I'll take your word for it," the chairman said. "Looks big enough to do more damage than that bomb."

Brown gave him a crooked smile, as if he agreed that, as far as destructive power went, he had the advantage on the bomber.

"More to the point," the chairman continued, "what're you doing with it?"

"He's guarding the vault," Finfrock explained.

The chairman edged past a piece of broken glass and stepped inside. There were papers everywhere. Deposit and withdrawal slips, receipts, and more he didn't recognize. "Guarding the vault? What would you want to do a fool thing like that for?"

Brown shrank a little. "I've got a duty to my investors."

"To risk your life? The money's insured, isn't it?"

"Yeah, but…"

"What the hell," Supervisor Haines said. "It's his life. Let him set in there by his safe if he wants to. No skin off our butts. We got more important business just now."

"They've been telling me," Brown said, leading the way back down the dusky hall toward his office in the rear of the building. "But there's some problems. You don't have that much money in your accounts. Not that's not borrowed against or that I know have got payments due."

Supervisors Babcock and Fair met them at the door. "Can you believe this?" Finfrock told the chairman. "This fool's saying he's not gonna let us have our money."

"You bet I'm not. I mean, you're askin' me to help you rob taxpayers and kite checks." Brown didn't raise the Smith & Wesson, but his knuckles got white around the grips.

"Now, let's not go calling each other names, here," the chairman said, wondering what they could do without Brown's cooperation. Kiss the Energy Cooperative goodbye, he supposed.

"Mr. Brown," Supervisor Haines said, "what we got here is a genuine emergency. Haven't you been listening to me and my fellow board members explain that to you?"

"Well, yeah, sure I have. But you can't go and spend money you don't have."

"Sure we can," Haines reassured him. "We're the government. Don't you know the United States is running a deficit?"

"Of course," Brown said, "only you're not the federal government."

"Actually, just now we are," Supervisor Haines continued. "I just got off the phone with the Homeland Security Department. Told them what's going on here. We've been delegated full authority. Donald Rumsfeld, himself, personally signed off on this thing. Until they can get a counterterrorism task force together and fly it in here, we got us a martial law situation. So you will release the money we tell you in the manner we specify, or we'll have your ass on the first helicopter out of here so's you can join the rest of the enemies of the state and see firsthand how you like the climate at Guantanamo."

The chairman was impressed. He would have believed Haines himself, but for the Rumsfeld bit. Rumsfeld was Defense. Tom Ridge was Homeland Security.

Brown wiped a sudden bead of sweat from his brow. He did it with the hand holding the fifty caliber and never seemed to notice when he dragged its blued steel across his forehead. He looked around the room and searched the eyes of each member of the board of supervisors. "Well," he told them, "you should have explained it real clear like that right off the bat. Now, how much do you need?"

◇◇◇

Judy had repacked her luggage at least three times. It was that or climb walls. Would she wear that little off-the-shoulder number if Englishman didn't come with her? Or was the black dress with the daring neckline a better choice? She packed one, then the other, then both.

What about bathing suits? Should she go with the conservatively cut Speedo or the bold bikini she'd bought a few years ago and never worn, except to model it for Englishman? The Speedo came out and the bikini went in. Or, did she even need a suit in France? Weren't there nude beaches everywhere? The bikini came out. Then both bikini and Speedo went back, along with doubts she would have the nerve to indulge in public nudity, even if it was the norm.

Was one pair of hiking shorts enough? And, considering how full her bag was getting, should she pack another?

She was anxious to head for Wichita's Mid-Continent Airport, now that she had her travel money and new hairdo. Especially since running those errands might have turned her into Buffalo Springs' most wanted fugitive. And it was almost noon. She started to call Englishman to tell him she was ready to leave, except she couldn't. The girls had taken the station wagon. They were supposed to be helping at the potluck. She could walk over to get the car easily enough, but she might be spotted and end up spending precious time explaining the incident at the Farmers & Merchants. And, she admitted to herself, she wasn't looking forward to telling the Heathers about her sudden vacation plans, especially if Englishman wasn't going. While there was a chance he might, she waited, and considered outfits and European weather patterns and her fantasies of what two weeks in Paris could be like. Until the headache started.

Damn inconvenient time for a migraine, she thought. She popped a couple of super-strength pain killers and got ready for it. She closed drapes and turned the living room into the quietest, darkest place possible, dampened a washcloth and filled it with crushed ice, then lay down on the couch with it draped over her eyes and forehead.

Was this the price of getting old? She wasn't even menopausal yet, but already her hormones were doing crazy things to her body—like throwing these migraines at her. They didn't last long—that was the bright side. She just had to wait them out. Then the pain hit and there was no bright side, except the arc of lightning that danced inside her head.

She had just reached the stage where she wondered if she would have the strength to make it to the bathroom if the nausea got any worse when everything got worse. Something screamed in her ears and, for a moment, it felt like her head must have shattered into thousands of pieces that would cascade off the sofa and litter the hardwood floor. She surprised herself. She managed to sit up. The agony of rising was worth it if she managed to keep the phone from ringing again. For a moment she just held the handset, savoring the fact that it couldn't continue making that titanic assault on her eardrums. One end of the phone was making softer noises at her, insistent ones. She finally held it near an ear.

"Judy?" It was Mrs. Kraus' raspy voice. "Are you there? Can you hear me?"

Making herself get the phone had carried her past the migraine's edge. She could handle the sounds Mrs. Kraus was producing if she didn't let the earpiece get too close. The dim light filtering past the curtains didn't blind her anymore, though she saw two of everything. Double vision—that would go away too, just like the nausea which had almost vanished. She thought she might be able to speak if she had to. Under the circumstances, she decided to give it a try.

"Yes." The effort nearly exhausted her. She wobbled a little, but she knew it was over now. In a few minutes she would merely have an awful headache. By the time she got to Wichita, it would have subsided to a dull throb. By the time she was over the Atlantic it would be gone entirely. Until the next one.

"Are you all right? You don't sound like it."

Judy concentrated. "I'm fine," she lied. "What can I do for you?"

"Well, Englishman asked me to call, see if you were still there." There was a space between the words and Judy's ability to comprehend them. And a moment more to decipher the hesitation in Mrs. Kraus' voice. Mrs. Kraus might have agreed to make this call for Englishman, but that didn't mean she was happy to get stuck with it.

"Englishman's not coming, is he?" Judy was suddenly sure of it. If he were, he would have called her himself.

"He's doing his best," Mrs. Kraus countered. "There've been three bombs in town today, Judy. Notes claiming they're set by al Qaeda. He's got two deaths to investigate. And there's been an attempt on Mad Dog's life."

"I'm still leaving by twelve-thirty, whether he's here or not. You tell him that. Then tell him I'll phone from Paris to let him know if I'll be back."

There was a long silence. Mrs. Kraus sighed. The poor woman must have known she was stepping in a hornet's nest, but she hadn't realized the hornets were already riled.

"Okay, Judy," Mrs. Kraus said. "I'll tell him he's got till just after midnight. Give him a little extra time if you can."

"Not midnight," Judy said. "Half past noon. I'm leaving here at half past noon."

"You can't."

"Why? Why can't I?" Judy was ready to argue.

"'Cause it's already five to one," Mrs. Kraus said. And then she asked Judy if she were all right again, only Judy didn't answer because she'd dropped the phone and sprinted to where she could see the clock on the kitchen wall. It was twelve-fifty-six and she still hadn't gotten the car. Hadn't changed and wasn't on the road somewhere between Nickerson and Hutchinson where she'd planned to be…because somehow those few minutes on the couch had turned into more than an hour.

◇◇◇

The sheriff was spotted with mud and mulched plant parts from the blast. So, he noticed, was Deputy Wynn, and neither of them had found anything in the ditch more enlightening than a discarded beer bottle and an empty chewing tobacco tin.

"That bomb's in a gazillion pieces," Wynn Some whined.

"Let's make one more pass through the crater in the ditch," the sheriff told him. He started to wade back down in order to lead by example when the woman who ran the cash register at the Texaco stuck her head out the door and hollered.

"Is Englishman still over there?"

He must be more of a mess than he'd thought.

"I'm here," he said, trudging back to the edge of the blacktop and waving.

"Oh, sorry, Sheriff. Mrs. Kraus is on the phone. Says she can't raise your cell anymore. Nor your deputy's neither."

The sheriff drew his cell phone and checked to see that it was still on. It was, but the display told him it was in desperate need of a charge, something he'd forgotten to give it last night.

"Thanks," he told her. "Wynn, you turn this ditch into a grid and go back through every bit of it while Mrs. Kraus tells me what new catastrophe has struck. And check your cell phone, see if it's on."

The highway was empty and there weren't any customers at the Texaco. According to his watch, the potluck had begun almost an hour ago. It didn't pay to be late to a potluck.

The front door was propped open to allow the woman at the cash register to share a day the sheriff would have described as perfect—but for its surplus of bombs and bodies. He paused to brush himself off and stomp the worst of the muck from his boots before he stepped in and took the phone she offered.

"Sorry," the sheriff told Mrs. Kraus. "Cell's lost its charge, and Wynn probably didn't have his on."

"Lots of people been trying to get you," Mrs. Kraus said in the dulcet tones of a metal file taking a burr off a plowshare. "Doc first. Your latest delivery isn't anybody local, far as he can tell. Says he's amazed at your powers of deduction, though. Your motorcyclist was a she."

"She?" That took the sheriff by surprise. The body had been badly mashed by the tree, but he should have at least considered the possibility. Too much going on, and all of it too fast. "What else? Any more bombs turn up?"

"Well, your brother just walked in with a hand grenade. Good thing I wasn't close to my Glock when he showed it to me or you might need to be taking him over so Doc could do his third autopsy of the day."

"Hand grenade? Mad Dog?"

"Yeah, seems Hailey uncovered a cache of weapons over at the Bisonte. Mad Dog and Janie Jorgenson brought it here to show you. Your brother, he's a wise ass. Said maybe we should call the White House and tell them we may have found where Saddam hid those weapons of mass destruction."

"Mad Dog still there?"

"Nah, sorry. Guess I should have kept him around for you to talk to, only I shooed them off. Thought maybe he and Janie might have some getting reacquainted to do. You know what a hopeless romantic I am."

"Mad Dog say what else they found? Bomb making materials maybe?"

"Don't know. I figured you'd want to look for yourself. Judge Livermore came by to drop me off a plate from the potluck and I had him draw up a search warrant."

"Good thinking." Benteen County had such a small population and so few major crimes that the sheriff's department often didn't trouble with the legal niceties. Folks trusted the spirit of the law rather than its specifics, and the fact that everybody knew each other meant public guilt didn't necessarily require a verdict to result in suitable penalties.

"I don't think Craig Finfrock's at the Bisonte just now. The supervisors haven't come back since they went to the Farmers & Merchants. Could be across the street at the potluck, or downtown still, checking to see if the bank robber cleaned out their personal accounts."

"They make that call for help Chairman Wynn promised?" A pair of butterflies fluttered in the Texaco's open door and landed on the paperback rack—on one of those romance novels that show a pair of impossibly beautiful people whose garments have been rent in tasteful but titillating fashion by their adventures. What one butterfly proceeded to do to the other would only be implied inside the cover on which they perched.

"Not that I know of. So, after I called Judy for you, I called the FBI."

"You got Judy? She was still there?"

"Yeah. You owe me for that one, Englishman. I know you're busy, but that's a call you should have made yourself."

"But she's waiting for me? She's not going?"

"I didn't say that. It was a peculiar conversation. She sounded preoccupied to begin with, then gave me a message to tell you she was leaving promptly at half past noon, only it was already later than that and when I told her so she stopped talking to me. That wasn't long ago, but I'd say she's probably on the road to Wichita, even as we speak."

"Damn," the sheriff muttered. "Well, the flight's not till four-forty. If this trip to the Bisonte breaks the bomber thing, maybe I can still catch her. Deputy Wynn and I came up empty here. We'll go to the Bisonte, now, and see if we can turn around our day. Call Wynn's cell if you need me. I'm going to relieve him of it."

"Whoa," Mrs. Kraus said. "Don't you want to know what the FBI had to say?"

The sheriff popped himself upside the head with the palm of one hand. "I'm sorry, Mrs. Kraus. Of course I do."

"I spoke to the Wichita office. I spelled it all out for an agent—pipe bomb, letter bomb at the Farmers & Merchants, third device at the Texaco. Told him how we got notes claimed it was al Qaeda."

"And?" the sheriff asked when she paused for longer than he liked.

"He said 'Yes, ma'am' and 'No, ma'am' and 'We'll get right on it, ma'am.' Real polite fellow, but I could tell he thought I was some fruitcake. I begged him to check us out and get back to me."

"And you haven't heard from him," the sheriff guessed.

"And don't expect to. Not soon, anyway."

"I'll try the KBI on our way to the Bisonte. They might take us seriously." He thanked her again and hung up and found something resembling the creature from the black lagoon standing in the door and dripping on the tiles while it tried to give him a hunk of metal with its outstretched hand.

"Could this be important?" Wynn Some asked.

The sheriff took it and decided it could. It was a battered timing device. The blast had bent it up pretty badly, but it was clear you couldn't set the thing for more than sixty seconds.

If Hailey's wound hadn't already been treated, the blood on the front seat of the Cooper would have panicked Mad Dog big time. Instead, even though the car still had less than four thousand miles on it, the damage to the upholstery hardly fazed him. He pulled out his handkerchief and cleaned the passenger's seat for Janie, let Hailey make herself comfortable in the rear, then demonstrated that the little car had room for big people by joining them.

"Where to?" Janie asked.

"We're kind of late for the potluck. If we go, I need to stop by Dillons and get a couple of pies from the deli. We could do that, then see if there are any leftovers in the park."

"Will the celebration still be on?" She shrugged and answered herself. "Of course it will. This is Buffalo Springs. If bombs are going off around town, people will want to get together even more so they can talk about them."

"I expect lots of your old friends are there. They'd love to see you."

She smiled. "That would be nice, but maybe not today. Can we get some sandwiches at that deli, put together a picnic lunch and go find a quiet spot where we can talk some more?"

"Sure," he agreed, pleased by her preference. He started the Cooper and guided it around the far side of the park, away from the lunch crowd. People waved and called to them. Mad Dog just beeped the Cooper's horn and waved back and kept right on going. He had to hurry when he got down to Main to beat the parade headed their way. Mad Dog was hard pressed to remember the last time he'd seen such a crowd in Buffalo Springs, or spent such an eventful day.

Janie broke their comfortable silence. "You should have told Mrs. Kraus about my...our son."

"Yeah, I know," Mad Dog agreed. "I'll let Englishman know, soon as I get a chance. I think the world of Mrs. Kraus, but somehow, everything she learns turns into communal knowledge. No need to expose you to more gossip than our being together today will have already started."

"I got used to some people thinking I was a tramp while we were dating. It wasn't much worse than just being poor with no father. But really, Mad Dog. You should have given her those pictures so she could make copies for your brother and his deputies. The more people keeping an eye out for him, the safer you'll be."

Mad Dog downshifted and pulled into the Dillons lot. He patted his pocket. "I looked at the pictures. I didn't recognize him. Most likely, that means he's not been around here long, and, like every stranger, he'll be treated with a healthy dose of suspicion by everyone in the community. Especially after what's been going on today. He won't be hard to find, Janie, though I'm not sure I want him found."

"I know," she said. "In spite of everything, he's still my son."

The parking lot was almost deserted. Everyone was watching the parade or enjoying the picnic. Mad Dog parked in the middle of the empty lot, where no one would pull in next to the Cooper and open a door into it, or bang their shopping cart against its pristine paint.

"What would you like for our picnic?"

"You remember that place on Calf Creek where we used to go swimming?"

Mad Dog remembered. They used to park his '57 Chevy near a bridge and hike through the shallow water around the first bend and out of sight of the road. There had been a beach-like patch of sand along the north bank under a clump of thick cottonwoods that ensured privacy. The water in Calf Creek, unless it was flooding, was never deep enough for swimming, but there'd been a spot where the current had dug out a hole at least three feet deep. In the summer, sitting in that hole had been like sitting in a hot tub. He recalled the gentle caress of the bubbling current, and similar ones exchanged with the girl in the seat beside him. He felt an almost forgotten stirring deep inside and his voice was a little husky when he said, "I remember."

"I'd like to have our picnic there," she said. Her cheeks were a little flushed and her eyes very intense.

Mad Dog cleared his throat. "I meant, what would you like to eat?"

Her eyes ran over him and she smiled. It was that wicked, elfin smile that had hung on his memory and made his heart ache for more than a decade after she left. "Anything you like."

"Uhh, right," Mad Dog gulped. He felt as clumsy as a teenager and practically tripped on the curb as he aimed for the Dillons entrance. In his head, he was eighteen again and there was a hot seventeen-year-old he loved more than life itself back in his car. This was time travel. It was too good to be true but he didn't care. He patted the back pocket of his jeans to see if he had a condom in there before he remembered he hadn't carried one for just-in-case in a long time.

"You're insane," he told himself. Himself agreed and wondered how fast he could get from the Dillons parking lot to their old swimming hole on Calf Creek. Not fast enough, a portion of his anatomy answered.

132 J. M. Hayes

"Hi, Mom," Heather said to her cell phone. She was helping move tubs of ice cream out of the freezer in the Buffalo Springs Non-Denominational Church. The ice cream social would begin when the parade ended at Veterans Memorial Park. Two of Two was out there already, filling balloons with helium and showing kids how to make squeaky voices. Entertaining that hunk who was home from KU for a few days, too, and who was seriously pleased with the outfit Two had chosen that morning. One of Two might have felt left out, except she wasn't so much moving ice cream as supervising its movement. A couple of guys who'd been so far ahead of her in high school that she'd gone unnoticed by them had belatedly discovered her at the potluck. One was a junior at Ft. Hays, the other a senior at K-State. Both were handsome and mature and she was enjoying the way they were competing for her attention.

"Why didn't you come to the potluck?" she asked, while each of the guys tried to carry more tubs than the other.

"Something came up," her mother said. There was a long pause as if her mom couldn't decide whether to tell her what that something was.

"What's that, Mom?" Heather asked. She had to stifle a giggle because the K-Stater was exaggerating his efforts to keep a gigantic stack of ice cream balanced, like some comedian from a silent movie clip.

"I, uhh…I need the car. Where is it?"

"You want me to bring it to you?"

"It'd probably be quicker if I came and got it."

"I don't mind," Heather told her mother. She didn't, really. It would only take a minute, and maybe her helpers, or one of them, might come along.

"Where is it, Heather? I'm late."

"For what, Mom?"

There was another pause and Heather thought she could feel the steam her mother was generating through the phone's receiver. "The car's just north of Bertha's on Adams, Mom. But you probably should let me get it for you. The parade's coming and that's where they'll end up. You might not have time to get here before they block you in."

"All right. Just bring the damn car. I've got to catch a plane for Paris."

"What?" Heather asked, suddenly oblivious to the guys vying for her attention. Her mother didn't answer. The dial tone suddenly hummed in her ear.

The Kansas Bureau of Investigation knew the state had a Benteen County, and that its sheriff was named English.

"How's the weather in Buffalo Springs, Sheriff English?" the agent asked as the sheriff dodged the parade on Main Street.

"Probably about as perfect as it is in Topeka."

"Which means we'll either have a hard freeze next week, or hit a hundred."

"Uhh, look," the sheriff said, anxious to get past the niceties. "We got a situation here."

"Yes, sir," the agent said, suddenly businesslike.

"We've had some bombings." The sheriff made a left on Pear so he could slip around the block and enter the Bisonte's parking lot via the alley instead of Main.

"Bombings? Plural, as in more than one?"

"Three so far, with notes that hint at an al Qaeda connection."

"You shoveling your barnyard on me?" the man in Topeka asked. The sheriff realized how crazy it sounded—al Qaeda in Buffalo Springs, Kansas. "How many killed?"

"Two," the sheriff said. "Though they didn't die in the bombings, actually. In fact, nobody's been hurt by the bombs, so far."

"Two dead, but not from your terrorist bombings?"

"That's right. One was shot by a Cheyenne arrow and the other lost control of a motorcycle. I think that one was the archer from the first death."

The sheriff paused to catch his breath and make another turn. The man in Topeka paused too. The sheriff could practically hear the silent disbelief halfway across the state. He slid into the alley and bounced to a parking spot beside the bar.

"Look," he continued. "I know the al Qaeda thing is unlikely, but we're a real small department and we're spread too thin for stuff like this and…"

"What's that noise in the background?" the KBI agent interrupted.

It took the sheriff a minute to realize what the man meant. He must have heard the Buffalo Springs High marching band, in the middle of a cacophony that faintly resembled something by John Philip Sousa.

"It's a band," the sheriff explained. "There's a parade for our Buffalo Springs Day festival. I tried to get the county supervisors to cancel it but…"

"Harley Beaudean, right? Jeez, Harley, you really had me going for a minute."

"This is no joke, agent," the sheriff said. "This is a legitimate crisis. A bizarre one I'll grant…"

"Harley, I got too much caseload to listen to any more BS just now. I'll meet you for a beer after work and you can tell me where you found that awful music."

"Don't you have caller ID or something?"

"Good one, Harley. Really good. You can scoop me more of this over at the Bullfrog about five-thirty." Then the man hung up.

The sheriff thought about hitting redial and trying to convince the KBI he wasn't a practical joker named Harley. Then he considered what might happen if he wasted time on the phone while a fourth device went off in the middle of that parade or during the festivities in Veterans Memorial Park. He had no time to argue, especially not if the source of their bombs lay behind the door to the adjacent bar.

The sheriff holstered Wynn's cell phone and drew his .38 Police Special, opened the cylinder. Five bullets, the hammer over an empty chamber, just the way he wanted it.

"Whatcha doin'?" Wynn asked. The sheriff wondered when Wynn had last seen him draw his gun.

"Lock and load," the sheriff said. The phrase surprised him as much as it probably did his deputy. Embarrassed him a little too, as he realized how much adrenaline had to be flowing for him to say something so Hollywood macho. "Let's see if Osama has moved al Qaeda headquarters right here to the heart of Kansas."

"So that's what the luggage was for. Do you know anything about this trip to Paris?" Two asked her sister as the girls made their way across the park to where they'd left the station wagon. Three decreasingly enthusiastic upperclassmen, volunteers for ice cream and balloon duty, watched from where the Heathers had left them with a half-hearted promise to be right back.

"Mom always wanted to go." Heather English dug keys out of her purse as they edged around a grove of evergreens. Little of the park's two square blocks was ever mowed or weeded because of the county's strained budget. They stayed on a path to avoid stickers and brambles. "You've heard her talk about it. Dad's always got some excuse to put it off. What's hard for me, though, is they made these plans without telling us."

"No way Englishman will go today." Two said. "I mean, Judy's going to have to wrestle him onto a plane even when he's ready to take time off. He won't leave while a mad bomber's running around."

"There were two sets of luggage, and Dad's passport. But Mom just said *she* had to catch a plane to Paris. She didn't mention Dad. You think Mom would go by herself?"

"Hey, you're the one who's known her all your life," Two said. "What do you think?"

"Paris," One said. "Jeez. If she's really mad at him, she might go alone."

The girls scrambled into the elderly Taurus as the Buffalo Springs High Band rounded the corner down on Main and headed their way. The Ford started without complaint and backed onto Jefferson, irritating a small group of citizens who had to make way by getting out of the middle of the street, thus giving up the prime locations they'd chosen to watch the parade approach.

"Mom sounded weird," Heather said, turning right on Cherry. Their house was at the end of the fourth block east of the park, just northwest of the Buffalo Springs Schools. "I mean, it was like she was trying to get the car and slip out of town, and when she had to tell me where she was going she hung up so she wouldn't have to explain."

"That's not like Judy," the second Heather said.

They pulled up at the stop sign at Adams. Not a rolling stop. The full thing, and checked carefully in both directions before proceeding. After all, their father was sheriff.

"Like I said," the original Heather explained, "if she's totally ticked at Dad, there's no telling what she might do. She didn't want me to bring the car. She wanted to come get it herself until I told her she might get blocked by the parade. That was the first she mentioned Paris."

"I don't get it," the second Heather said. "This is like too weird."

And it was.

They stopped in front of the house and parked under the shade of a pair of elms that flanked their walk. The Heathers were out of the car and going through the front gate, side by side, when the door opened and a stranger came out carrying a pair of suitcases.

"Help me with these, will you girls?" the stranger said with a familiar voice.

"Mom?" Heather said.

"Judy?" Heather echoed.

Then in chorus, the girls demanded, "What have you done to your hair?"

◇ ◇ ◇

"Finfrock in?" The sheriff asked the bartender. The man slouched in the Bisonte's front door, sucking a toothpick and watching a series of convertibles pass. The cars were filled with pretty girls waving to the sparse crowd. Normally, those girls would have been flanking each of the Benteen County Commissioners and the sheriff would have been out front, in the county black and white, leading the procession with his light bar blazing.

"Aw, damn," the man said, straightening and displaying enough muscle inside his tight tee shirt to cause Deputy Wynn to back-pedal a couple of steps and put his hand on the butt of his gun. It didn't matter. The sheriff had disabled the deputy's service revolver years ago, after it became clear that an armed Wynn was a threat to public safety. The sheriff made him turn it in at the end of every shift and kept it locked in a drawer in his desk so his deputy couldn't take it out for target practice and discover it had been rendered merely ornamental. The sheriff had worried about leaving Wynn defenseless in case of a real emergency, but there had been no more than a couple of those in Benteen County since he'd become sheriff many terms ago. Besides, he only had to recall the time Wynn Some drew down on a crowd of senior citizens because he thought one of them had hit him with a snowball. One had, but the sheriff never let Wynn carry a gun with a firing pin again.

"Mad Dog actually went and told you, didn't he?" the bartender complained. "I was hopin' he was joshing me. I know he's got kind of a liberal outlook on guns and all, but I didn't think he was a tattletale."

"That was a hand grenade he brought to my office," the sheriff countered, "not a gun. And we've had three bombings in Buffalo Springs this morning. It would take one hell of a bad citizen not to tell me about discovering illegal explosives today."

"Illegal. Sheriff, ain't you read your Second Amendment?"

"Many times. It doesn't mention hand grenades."

"Thing was just innocently lying back there in Mr. Finfrock's private collection. I mean, it was more like it was in a museum until that wolf of Mad Dog's let herself back there and brought it out into the bar."

"Which brings me back to my first question," the sheriff said. "Finfrock here?"

"Nope. He's not. I figured he'd be in one of them convertibles that just went by."

The convertibles had been replaced by the clowns and the man on stilts. Next would come the horseback contingent. From marching band to the last of the pretend cowboys, the whole parade would have passed in under five minutes.

"I want to see this museum," the sheriff said.

That's when the bartender should have asked to see the search warrant that was still with Mrs. Kraus back over in the courthouse, but he didn't.

"Sure," he said. "Normally, I couldn't show you. Mr. Finfrock, he keeps it locked up in that back room of his. Only this morning, for some reason, seems he went off and left it open. Had to be, right, else how'd Hailey get in there to steal that grenade in the first place?"

The bartender stepped aside and held the door for the sheriff and Deputy Wynn. "Can I get either of you gentlemen anything?" he said, as he escorted them toward the bar. The place was empty. "Hardly anybody been in this morning," he explained when the sheriff declined the offer and before Wynn could ask for a free soda pop. "You'da thought Mr. Finfrock would just leave us closed till this afternoon. Hard to compete with a potluck and free ice cream. Should do real good later on."

The sheriff agreed. Buffalo Springs Day got him an occasional rowdy drunk whose expectations of coming home for the reunion didn't match the reality. The sheriff followed the bartender and Wynn followed him and they made their own little parade to Finfrock's office.

"You're lucky I didn't lock this back up after Mad Dog and that pretty lady left. Only I wanted to show Mr. Finfrock how I found it, and how that wolf got back here. See, I don't got keys to his collection room, though he lets me in most times I want."

The man opened the last door and stepped inside, reaching over and snapping on the lights. Museum, the sheriff decided, had been an accurate description. There was enough weaponry to outfit one of those second-amendment militias the bartender seemed to favor, but it was all lovingly displayed in cases and shelves covered with soft cloth. Some of the more exotic stuff was in glass display cases.

The sheriff was no arms expert, but he recognized a Browning automatic rifle, an M16, several varieties of AK47, a MAC-10, and then some heavier stuff including a .50 caliber machine gun. The row of grenades, minus the one with Mrs. Kraus over in the office, was right where she'd told him to expect it.

Only a few feet away was an ancient rifle. It lay atop a glass case filled with sabers and epees and such. It was a Sharps buffalo gun, just like Mrs. Kraus had reported Mad Dog found—and just like the gun Bradley Davis, director of *This Old Tepee*, had said was stolen from the same locked cabinet as the Cheyenne bow and arrows connected to the two corpses in Klausen's Funeral parlor.

"What about this?" the sheriff asked, pointing out the antique atop the display of edged weapons.

"The buffalo gun? That's new. Mr. Finfrock, he traded for it just last night."

"Who'd he trade with?" the sheriff demanded.

The bartender shook his head. "I don't know. Was my night off. But I heard Mr. Finfrock grousing about what he had to give for it." The man crouched down and opened the door to a cabinet under a row of modern machine pistols. He reached in and hauled out a small drum and showed it to the sheriff and his deputy proudly.

"We used to have two of these."

The sheriff bent and took a closer look. The drum was stenciled with a complex series of specifications. Most of the numbers meant nothing to him, but one caught his eyes. It read, "TNT equivalence: 118%."

"Is this…" The sheriff had a sinking feeling that he knew what was inside.

"That's right," the bartender nodded, enthusiastically. "It's C4 plastic explosive. Plastique. I betcha there's enough in here to level most of Buffalo Springs."

Janie Jorgenson was aroused. It surprised her when she finally recognized the feelings. She thought she was panting nearly as hard as Hailey, in the back seat, as she watched Mad Dog's still cute butt disappear into the Dillons. She hadn't felt this way since…well, not for a long time. Not since the hot flashes and the insomnia and the mood swings came along. Thank goodness those were past her now, but with them had gone her femininity, or so she'd thought. Until she'd seen that familiar look in Mad Dog's eyes. Was that part of what brought her back here?

She remembered their visits to that swimming hole on Calf Creek like they were yesterday. Hot sun, hot water, hot bodies pressed against each other. They had been drunk with the need for each other then. She flushed and tried to make herself sober up and return to here and now. She wouldn't be wearing that same svelte body to Calf Creek today. Of course, neither would Mad Dog, though she thought he might still look pretty good at a skinny dip. All she'd meant to do was get him out of town for a few hours. Get him off the streets and away from danger until…

Janie was fifty-seven years old, and though she swam at least an hour four days a week, she was carrying a lot more flesh these days. And not where the girls in the centerfolds or on the movie screens carried it. She had cellulite and stretch marks and varicose veins, to say nothing of boobs that were more pendulous than perky. She couldn't imagine how Mad Dog would be able to look at her without cringing if she shucked out of her clothes the way she found herself wanting to.

And there was Sam to deal with. Running off to indulge in a fantasy frolic while trying to pretend the last forty years hadn't happened wouldn't do a thing about Sam.

Hailey stuck her nose in Janie's face and licked her, as if she'd been following this internal dialogue and wanted to offer encouragement. And then, with surprising agility, Hailey hopped into the driver's seat, scooted around to face out the driver's window, and launched herself into the parking lot.

"Hailey, come back," Janie called.

Hailey, of course, paid her no attention, except for a reassuring glance over one shoulder as if to say, don't worry, I know what I'm doing.

An old Ford pickup with a camper shell on the back pulled into the Dillons lot. A pair of dark-skinned women, Hispanic maybe, with long shiny-black hair popped the doors and got out and waved toward the grocery store. Janie turned and looked in that direction. She hadn't noticed him before. He was sitting against the wall, legs folded underneath him. He waved casually back, unfolded those legs, and stood. He was a big man with steel gray braids hanging beneath a billed cap. Not Mexican, she decided, Native American.

The man started across the parking lot toward the truck. He didn't get far before Hailey trotted over and sat in front of him, directly in his path. Most people would have shied away from an animal they feared might bite, or sidestepped her, knowing she was somebody else's responsibility. The man with the braids stopped dead still and considered her. He said something that Janie couldn't hear and reached out and presented his hand for her to sniff. Hailey accepted the offer, let him pat her on the head, then lay down. It wasn't a casual on-her-side sort of down, but perfectly straight, legs neatly balanced on either side of her body so that you could picture her being up and about her business—including tearing out his throat if that were what she wanted—in an instant.

The old Indian gently lowered himself to the asphalt and sat, cross legged again, in front of her.

That was when Mad Dog came out of the Dillons. He had a couple of paper bags in his arms and a big silly smile on his face as he glanced at where Janie sat in the Mini. And then he noticed the tableau a few yards away. His smile disappeared and his face got serious. He walked by Janie without a word.

Just before he got there, Hailey stood and circled slightly and then lay back down in that relaxed but dangerous looking way of hers. Mad Dog put the paper bags on the ground in front of the old man and sat on the pavement as well. The three of them formed a little circle, the bags of picnic makings in the middle. Mad Dog said something. The old man answered, then bent and touched the ground and the bags four times. What he was doing seemed formal and solemn. Hailey opened her mouth. She looked from one man to the other with what Janie thought was a wolfish smile. Janie couldn't hear them from the car. There was just enough breeze to carry their soft voices away, and just enough echo of something nearly recognizable being played by a distant band to drown them out.

Janie Jorgenson watched, trying to understand what was going on. Mad Dog, it seemed, had given their lunch to the old man. At least when the two of them got to their feet, the Indian gestured and one of the women from the truck came and took the paper bags. Then Mad Dog pointed toward the vacant lot next door. There was a little picnic table just off the edge of the parking lot where it appeared people could take food from the deli. The two of them seated themselves there and Janie began to wonder if Mad Dog had forgotten all about her.

Still, she was fascinated when the Indian pulled cigarettes out of a pocket and lit one and passed it to Mad Dog like he was passing a joint. Mad Dog didn't smoke. The ashtray in his car had never been used and she would have smelled it on his clothes if he were a smoker.

Mad Dog didn't look her way, hadn't since he came out of the grocery store. She was starting to get a little angry. She got more so when they lit and shared a second cigarette.

Eventually, she let herself out of the Mini Cooper and stomped across the parking lot, following Main back to where she'd left her rental car. Mad Dog didn't seem to notice. Hailey did, but Hailey didn't come after her.

So much for the potency of her revived feminine charms, and her ability to lead Mad Dog around by his…Well, she wouldn't need to worry about going skinny dipping on Calf Creek today. The hell with the hunt for Sam, she thought. Mad Dog deserved whatever happened to him. This was just like when he'd sent her to get an abortion while he met a football recruiter. Something had come along that interested him more than she did. Her first true love had abandoned her once again.

Chairman Wynn knocked on the jamb beside the open door to the sheriff's office. Mrs. Kraus looked up from her desk and put a hand over the phone. It wasn't like the chairman to knock, not even on closed doors. "Yes, sir?"

"Any word on our bomber?" The chairman edged inside and then slouched his way to the counter.

"Let me put you on hold," Mrs. Kraus told the phone. The chairman could have just listened while she continued trading gossip with a friend to find out what he wanted to know, but she preferred to maintain the illusion that she was a woman whose dedication to her job was constant. "I'll take that report on your missing parakeet in a minute."

She put the phone back in its cradle and faced the chairman. "Englishman and your boy are following leads," she told him. She wasn't sure whether she should mention where those leads had taken them. "Weren't you with the rest of the board? They all back there in the courthouse now, or have they gone over to the ice cream social?"

"Fair and Babcock are in the park. Haines and Finfrock are making some arrangements. Should be done in a minute and then we'll go over and join the festivities."

Chairman Wynn was a nice enough fellow, once you got past his tendency to treat everyone who worked for the county as a personal servant unless an election loomed. If you were in legitimate trouble, you could count on him being there for you, even if it meant cash out of his pocket. But Mrs. Kraus couldn't remember the last time he'd acted like this, almost subservient to her. It was weird and she tried to think why this was happening. Then it dawned on her.

"You couldn't get us any outside help, could you?"

The chairman shuffled his feet and chewed on his lip. "Well, no," he admitted. "I tried, but everybody seems to think it's a practical joke."

Mrs. Kraus remembered her own efforts and sympathized. But here was an opportunity to remind the chairman that big fish in little ponds could get lost when they tried to play in the ocean.

"What about your political connections? I thought, you being such a force in the Kansas Republican Party, you could get straight through to the folks in Homeland Security."

The chairman blushed. "So did I. National folks treated me like a prankster, or worse. I did get one of the bigwigs at state level to pay attention. Finally convinced him I was serious and then he up and asks me what I expect him to do about it. Whose budget's gonna cover the cost of say, sending us a Kansas National Guard unit, and where do I think I'm going to find one with explosives experts anyway. They're probably all deployed in Iraq, he told me. He said, unless we're starting to stack the dead up like cordwood and CNN is flying in a team to give our terrorist attacks live coverage, we're pretty much on our own. Lord, last thing we want is media coming here."

The blow to the chairman's ego must have been substantial. Mrs. Kraus thought back to her conversation with the FBI agent that, so far, had produced no response. "Well, hell," she growled. "You tried. Besides, there ain't been any more bombs."

Her little pep talk put some starch in the supervisor's spine. He wandered over to where the front windows opened on the park and gave the office some much needed aromatherapy. The sounds of happy people enjoying mountains of frozen cholesterol wafted in. He bent and smelled the honeysuckle vines that bracketed the windows and took a long look at the glorious day outside. When he turned back into the room, he seemed pretty much himself again.

That was when Haines and Finfrock came in. And when the second phone line rang. "Sheriff's office," she said.

"Finfrock there?" Englishman's voice was weak and interrupted by enough popping sounds to remind her she wanted to pick up some Orville Redenbacher's at the Dillons.

"That you, Englishman? You're breaking up bad."

"We're all set," Finfrock told the chairman. "Got airline reservations to put Haines in Denver in time to meet with Windreapers. We could still pull this off."

Haines wandered over by the sheriff's desk and leafed through the faxes that had come in this afternoon. Junk faxing was a fine art that cost the county lots of waste paper. Mrs. Kraus hadn't gotten to them on a busy day like this.

"We damn well better pull it off," the chairman said.

"Finfrock?" the sheriff asked Mrs. Kraus. "Where is Supervisor Finfrock?"

"Finfrock's right here. Wanna speak to him?"

The supervisors caught her reference and their own conversation switched topics. "That the sheriff?" the chairman asked.

"He want me?" Finfrock said. "Give me the phone."

"Got my confirmation," Haines said, folding some faxes and stuffing them in a jacket pocket. He started edging toward the door. "Look, I've got a long drive and they want you to check in early these days. I'll call, soon as the deal is signed. Wish me luck."

"No," the sheriff told Mrs. Kraus. "I don't want to speak to Finfrock. Just keep him there. I'll be right over." Or that's what Mrs. Kraus thought he said. She hated cell phones. Their batteries were always giving out or they constantly slipped in and out of spots where they got good reception. She wouldn't have one of the fool things.

Finfrock came around the counter and tried to take the phone out of her hand.

"Hang on," she told him, yanking it away.

"Wait," the chairman said to Supervisor Haines, grabbing his arm before he could get to the door. "We'll give you a ride."

"No need," Haines said, trying to draw free. "You've got to stay here for the festivities and in case there's more trouble. I'll just use long term parking. Then my car will be there when I get back."

"I thought Englishman wanted to talk to me," Finfrock said, grabbing for the phone again.

"You let go now." Mrs. Kraus curled over the phone like it was a football and Finfrock was trying to cause a fumble. She lowered her head and swung around and popped him in the nose, not entirely by accident.

"I really need to get outta here," Haines told the chairman, pulling toward the foyer.

"Stop that," the chairman said, though Mrs. Kraus wasn't sure which of them he was addressing.

"Pop, pop, hiss," said the line the sheriff had been on.

Finfrock confined himself to a succinct "Ouch." He stumbled back against the counter and knocked over a stack of papers, a cup filled with pens and pencils, and the hand grenade Mad Dog and Janie Jorgenson had brought to the sheriff's office from Finfrock's bar.

"What's that doing here?" Finfrock's voice had turned suddenly nasal.

The chairman echoed him, and Supervisor Haines bent and picked the grenade up and said, "Just what we need."

"Careful with that," Mrs. Kraus said. She put the phone back to her ear to tell the sheriff what was going on only there wasn't even static there anymore.

Haines turned it over in his hands, looking at it closely. "It really is a hand grenade, isn't it? Like the ones in those World War II movies."

"Set it down," the chairman said. "Don't touch a thing on it. The pin might come out."

"Oh hell, that pin's not gonna come out," Finfrock said. "Been in there for sixty years. Won't just pop out now."

Haines touched it with a finger, as if to test the theory. The pin dropped free and bounced across the worn linoleum.

"Uh oh," someone said.

Mrs. Kraus thought the comment failed to do the situation justice.

◇◇◇

"Daddy, where are you?" Heather asked her cell phone. "Call me. Mommy's gone."

Deputy Parker looked up from an abandoned cardboard box that had been left between a pair of ice cream-stained tables. It contained dirty paper plates and wadded napkins and no explosive devices. She'd been through so many boxes and bags in the park that she was no longer expecting each to erupt in flame and fire and splatter her over several blocks of downtown Buffalo Springs.

Daddy. That meant this was Heather English. Number One. Two was just behind her and both of them looked upset. Parker had begun to notice some differences in the girls. One was a little shorter than Two, her cheekbones a bit more pronounced, her complexion just a bit darker. And One was dressed in shorts and a bare midriff blouse while Two had styled herself as a cowgirl.

Daddy. From her own experience, Parker knew girls in their late teens seldom called their parents Mommy and Daddy anymore. Later, they might go back to it. But at the border to adulthood, teenagers consciously put away childish mannerisms. It was Mom and Dad at this stage, or sometimes even their parents' first names. Childish endearments were reserved for moments when a bit of begging might get something they wanted that their parents still controlled. Like when Parker just had to have that convertible she couldn't afford yet. Or, when things went awry. Badly, and the incipient adult was ready to return control to parents and let them fix everything. From the tone of Heather English's voice, that seemed to be the cause of her reversion. Something had gone wrong.

"Heather," Parker said. And then again, "Heather," because there were two of them. "Is there a problem?"

One composed herself. "Yeah. I can't get Dad on the phone. First his cell was busy, now he's not answering. I keep getting his voice mail and he doesn't call back."

"Is it something I can help with?" Parker asked. Food and ice cream were nearly exhausted in the park. As a result, people were forming clumps around a variety of class and family reunions, or gradually beginning to drift away. The park wasn't as attractive a target for terrorists as it had been. Parker longed to be relieved of this duty and get back into the investigation. Maybe this was an excuse.

"Have you tried the office?"

"A minute ago. Got a busy signal."

That meant both lines were tied up. And if the sheriff was too involved to answer his cell phone, maybe things were happening out there. Maybe she was needed.

"What's up? Why do you need to get in touch with your dad?"

One hesitated, but Two didn't. "Mom's acting really weird," she said. Clearly, both girls were upset. Two usually called her new mother Judy, not Mom. "She's cut off all her hair and bleached what's left and she's packed her bags and taken the Taurus and headed for Wichita."

Short blond hair. Parker knew that was what the Osama lookalike had been wearing when he robbed the bank this morning. And the hussy the farmer in the truck claimed to have seen about the same time had a platinum bob. Could one of them have been Judy?

"Wichita?" Parker asked. If Judy English had flipped out and robbed the bank, why would she head for Wichita?

"To catch a plane," One said. "To Paris. I mean, she's always wanted to go. But now she's doing it out of the blue. And she never said a word to us till just this afternoon when she was throwing bags in the car."

"Paris." Parker thought that made more sense. Rob a bank and blow the country. But she would have picked another country. France would extradite, ship her right back to face charges. Not, Parker thought, that Judy seemed the type to go off the deep end, or do anything without careful planning. Nor, more to the point, had Judy struck her as someone who would rob or lie or steal under any circumstances. Make trouble for her husband, oh yeah, but not this kind of trouble. Not rob a bank in the town where he was sheriff.

"She's always dreamed about going," One said. "Now she's doing it."

"And she said she might not come back unless Englishman gets off his butt and goes with her," Two added.

Whoa, Parker thought. If their marriage was so troubled that Judy English was ready to run off to Europe and never come back, that could put a different twist on things. An angry wife might want to do something wild and crazy to hurt her husband before she went. But Judy…rob a bank?

Parker pulled her own cell phone off her belt. The sheriff's office buzzed an angry busy signal at her. The sheriff's cell got voice mail, just like the Heathers had said. Deputy Wynn's cell got an "unavailable" message that meant his phone must be turned off. "Let's go to the courthouse," Parker said.

The three of them began threading their way through the remnants of Buffalo Springs Day celebrants. The courthouse dominated the street across from the park, a Victorian brick promise of stability and calm. A promise broken as Supervisor Haines came flying through the screen over the window to the sheriff's office, grabbing honeysuckle and letting it slow his drop to the lawn. He hit the ground running as Chairman Wynn and Supervisor Finfrock bolted out the front doors, moving as if the hounds of hell were on their trail. It was like the scene had suddenly morphed from tranquil bucolic bliss to Keystone Kops absurd.

Wynn and Finfrock, shouting something unintelligible, flew down the steps and sprinted across the grass and dove into the ditch at the edge of Madison. Haines had already disappeared around the south side of the building. The sheriff's truck came slewing around the corner down by Bertha's, light bar blazing. It skidded to a stop in front of the courthouse and began drawing a crowd, all of them watching the building as if something even more dramatic must occur there at any moment.

And it did. Light and smoke and sound erupted from the windows to the sheriff's office.

Parker sprinted toward the sheriff's pickup. She was a little slower than the Heathers.

"What…" she began, but there was such a confusion of voices that the only word she caught that mattered was the one Finfrock and Chairman Wynn were shouting. "Grenade!"

The word brought her up short and silenced everybody else.

The front door to the courthouse opened again. More slowly this time. Mrs. Kraus, hair wild and her body covered in soot, advanced onto the top step—center stage before the audience this madness had drawn.

"Whatcha gawking at?" she demanded. She held up her hand. The grenade was in it, a trickle of smoke still rising from a neatly drilled hole in its bottom. "Nothing to see. Thing was a dud." And then she sat on the top step and the grenade slipped from her fingers and bounced down to the sidewalk, and rolled off into the grass.

The courthouse still stood. No one was dead. Apparently, Parker decided, Mrs. Kraus was right.

"You are a man with many questions," Bud Stone said. Mad Dog silently agreed. "I may be able to help you," the Cheyenne continued from across the picnic bench, "but I have no simple answers and your attention is required here for now. Besides, my daughter and granddaughter wait for me. We have a long drive home. This is not the time for us to speak."

"No?" Mad Dog said. His voice was heavy with regret. He'd been dreaming of a moment like this, a chance to seriously discuss Cheyenne beliefs with a man who understood them intimately, ever since mild curiosity about his mother's heritage turned into an obsession to know who and what he really was.

"It is an old man's duty, when a young man asks, to try to answer his questions. I will do that. When you are ready, come to Oklahoma. I live just outside Clinton. Anyone can tell you how to find me. Then, you and I will sit and smoke again. And we will discuss the things which need to be considered."

"That would be great," Mad Dog said. "But I was down there a couple of times. I kind of felt like I got blown off. Like people didn't take me seriously. The only ones who would talk to me, they didn't know as much as I did, just from reading books."

"And those who talked to you, they didn't understand the little they knew," the old man said. "Yes, I am sorry. Few come to us honestly wishing to learn. Especially from those who are not clearly of our people. I heard of you when you were there. And I avoided you. Then I began to dream of you and wonder if that might not have been a mistake. It is why I looked for you before I left."

"Thanks for that," Mad Dog said. "I'll come visit as soon as I can."

"I know you will." The old man reached inside his shirt and pulled out a small yellow buckskin sack about the size of Mad Dog's thumb. He drew the leather thong that secured it over his head and offered the sack to Mad Dog. "You should keep this with you until you come. It is a good thing for a Cheyenne to have. Inside, there is red earth. It is from Bear Butte in South Dakota. A holy place."

Ochre, Mad Dog thought, accepting it as reverently as a Christian might take communion. "I can't thank you enough," he said. He couldn't imagine a more precious gift.

Bud Stone climbed to his feet and brushed cigarette ashes from his Levis. "And now," he said, "we must each go about our business."

"Yes, I guess so," Mad Dog reluctantly agreed.

"Besides," Stone said, "you don't need me as much as you think. Not when a *nisimon* has adopted you."

"*Nisimon?*" Mad Dog didn't know the Cheyenne word.

"A guardian spirit, what the White Men call a familiar."

"I don't understand," Mad Dog said. He knew he had a shaman's power. He could send his soul traveling through time and space when he prepared himself and concentrated properly.

He could connect with the spirits that controlled the universe, sometimes manipulate the forces that operated it. But he wasn't aware of any spirit entities having adopted him.

"We will talk of that when you come to Oklahoma." The old man settled his cap back in place. "In the meantime, she will look after you and reveal herself if she wishes." He turned and strode across the parking lot to the waiting truck. Mad Dog, more puzzled than ever, watched him go. Stone never turned or looked back. He went around the pickup and Mad Dog heard the door on the far side slam. The truck's engine coughed to life. The woman driving it swung in a lazy circle and headed toward Main. Mad Dog's Mini Cooper was at the edge of that circle. He was shocked when the truck brushed the Cooper and continued on. What shocked him more was that he wasn't upset about the Mini's first ding. More like honored, as if his car had been blessed as well.

The truck paused at the edge of the street, then went to the four-way at the Texaco, turned south, and headed for Oklahoma. The woman didn't stop to see if she had damaged his Mini and Bud Stone didn't look back or wave goodbye.

Mad Dog had expected to be horrified when his new car got its first scratch, but he couldn't work up even the slightest anger in light of what had just happened. Not after the gift he'd been given, and the promise of one even more valuable—knowledge.

Besides, he discovered, the truck had brushed his car so lightly that the scratch on the rear bumper was almost invisible. More troubling was that something appeared to be hanging from underneath. He was about to bend over and inspect it when he heard a siren coming down Main. He stood in time to see his brother throw his truck around the corner toward Bertha's and the park. At that same instant, Mad Dog noticed Janie wasn't waiting in his car anymore. His curiosity about what Englishman was up to evaporated in an "Oh shit" moment. He had completely forgotten Janie.

He looked around. She was nowhere to be seen. Neither was Hailey. He folded his frame behind the steering wheel and the Cooper's little engine growled as its tires bit macadam and took him flying into the street. Janie had been in front of her old house on Jackson when he found her. She had probably gone back. Maybe she'd left a rental car there. He blasted out of the parking lot and the cloth wrapped material under his newly scraped bumper bounced and hung closer to the street.

Jud Haines' red Buick ran the stop sign at Madison and careened onto Main. Hailey was close behind it. Mad Dog nearly climbed the sidewalk avoiding both before he got the Mini stopped. Haines accelerated full throttle, going east. Hailey gave up the chase, if that's what it was, and came back and jumped aboard when Mad Dog opened a door for her. As soon as she rejoined him he screeched tires and headed toward the old Jorgenson house.

Whatever had been hanging below his bumper stayed behind on the asphalt. It was sausage shaped, a small bag. Mad Dog would normally have been curious enough to go back and see what it was. But not after letting Janie get away again.

Mad Dog knew he had a major problem. If he was lucky enough to find Janie, how would he even begin to explain? He could use the help of that guardian spirit Stone had spoken of. She, Stone had said. Mad Dog wondered where she was and what she might be…and if he could ever persuade Janie to speak to him again.

Mrs. Kraus sat on the courthouse steps and thought she should have left the grenade in the sheriff's office. She was pretty sure it wasn't going to do anything else, but it didn't need any more chances to kill her. Chasing it around the floor so she could toss it out the nearest window had been opportunity enough.

Before she could corral the fool thing, it exploded in her face. She'd thought she was dead for a minute, but there was just a lot of noise and smoke and she was still there in one piece.

Haines was long through the window by then. Finfrock and the chairman had taken a more conventional exit and were outside shouting "Grenade!" for all to hear. So she'd tried to disguise her distress and carried it out there where she could make the supervisors look bad for leaving her to deal with their problem. And then, all the strength had gone out of her, and the thing rolled down the steps where she'd had to sit before she rolled down after it.

Finfrock was the first to recover. He rose from the ditch and stomped across the courthouse lawn to where the grenade lay. "Damn," he muttered. "I got ripped off. I gave that guy a perfectly good Uzi for this and the sucker turns out to be a Hollywood fake—all smoke and noise. Wait'll I get my hands on him."

Finfrock's voice penetrated the ringing in Mrs. Kraus' ears and she found herself sputtering with outrage. "When you do," she croaked, "you best get down on your knees and thank that man for playing you the fool, Craig Finfrock. 'Cause, if he hadn't, we'd all be hunks of raw meat lying in the rubble of what used to be the sheriff's office about now."

Trouble was, what she'd said was a gross exaggeration. Everybody else had shown the good sense to run for their lives. She was probably the only one Finfrock's folly actually saved.

Finfrock's shoulders slumped. "Well, I guess that's true," he admitted.

The sheriff pushed on the door of his Chevy and stood in the opening, hauling himself up so his head was above the level of the truck's roof. "It's all over, folks. Go on about your business now."

Mrs. Kraus watched as people began muttering among themselves. There wasn't any blood and it didn't seem likely any would soon flow. That made the spectacle at the courthouse less interesting, maybe not even up to the reminiscing they'd been doing. They began to break up into distinct groups again—classes, families, long-lost friends—and drift back into the weedy confines of Veterans Memorial Park.

The sheriff climbed down from the truck, marched toward the courthouse, grabbing Finfrock's arm along the way and removing the grenade from his hand. The sheriff and the supervisor came to a stop at the foot of the steps.

"Mrs. Kraus," the sheriff announced. "I want you to get me the Bureau of Alcohol, Tobacco and Firearms on the phone. We've found a cache of weapons over at the Bisonte that would do downtown Baghdad proud."

"Uhh," Finfrock said, "that's a private collection. No threat to anybody. No need to bring in a bunch of government bureaucrats to make a big thing over my little collection."

The sheriff stuck the grenade under Finfrock's nose. "You don't think this is a big thing?"

"It didn't hurt anyone," Finfrock whined. "And just because one little bitty explosive device managed to get out of my locked storage vault, that's no reason to bring in the feds. I mean after all, Englishman, this is Kansas. Folks here mind their own business. Pretty much everybody's got a few guns around for just in case."

"For just in case of what?" the sheriff demanded. Mrs. Kraus couldn't remember seeing Englishman so mad since the supervisors slashed his last budget request. "You've got enough firepower there to hold off a full scale invasion. And, from what I hear, it wasn't just a bogus grenade that got out of your vault. We need to talk about a Sharps buffalo rifle and a drum of C4 plastic explosives."

Finfrock's jaw dropped. Mrs. Kraus thought there was room in his mouth for that grenade. And good cause to shove it there.

"Don't say a word, Supervisor Finfrock," the sheriff demanded. "Not before I tell you two things."

Finfrock blinked. She could see he wanted to ask what they were but he was taking the sheriff's injunction to heart, so she helped out. "What's that, Sheriff?"

"First," the sheriff said, "my name's English, not Englishman and you will call me that, or Sheriff, or simply shut up. Got that?"

Finfrock nodded.

"And second, you have the right to remain silent…"

◇◇◇

"Daddy, we've got to talk to you," Heather English said. "Not now, honey." Englishman had sent Deputy Parker to lock the grenade in one of the cells back in the jail and was handcuffing Supervisor Finfrock to a heavy wooden chair in the sheriff's office. "I'm kind of busy."

Heather understood that. In all her eighteen years, she couldn't remember her dad handcuffing anyone, other than the occasional rowdy drunk, much less a pillar of local government.

"We know," Two said, "but this is really important."

He wasn't really listening to them. "Mrs. Kraus. I want everybody kept out of the office while I question this suspect. Chairman Wynn can stay. He's a witness to some of it and I may not have time to fill him in otherwise. And Deputy Parker, when she comes back up front. Nobody else." He fumbled through the drawers of his desk while Finfrock protested being labeled a suspect.

"You have any idea what I did with that little tape recorder of mine?" Englishman continued. "I want a record of this since the feds will probably end up prosecuting his case."

"Whoa, now," Finfrock said. "Slow down, Sheriff. I haven't done anything to cause you to bring the feds in. All we're talking about is a couple of little explosive devices and a few minor automatic weapons in a private museum."

"None of it properly licensed. See, I want that on tape," Englishman said.

"Please, Daddy," One begged. She was close to tears when she grabbed him by the arm and made that heart wrenching plea. It finally got his attention.

"What is it, Heather? What's the matter?"

"It's Mommy. She's gone."

"Catching a plane for Paris," he said. "Yeah. I know. And I'll deal with that just as soon as I can. Right now, honey, I've got some dead people and some bombings I need to sort out. And a bunch of explosives still floating around. I have to learn who's got them before we get more dead people."

"We really need to show you this," Two said.

He found the recorder and turned it on and did the testing-one-two-three bit. It worked when he rewound and played it back. He stopped then, and looked into his daughters' anguished faces. "This really can't wait?"

One shook her head and Two said, "No, it can't."

"Okay," he said. "Let's step out into the foyer for a little privacy."

That was ironic, leaving the sheriff's office for the entry to the courthouse to find privacy, but right now the office was where the crowd was.

The iron door behind the main staircase clanged and Deputy Parker emerged from the cell block in the rear. "I put it up on the third tier," she said, "in a cell that's far from any load bearing walls or the fireworks."

"Good," he said. "Go on in the office and make sure Supervisor Finfrock doesn't try to leave and take my chair with him. I'll be right there with some questions for him. What I ask should let you know what's going on."

She raised her eyebrows, but she was professional enough not to inquire what he was doing out here with his daughters. Besides, Heather thought, Parker sort of knew already.

"Now, what's this about?" he asked, ushering the girls into the far corner, away from his office and the front door and the likelihood of interruption.

"You already knew she was leaving?" Heather asked.

"And you didn't try to stop her," her sister added. The way Two put it was less question than accusation.

"I knew and I tried," he told them. "But you girls know what your mom's like when she sets her mind on something. And I haven't had much time to argue with her today."

"Did she tell you she might not come back? Not unless you go with her?" Two seemed more than a little angry because he hadn't fixed this family crisis already. Heather wasn't surprised, considering how fatally tragic the family crisis that brought her to them turned out to be.

He sighed. "Yes. She told me. I don't think she means it, or I don't think she will mean it when she cools down. If I can just get things under control here, maybe I can still talk her out of taking that flight. Or maybe I can join her in a few days. I don't know. Girls, I really don't have time to worry about this right now. It's not like we had some big fight or our marriage is coming apart. She isn't gonna just up and leave us and spend the rest of her life in Europe."

Heather dug into her pocket. She pulled out a couple of crumpled email printouts and handed them to her Dad.

"What's this Bloodlines thing?" he asked, pointing at the "From" line.

"You know that singer/songwriter you guys like so much?" Heather said. "I'll bet you've got one of his CDs in your truck right now."

"John Stewart," he said.

"Right," Heather continued. "Well, Bloodlines, that's the name of the internet discussion group about him and his music. Mom subscribes to it."

"Okay, right. I knew that." He got silent a minute as he read, first one and then the other. "I don't understand. These seem like some kind of prayer circle stuff. Nothing to do with John Stewart."

Heather took them back. "That's what '0% JS' in the subject line means. Right after where they say 'Prayers, Pixie Dust, and Good Thoughts.'"

"I still don't understand," he said. "I mean it looks like a couple of people calling themselves Angelbravo and Lordfrench are expressing their concern about someone facing a life threatening illness. What's that got to do with your mother?"

"Dad." Heather was totally exasperated. "Look who they're addressed to?"

"Some other computer handle," he said. "How would I know who Englishwoman…" Then he got it. "Oh shit," he said. "Your mother's calling herself Englishwoman? That can't be. This Englishwoman has some sort of terminal disease."

Heather watched his face turn the color of ash as the other shoe dropped.

◇◇◇

Jackson Street was deserted, or nearly so. Mad Dog spotted an elderly Chevrolet parked near where the street ended at a field of ripening wheat. It had Kansas plates and was too old to be a rental. Mad Dog thought he remembered something new and shiny parked across from the house with the peonies. It was gone now, leaving a clear view of the red, white, and pink blossoms bobbing gently in the dappled sunlight that penetrated the leafy canopy above.

He had missed her. She had already collected her car and gone. And he didn't have a clue where. He didn't know whether she was planning to stay around, or if what he'd just done to her might have changed her plans. She could be on the road back to Wichita and a flight out of Kansas already. Hell, he didn't even know if Jorgenson was the name she actually went by these days. He might never find her again.

He was feeling pretty sorry for himself when Hailey stuck her head out of the back seat and planted a slobbery kiss on his right ear.

It was a little like a gentle slap in face, albeit a very wet one. Still, it broke the woe-is-me chain of thoughts he'd been indulging. He reached around and gave Hailey a big hug. "That's right," he told her. "We've still got each other." She whined and pulled free of him and turned and looked out the back window like she wanted to go somewhere.

"What, babe? Do you want to go home?" And then he had it. Janie might want to go home, but she wasn't going to do that before she saw her granddaughter. That meant the site where *This Old Tepee* was being filmed. That's where the girl who was also his granddaughter would be staying. And if, by some chance, Jackie wasn't there, her employers would surely know where to find her. It was a link. Janie might have gotten away for the moment, but he was suddenly sure he could find her again.

Mad Dog whooped and did a U-turn that would have slammed Hailey against one of the windows if she hadn't braced herself, like she was expecting it. The Mini charged out onto Main, stopped at the four-way next to the Texaco and the Buffalo Burger Drive In, and turned south.

"You aren't free of me yet, Janie Jorgenson," Mad Dog shouted. Janie wasn't in hearing range and neither was anyone except Hailey, who had her head out the window where she could take full advantage of the breeze.

He smiled. "You just think you were stalked before," he yelled to the missing woman.

◇ ◇ ◇

"My cell's dead," the sheriff said. "Either of you girls have yours?"

They offered them simultaneously and he took Two's because she practically forced it on him. He punched in a number and got the standard "not in service" message.

"Your mother apparently has hers turned off."

"We know," One told him. "We've been trying to call her ever since we found these emails at the house."

The sheriff tried a second number. "Busy," he said. "That was Doc Jones over at the coroner's office. He's either on the phone or he's got it off the hook. Since he's our family physician, I'll bet he knows what's going on. I think he's been hinting around about it all morning. I was too preoccupied to catch on."

The girls nodded and Mrs. Kraus came and stuck her head out the door to his office. "You best get yourself in here if you want to talk to your suspect. He's making noises about a lawyer."

"Yeah, be right there," the sheriff said. He fished in his hip pocket and came out with the keys to his pickup. "Take the Chevy," he told the girls. "Go to Klausen's and see if you can find Doc. Have him call me right now. Don't let him give you any bull about doctor/patient confidentiality."

"Right," the Heathers chorused, much happier since someone was taking responsibility for making things right again. The sheriff didn't share his concern that this might be beyond his ability to fix.

"If he won't call me, you do it. Soon as you find him."

"We're on our way," and they were, clearing the front doors before he could turn to the business that awaited him across the foyer.

"If I'm a federal suspect," Finfrock was saying as the sheriff came in and closed the door behind him, "I want to talk to my lawyer."

"Okay," the sheriff said. He went over and sat in his old wooden swivel chair. It groaned and he felt like harmonizing. Judy, sick. Not just sick, dying maybe. He couldn't get his mind around it.

"Okay?" Finfrock said. He sounded puzzled, like he'd been expecting an argument. "Whadaya mean okay?"

"I mean call your damn lawyer," the sheriff snapped. "You think I give a fuck?"

Everyone in the office looked at him, mouths agape. The sheriff seldom cursed and never used the "f" word. They were probably shocked by his behavior. Hell, they had every right to be. He knew he should be pushing Finfrock about the stolen Sharps and the drum of plastic explosives he'd apparently traded for it. That might lead him to Buffalo Springs' wannabe al Qaeda cell. But right now he was waiting for a call from the coroner's office, and confirmation of, or release from, Judy's death sentence.

"Uhh, look," Finfrock whined. "Those guns, the grenades. I keep them all behind locked doors. I don't let anyone else play with them." The sheriff didn't want to listen, but he'd been re-elected in spite of his party registration because he cared about this community and its safety. He'd given years of his life to maintaining Benteen County as one of those pastoral fantasy worlds urban folks dreamed about—a place where people seldom locked their doors, parked their cars and left them running with packages on the seat while they ran a quick errand, and hardly ever paid a penalty for what town folk would call their foolish innocence. Almost unconsciously, he reached up and turned on the tape recorder.

"Now, I'll admit some of my collection may not technically meet guidelines for private ownership and registration," Finfrock said. "But, where's the harm?"

"Thought you wanted a lawyer," the sheriff said.

"Well now, hey, we're all friends here aren't we?" Finfrock looked around at the room's occupants and smiled hopefully. "I think, if you'll just be reasonable and not start calling in federal agents, we can work this out."

The sheriff reached up and massaged his temples. Until he touched them, he hadn't even realized he had a headache. Stress, he thought. He looked at his watch and recited the time and date into the recorder, then told it who was present. "You been read your rights, Mr. Finfrock?"

"Yeah, sure," the supervisor agreed, "but just call me Craig."

"And you understood those rights? You understand you have the right to an attorney and if you can't afford one, we'll provide one anyway? You understand all that, Mr. Finfrock?"

"Craig, really. And yeah. I understand. I don't need a lawyer. You go ahead, ask me what you want."

"All right, Craig, who'd you give the can of C4 explosives to?"

Finfrock twisted miserably in his chair. "Well, it was just a trade is all," the supervisor said. "You know, like I'll trade you an entire set of 1961 New York Yankee baseball cards, starting players, including right- and left-handed pitchers and one reliever for your autographed Babe Ruth bat. That's all. And I've been looking for a Sharps buffalo gun for years."

"Who?" the sheriff repeated.

Finfrock looked uncomfortable. "You're thinking that the guy I traded with, he's the one been bombing Buffalo Springs, right?"

"Who?"

"Well he can't be. I mean, really, he wouldn't. He's completely trustworthy. You're all gonna laugh when I tell you who it is."

The sheriff opened his mouth to ask it one more time. And the phone rang.

Wynn Some, Lose Some began getting bored after turning away the first few customers from the Bisonte. Once the new wore off, he let the bartender handle it. The man seemed glad to assume the responsibility. He'd complained that telling customers the place was closed by order of the sheriff might set them to thinking it was for some sort of health violation. Now, when folks dropped by for a drink or to ask about happy hour, he was saying they'd had to lock up on account of the bombs in Buffalo Springs, to check back in an hour because he was sure they'd be open again by then. Wynn, having seen what was in the room behind Craig Finfrock's office, didn't think so, but he didn't bother arguing about it.

Main was busier than usual, especially as folks headed home, or elsewhere, after the parade climaxed the potluck and ice cream social. But busier than usual meant a car every five minutes instead of one every half hour or so.

The biggest excitement was when Jud Haines' red Buick went by hell bent for leather. Wynn had made slow-down motions at the supervisor, but Haines either didn't see him or ignored him. If Wynn Some had had access to the county black and white, he would have taken great pleasure in writing up the cocky supervisor for speeding and maybe reckless endangerment and, if the supervisor got sassy with him, might have hauled Haines off to sit in one of the eight-by-eight cells in the back of the courthouse until he learned proper respect for officers of the law. Or so Wynn Some fantasized as he killed time, sitting on the edge of the curb by the entry to the Bisonte's parking lot on the kind of spring day that fairly begged you to play hooky.

He'd first noticed Haines because of all the tire squealing a couple of blocks down where either the supervisor or Mad Dog must have gone through a stop sign and damn near run over each other. He'd seen Haines come roaring his way while Mad Dog swerved around on the street and something fell from his car. Then Haines went by and failed to obey a duly constituted officer of the law and Mad Dog stopped and let Hailey join him in his new Mini Cooper—which Wynn thought looked mighty snappy but was sure couldn't hold a candle to his Lexus, no matter what Mad Dog claimed. Mad Dog didn't go back after his package.

Littering. There was another crime the deputy might have done something about if he'd not been firmly instructed to stay here and make sure no one entered or left the Bisonte, especially with any of Finfrock's toys.

The deputy got excited when he saw the sheriff's truck come down Main. He was sure he was about to be relieved of this monotonous duty and he started walking to meet it, only it was the Heathers in the truck and not Englishman, and they turned in at Klausen's Funeral Parlor instead of coming the extra block toward the Bisonte.

Wynn knew he should go back and keep an eye on the bar, like he'd been told, but he was awful curious why the Heathers had their dad's truck and what they were doing at Klausen's. He stood in the street, wracked with indecision.

Traffic on Main had thinned, so he watched with interest as Cletus Thornburg pulled off a side street and came toward him. Cletus was towing his boy's old GTO with a not much newer GMC. They hadn't done a neat job of tying off the tow chain. It dragged along the street, ringing like some insane Salvation Army solicitor and giving off sparks. Down by the Dillons, the chain hooked on Mad Dog's package and began pulling it toward the Bisonte. Deputy Wynn stepped in front of Thornburg and thrust out a hand in an obvious order to stop.

"What's the trouble, Deputy?" Cletus asked, affable as always.

"Your tow chain's loose. Might take a chunk out of the asphalt or, way it's making sparks, start a fire under your boy's car. You got to fix that."

Cletus thanked him and had his boy climb under the GTO and rearrange the chain, freeing Mad Dog's package in the process.

"I'll take that," Wynn told them. He stepped under the shade of an elm and tried to figure out what Mad Dog had lost. There was something soft and pliable inside a filthy cloth sack that probably had been clean enough before it was dragged along Main for a couple of blocks. Wynn untied the string that closed it and found a paper sack inside. He tugged at the package within and tore a seam in the paper instead of drawing it free. There was something dough-like within. He pinched off a chunk and tasted it. Mad Dog, he decided, wasn't much of a cook.

◇◇◇

"Oh, wow! A Mini Cooper! Can I have a ride?"

She looked like a model from a beer commercial—perky and cute and exposing lots of flesh on a figure of the sort seldom encountered in the real world. Mad Dog guessed she was used to getting her way with men because she didn't wait for him to answer before grabbing the passenger's door handle to let herself in.

Hailey growled, something she rarely did, and the girl stepped back.

"Not right now," Mad Dog told the girl, more politely than Hailey had. "We're in the middle of something."

"Hey," she said. "I know you. You're the jogger—the guy that archer was shooting at this morning. This must be your wolf." She hadn't opened the Cooper's door, but she hadn't put much distance between herself and Hailey's grumble of discontent.

Several handsome young men had followed her from where they'd been loading the ring of trucks and RVs that formed the PBS encampment. None threw themselves between Hailey and the stunning blond, no matter how good she looked in those short-shorts and that skimpy halter. Discretion, Mad Dog thought, a wise decision pending a proper introduction.

"That would be me and Hailey," Mad Dog confirmed. "And you must be Daphne. I'm looking for someone. A woman, pretty, about my age. She would have driven in here in the last few minutes to see her granddaughter Jackie, a crew member."

Daphne shook her head. "No. People have been leaving, not coming. Not until you." She looked at her band of followers as if for reassurance that she hadn't missed something. Mad Dog felt a sharp pang of disappointment. He'd been sure this was where Janie would come next.

"Could I talk to Jackie?" he asked. Maybe she'd heard from her grandmother. Maybe the girl knew where Janie could be found.

"Jackie's been gone all day." It was one of the girl's entourage, a tall guy with a stud in one eyebrow and a pair of hoops in the opposite ear.

"I saw her this morning," Mad Dog told the man. "She was with another guy. They had a flat tire and they told me they were on their way here."

"Yeah?" the kid with the earrings said. "I haven't seen her. Why don't you ask her old man?"

Mad Dog knew who Jackie's father had to be. That couldn't be who the kid meant. "Her boy friend?" Mad Dog asked. "Where can I find him?"

"That's right," the kid grinned. "I remember, you hippie generation people referred to your significant others as old man and old lady didn't you?"

Wow, Mad Dog thought. Revenge on the time traveler. He had, in fact, had an old lady for a few weeks when he experimented with that commune on the Kansaw near the Oklahoma line in the late sixties.

"Nah," the kid continued. "I meant her dad, Brad Davis. He's the chief honcho here, the director for *This Old Tepee*."

How could that be? How could a sociopath, a would-be-patricide, have managed to get himself put in charge of a major Public Broadcasting project? "You're sure?"

"Hey man, no way an undergrad with a weakness for tar like Jackie could have gotten on this crew otherwise. Ask anybody."

The rest of the crowd seemed to agree.

Mad Dog wasn't sure what tar was, but he didn't think it was good. He reached in his pocket and fished out the envelope with the pictures of his son Janie had given him. "Could this be Davis when he was young?" he asked, passing a couple around.

No one seemed to think so. "Why not ask him yourself?" the man with the eyebrow stud suggested. "That's him, packing the sedan on the other side of the stuffed buffalo. He's the guy with the graying hair and the long face watching his cell phone. I might look like that if I'd lost half my cast a week into production. He's hoping to get us a stay of execution. But it won't happen. This thing died with that kid this morning."

◇◇◇

"Jud Haines," Supervisor Finfrock said. "That's who I traded the C4 to. Who could be more trustworthy than that? Hell, we just trusted him with three million dollars, didn't we?"

The sheriff barely heard. The phone was ringing and he reached for it.

"Say, where'd Jud get to?" Chairman Wynn asked.

"And if he's so damned trustworthy," Mrs. Kraus wondered, "why'd he pull the pin on that grenade?"

Finfrock shrugged. "Well, it was just a Hollywood fake."

"But he didn't know that," Mrs. Kraus shot back.

"Everybody, shut up!" the sheriff said. From their expressions, it shocked them as much as his obscenity had a few minutes before. But it worked.

"Sheriff's office," he said to the phone.

"She told me, specifically, not to let you know." It was Doc Jones calling because the Heathers had forced him into it.

"Let me know what?" the sheriff asked.

"Englishman, I can't tell you a thing about Judy's medical condition. No matter how much I sympathize or how bad I want to help you and the girls. I took an oath and this is a matter of professional ethics."

The sheriff knew Doc. They'd pulled charred bodies out of twisted wreckage together, been through a couple of murder investigations. If Doc said he wasn't going to talk, he meant it.

Oh, they were close friends, close enough so the sheriff let him use that damn nickname. The sheriff could probably wheedle a few hints if he had long enough to work on Doc's sympathies. But he didn't. It was three already. Even with lights and siren, it would take him more than an hour to get to the Wichita airport. With her flight scheduled for four-forty, he had to leave soon.

Or, he could still call Wichita and have her stopped. That was an option. Not one he liked, but it gave him an idea.

"Doc, this is not a personal matter. It's police business. Judy has been acting irrational all day. You know what happened at the Farmers & Merchants, right?"

"I've heard," Doc said, "but I don't see how that…"

"It was Judy," the sheriff told him. "She needed cash for this Paris trip. She was the one who took the bomb in there and stole five thousand dollars."

The sheriff believed Judy's version of what had happened. It made sense, especially in light of the courthouse bomb, but blaming her gave him an excuse. "I've got to arrest my own wife, Doc, so if you know anything about why she did it, you've got to tell me. If she needs help, I want her to get it. But I aim to make sure she doesn't hurt herself or anyone else."

There was a moment's silence on the phone. Chairman Wynn and Mrs. Kraus exchanged whispers on the other side of the office and Craig Finfrock looked like he wanted to get up and carry the chair he was handcuffed to over so he could get involved in their conversation. Only Deputy Parker appeared unfazed. She hardly knew Judy. She might not have an opinion, one way or the other.

"All day, you said. So what other irrational behavior have you witnessed?" Doc asked. The sheriff could hear it in Doc's voice. He was about to get an answer. He didn't know how he felt about that. None of this fatal disease shit seemed real as long as a name hadn't been put to it. But he had to know.

"There was some strange stuff at home this morning," the sheriff said. He decided not to elaborate on that, especially in front of an audience. "Wild emotional flip flops. She arranged this Paris trip before dawn and without telling me about it. Then she went and got a haircut. An extreme one, and a bleach job. She's running around with a platinum crew cut now. She went over and robbed the bank right after she did her hair."

"Hold on now," Doc said. "You don't really believe Judy robbed that bank. I sure don't. You tell me something like that, you better have proof."

"Doc, she confessed it. She told me over the phone just before she left town."

"Oh," Doc said. There was a pause before he continued. "Well, some erratic behavior is to be expected. She's on an emotional roller coaster. And I understand about France. She's always wanted to go and she's probably thinking now or never. There's a chance a thing like this can affect a person's thought processes, but I didn't see any signs of that when I gave her the test results yesterday. She seemed normal enough, under the circumstances. Absolutely no evidence of personality change. I would have laid odds she'd be physically incapacitated long before anything like that could happen."

"Damn it, Doc," the sheriff demanded, "what's wrong with my wife?"

"Tumor," Doc said. "Brain tumor, deep in the cerebellum where it's probably inoperable."

"Good God," the sheriff said, but even as he said it he knew he no longer had any faith in a benevolent deity.

"Mr. Davis? Brad Davis?" Mad Dog approached the man with the long face stuffing a suitcase in the trunk of a rental car.

"We're not hiring."

"And I'm not job hunting. My name's Mad Dog," he paused and watched for a reaction. He got one.

"Oh yeah," Davis said. "I remember. You're the guy with the buffalo we were going to rent. And you wanted to talk with Bud Stone, didn't you. Sorry, we're out of business and Stone's already gone."

"That's okay. Actually, I wanted to talk to you about your mother."

Davis glanced at his watch. Mad Dog had never seen one before, but he thought it might be a Rolex. "I can give you maybe five minutes," Davis told him. "Now, what's this about my mother?"

"Your mother is Janie Jorgenson, right?"

"Did you know her when she lived here?"

Mad Dog nodded. "Has she ever mentioned me?"

Davis shook his head. "She never talks about Buffalo Springs. She wasn't happy here." He looked at Mad Dog and reached up and rubbed a hand across his cheeks and through his prematurely graying hair. "Is something wrong with me? Have I got something on my face?"

Mad Dog realized he'd been staring intently. He couldn't see any of himself or his family in the man. If this were the son Janie had told him about, he didn't resemble his father. He didn't look like the pictures Janie had given him either, though a lot could change in twenty years.

"No, I'm sorry. I was just trying to see Janie in you, Mr. Davis. And, excuse me, but I'm curious about the names. She's going by Jorgenson but you're Davis?"

"She's Jorgenson again all right. She and my father went their separate ways. I got his name, but she stopped using it long ago."

"Did she tell you anything about your father?"

"She didn't have to. He and I see a lot of each other."

Mad Dog couldn't hide his surprise.

"What's this about, Mister? Who are you and why are you so interested in my family?"

Mad Dog scrambled for an answer. "I was a good friend of your mother's when she lived here," Mad Dog explained. "Indulge me, please. How old are you, Mr. Davis?"

"I'm thirty-seven, or will be next month. I hope you're going to explain this."

Thirty-seven wasn't possible. Nor was a June birthday. If Mad Dog were Brad Davis' father, the man would have to be forty. By their calculations, Janie had gotten pregnant in June. If she'd had a baby, it would have been due around March of 1963. Davis hadn't been born until more than three years later. The man couldn't be his son.

"I'm sorry," Mad Dog said. "I must have you confused with your older brother."

"What older brother?" Davis said. "I'm an only child."

Heather Lane was on the verge of losing it.

"You have to go after her," Two told her father. She was on a cell phone in Doc Jones' office and Englishman was still at the courthouse.

"Calm down, Heather," Englishman said. "I will if I can. Things may be coming together here. I only need a couple of answers to wrap things up. Don't worry. I won't let her get on that plane."

"No, Englishman, *you* have to do it." Memories of the bizarre conflict that tore her parents from her only six years before were suddenly fresh and painful again. She couldn't lose a second family, could she?

"You can't let a bunch of storm troopers from Wichita humiliate her in front of all those people at the airport. They'll treat her like a common criminal. She needs someone who loves her, someone who cares about her."

"I promise," Englishman said. "I'll only call as a last resort, and I'll explain the circumstances to them. They'll treat her right."

"Oh yeah, sure." Two threw the phone at the wall and missed. It hit the couch in Doc's office and her sister rescued it.

"Dad?" The other Heather put the phone to her ear and checked to see if they were still connected. "But Dad…" One continued, then paused to listen to his excuses, or so the expression on her face indicated.

"Dad, if you don't go get her, we will," Heather English interrupted. Then her eyes got wide and angry. She turned to her sister and said, "He told me not to throw a temper tantrum and hung up on me."

"I'll go along, if you want," Doc offered.

"No," both Heathers said.

"Just us," Two told him.

"And Dad, if he cares enough," One agreed. They turned for the door.

"If it wasn't for this bank robbery thing," Doc called after them, "I'd tell you to let her go. A few days in Paris might be just what she needs to sort things out. Half of her battle will be how she feels about herself and her life. Only I wish Englishman was going with her."

If Doc said more than that, Two didn't hear it. She and Heather were out the back door to the mortuary and on their way to Englishman's truck. Two, though more tenuously connected to the English family, was in the grip of a more demanding terror. It wasn't just Judy she was worrying about. It was also her place in the universe. She grabbed the keys and said, "I'm driving."

One didn't argue. The girls piled into the truck and Two squealed out of the parking space, laying rubber all the way to the street. One got her seat belt fastened just before they turned onto Main. She reached over to switch on the lights and siren and noticed something else.

"Look out," One howled. The truck's brakes cried in echo to those of an aging Nissan Altima that caught the Chevy's rear chrome-step bumper and sent them spinning in a perfect three-hundred and sixty degree circle, right in the middle of Main.

Two checked her rearview mirror. A man and his female passenger stepped out of the Altima into the street. Clearly, neither was hurt. She slammed the truck into gear again and popped the clutch. They were pointed in the right direction.

She was still smoking tires when the Chevy passed Deputy Wynn, standing by the curb in front of the Bisonte, eyes nearly as wide as his mouth. Two glanced in the mirror and watched him recede.

"There's no real damage," her sister told her, "so step on it."

Heather Lane needed no encouragement.

"Look," Mad Dog said. "I just spent most of the afternoon with your mother. She told me she had a son named Sam, Samuel." He could see from Davis' eyes that the name meant nothing to him.

"No way," Davis said. "My mother and I aren't close. But she's always been pretty open about things. Even difficult stuff. I think she must have been spinning you some kind of tall tale, though I can't for the life of me think of why."

Mad Dog decided straight out and honest was the best approach. He wasn't much good at anything else anyway. "She told me I was that boy's father," he said.

"Oh," Davis said. "You're the football player, aren't you."

"Then she did tell you about me."

"No, sir. She didn't. But she told Dad and he told me."

Mad Dog ran a hand through his non-existent hair. "I don't get it," he said.

"Me either," Davis said. "I'm not sure what to tell you, or if I should tell you anything. I'm surprised mother's been here. I would have bet she'd never come back unless it was to blow this town off the face of the earth."

Considering what had been going on today, Mad Dog didn't like the way he'd put it. "What makes you say that?"

Davis took a deep breath and let it out with a sigh. "Dad tried to explain her to me once. If you knew her while she was here, you must remember her father ran off and abandoned her and her mother. People treated them as second-class citizens because of that."

"It's not true…" Mad Dog began. Though, on second thought he had to admit it might have seemed that way to Janie and her mother. Folks in Benteen County were slow to accept strangers, and inclined to discuss their strangeness. Hell, they were inclined to discuss everybody's strangeness, as Mad Dog knew from years of testing their limits. Janie and her mother hadn't been treated like pariahs, but they hadn't stuck around long enough to win real acceptance either. Janie had been a top student and a cheerleader at Buffalo Springs High, but he supposed she'd had to be twice as cute and vivacious and to work twice as hard as anybody else in order to accomplish that. Mad Dog had only noticed the cute and vivacious parts, then the loss of his heart.

"Well, she thought so," Davis continued. "She hated this place. Dad told me she ran away from here because she was pregnant and abandoned." He gave Mad Dog a hard look with this disclosure and Mad Dog decided not to argue the point. "You got any idea how a seventeen-year-old high school-drop out supports herself?"

Mad Dog didn't, and wasn't sure he wanted to know. He avoided the man's eyes, looked down at Davis' shoes instead— good ones, hiking boots with a footprint that even looked expensive.

"She only had one commodity. Her body. That's how Dad met her. He was a city prosecutor. She'd had a couple of years in the life by then, but she still had an innocence about her, or so he told me. He rescued her. At least he thought he did. I was the result. I was her first and only child. She had an abortion when she left here because she had to keep her figure to market it. But I guess she never really loved Dad, or not as much as she loves money. They split after she finished her MBA. I was seven. Since then, she's passed in and out of my life on her schedule. Oh, she loves me in her way, but she loves besting the opposition in a business deal more."

"I'm sorry," Mad Dog said, forcing himself to meet the man's eyes again. "I had no idea. But what you said about her wanting to blow Buffalo Springs off the face of the earth, that was an exaggeration wasn't it?"

"Not an exaggeration," Davis replied. "Just a figure of speech. Do you know who my mother is? What she does?"

"Obviously not," Mad Dog said.

"She's Chair and CEO of one of the most innovative energy corporations in the Americas."

"Oh Jeez," Mad Dog said. "Not Windreapers?"

Davis nodded. "The only reason I can imagine her coming back to Kansas would be to wipe your hometown off the map and replace it with a wind farm."

It was starting to make sense. "How about your daughter? Would she know where Janie is? Your mom talked about being in touch with Jackie. She said part of the reason she came back was to visit her. Could we ask?"

"We could if I knew where Jackie's got to," Davis said. "She's been missing from here all day."

"But I saw her this morning. She and some guy were bringing in a pickup load of stuff."

Davis shook his head. "Only load we had come in today was that stuffed buffalo Chad drove up from Pretty Prairie." He glanced around, located a couple of guys sorting through piles of leather and fur under a tarp, and shouted, "Hey, Chad. Did Jackie go with you to get the buffalo?"

Chad wandered over. He smiled at Mad Dog and acknowledged him with a, "Hey, man." Then he turned to Davis. "She didn't go with me. I thought you knew that. I found her walking along the road as I was coming back. She'd run out of gas and asked me to drop her at the filling station in town."

"You seen her since?" Davis asked.

"No, sir. And, actually, I didn't get her to the gas station. Just after this gentleman helped us with our tire, we passed a red Buick. She waved it down and told me to let her out."

The kid had Mad Dog's attention now. "The Buick, do you have any idea who was driving it?"

Chad wrinkled his forehead and put a finger to his chin. "You know, there were two people in the car. When she saw them she stuck her head out of the truck and waved and shouted at them. She called one of them 'Gran,' the other one, I thought his name would have been more appropriate if we were in Oklahoma, since that musical is the only time I'd heard the name used before."

"Oklahoma?" Davis asked.

"Yeah," the kid replied. "Rod Steiger played the role in the movie…"

Mad Dog didn't have to wait for the boy's answer. "Jud," he said. Jud Haines was the principal backer of the Benteen County Energy Coop and its impending deal with Windreapers. And Janie was Windreapers. God, Janie must really hate him, and this community, to have planned such an elaborate revenge. Englishman had to be warned.

It left the sheriff feeling like that time just after he was first elected. He was called out to an accident on the blacktop east of town. A bad one. The car was crumpled under the cattle truck that had broadsided it, then dragged the remains more than a hundred yards beyond the intersection. He hadn't recognized it as his mother's until he wrote down the plate number. That was long after he'd determined the truck driver was the only survivor. And then, he'd had to carry on, because the trucker had two broken legs and there were dead and injured cattle everywhere.

The sheriff shook his head—like he was trying to shake off his need to deal with Judy the way he shook water from his short cropped hair. The aquatic metaphor was all too apt. He felt like he was underwater, struggling desperately to reach the surface. He forced himself to take a couple of deep breaths and then turned to his attentive audience.

"I guess you all understand I don't have time to spare for this. But several bombs have gone off this morning. I lied to Doc so he'd tell me what's going on with Judy. Somebody else left that bomb stuffed in the deposit box. Judy took it inside, but she didn't know what it was. So, tell me again, Mr. Finfrock, who did you give that C4 to?"

Finfrock seemed anxious to please. "Haines. I gave it to Jud Haines."

"In trade for a Sharps buffalo rifle?"

"Yeah, that's right."

"And how would Supervisor Haines come by an antique buffalo gun?"

"A garage sale?" Finfrock fidgeted in his seat. "That don't sound too likely, does it? But it's what he told me."

The sheriff didn't bother with that one. "He tell you why he wanted the plastic explosives?"

"Tree trunks," Finfrock said around a sheepish grin. "Look, I guess this all sounds pretty wild, now I hear myself saying it, but I've been looking for a Sharps for years, and when he came in the bar with it, well, I pretty much gave him everything he wanted. But it's Jud Haines we're talking about. He wouldn't hurt anybody. I mean, he's a supervisor, just like me and Chairman Wynn here."

"We just gave him three million dollars," the chairman said. From the sound of his voice, he didn't seem as sure of Haines' innocence as Finfrock.

The sheriff ignored the chairman and concentrated on Finfrock. "And you didn't think anything of it when bombs started going off all over Buffalo Springs the morning after you made that trade?"

"How'd you know it was last night?"

"'Cause that's when someone went into one of the RVs where they're shooting that PBS special and stole a Cheyenne bow and some arrows…"

"And a Sharps," Finfrock finished for him. "I shoulda known it was too good to be true. But I was with him when we found that bomb over at the Texaco. He couldn't have planted it, could he?"

"We found the remains of a timer from that bomb," the sheriff said. "It couldn't have been set for more than sixty seconds. That means somebody who was still at the station had to have dropped it there, or…"

"Haines brought it there himself," Finfrock said. "Shit. I gave him a whole range of timers and radio controlled switches along with a bunch of detonators. He said he wanted to experiment and I sure wanted that Sharps."

"Three million dollars," the chairman wailed. "We just transferred three million dollars into the control of a terrorist bomber."

The sheriff swiveled his wooden chair in Chairman Wynn's direction. "Where the hell could you get three million dollars?"

The chairman and Craig Finfrock exchanged worried glances.

"You know," the chairman said. "Maybe Craig and I oughta talk to a lawyer after all."

"Was that a law enforcement vehicle?" The man who'd been driving the Nissan was pointing down Main, out of town toward where the Heathers had disappeared from view only moments before.

Deputy Wynn chewed his lip for a moment as he decided how to deal with this. The man had walked around his Altima just fine, until he spotted the deputy. Now he had an exaggerated limp and was feeling his neck like he was considering what the symptoms of whiplash should be.

"Was that your county's vehicle?" the man asked, "'Cause it just left the scene of an accident with injuries. I mean the wife and I are banged up pretty good here, aren't you, Hon?" The woman looked confused for a moment before the light bulb went on.

"You know, I should probably see a doctor," she said.

"Yes, sir, it was official," Wynn told them. "Looked like you done it some damage in the back there, too."

"I damaged it?" The man's voice was filled with moral outrage.

"Yup," the deputy continued. "It came onto the street with light bar flashing and siren blaring. Don't you know you got to yield the right of way to an emergency vehicle, sir? Especially one involved in such an important errand."

"But it never gave us a chance to stop. It caused the accident, not us."

"No, sir," Wynn proclaimed. "I could see you were speeding. Outsiders like you got to pay attention to our traffic signs. Serious accident like this, I probably couldn't find a judge who could get around to setting your bond before Monday. Have to hold you over the weekend."

"Now wait a minute. I wasn't speeding."

"Course you were. That's why I run out in the street here and tried to wave you down. I sure hope you're insured," the deputy continued. "I hate to think of the damages you might be responsible for if our truck can't deliver that heart in time for the transplant."

"Heart transplant?"

"And look here," Wynn said, showing them the battered sack containing Mad Dog's dough. "You made them drop the liver. I'd ask to see your license and registration only I got to arrange fresh transport for this right now."

"Uhh, sure," the man agreed. "Don't let us keep you. We're feeling a lot better. We'll be on our way." He wasn't limping as he hurried around his Nissan and got behind the wheel. His wife was already belting herself in.

"You guys keep a close eye on your speed now, you hear?"

"Sure thing, deputy," the man called. The Altima was already rolling. "Thanks for the warning."

Wynn watched as the man headed out of town as fast as five miles below the posted limit could take him. The deputy was feeling mighty proud of himself until he heard the squeal of another set of tires. He jumped onto the curb and whirled to see who had nearly run him down. It was a car with out-of-state plates, a rental, from which an attractive middle-aged woman emerged.

He was on a roll. He was still planning how he would put the fear of small town cops into her and send her on her way when she marched up and yanked the sack from his hands.

"What are you doing with that?" she demanded.

"Well I…" Wynn took a step back and wondered if he ought to draw his gun and show her who was in charge. It obviously wasn't him. She tore into the bag and he was surprised to see a small timer attached to one end of Mad Dog's dough. He'd heard you had to let dough rise before you baked it. Maybe that was why it tasted so bad. It wasn't ready yet, though the numbers on the timer indicated it was mighty close.

"Hey, that's Mad Dog's dough. And not very good from the taste of it, but I was gonna give it back to him."

She paused and gave him a peculiar look.

"You ate some of this?" She seemed incredulous. "This isn't dough. It's C4 plastic explosive. Maybe you should see a doctor." She shook her head as she jumped back in the car, popped it into gear, and headed east on Main as fast as the driver of the Nissan had wanted to go. Almost as fast as the Heathers.

"No," Wynn said to her rear bumper. "She was kidding," he muttered. But he had the sinking feeling she wasn't. His stomach rumbled. He felt a burp coming on. It made him very afraid.

M rs. Kraus thought it was like when the second Heather appeared on the scene. The girl's crazy father had come looking for her, not because he wanted to take care of her himself, but to use her as a weapon against her mother. He was fresh out of prison. Hadn't seen his daughter in years. So he kidnapped the wrong Heather and threatened her life as a way to get at Two's equally loony mom.

Since he first got elected, Englishman had always tried to be a good lawman, even if he'd never had any formal training for the job other than a brief hitch in the army that sent him home with a Purple Heart and a cynical view of the world outside Benteen County. But when his own daughter's life had been on the line, he'd stopped being Sheriff and started being Dad.

This time it was Judy, and though the sheriff's bride might not be in quite such immediate danger, she was apparently running away—headed for Wichita and a flight to France. Mrs. Kraus could see Englishman wrestling with his duty—the threat to his community—and weighing it against his responsibility to Judy. She felt pretty sure the community was about to lose out.

"What's this lawyer crap?" Englishman was in the chairman's face and Mrs. Kraus wasn't at all sure he wouldn't be grabbing the man by his throat if he didn't start answering questions right now. Time for a little meddling, she thought.

"How you gonna feel, waiting on a lawyer if another bomb's out there and somebody gets killed?" she asked Chairman Wynn. "You ain't been Mirandaed. What you say can't be used against you. Strikes me, it'd be in your best interest to explain right quick."

"We haven't done anything that bad," Supervisor Finfrock said. "We maybe bent a few rules and regulations, violated the open meeting law, but it was a genuine emergency and for the good of the county. We don't need a lawyer unless Jud Haines isn't on his way to close that Windreapers deal."

"My God, man," the chairman said. "Haven't you been paying attention? Jud Haines is our bomber. Jud Haines pulled the pin on a grenade right here in this office so he could make a clean getaway. That money's in electronic limbo right now, and we let him code in the password that will transfer it wherever he wants, including countries that don't share information about banking transactions."

The sheriff turned to Finfrock. "Right now, I don't care if you robbed the county blind to come up with that money. All I care is where it's supposed to go. Where Jud Haines has gone."

"We needed three million to guarantee the construction of the transmission lines and the infrastructure for the county's wind farm," Finfrock explained. Mrs. Kraus could tell he didn't think he'd done anything seriously wrong. Of course, he didn't seem to think collecting weapons of mass destruction was a problem either. "After the bombings this morning, we knew the deal was dead if word got out. Jud contacted Windreapers and told them we got a counter offer. That, if they wanted to build their farm here, they had to close the deal today."

"That don't make no sense," Mrs. Kraus said. "You don't even have all the land lined up. You're lacking three sections in the middle, last I heard, including Mad Dog's."

"I really don't think you should say any more," Chairman Wynn suggested. It earned him a glare from Englishman hot enough to raise blisters. The chairman wilted under it.

"Okay," he said. "It's like Finfrock told you. We're facing an economic crisis in this county. If we don't close the deal on that wind farm, we're likely to be closing up government here in the next few years. May have to merge with another county or two, just to supply basic services."

"Who cares how you rationalized this," Englishman said.

"Well," the chairman continued, "we acted to seize those properties this afternoon. Eminent domain. We'll pay the owners a fair price but, to have that wind farm, we had to have that land."

Mrs. Kraus was shocked when Englishman responded with a laugh instead of rage. "You seized Mad Dog's section?"

"It's legal. We got the power to do that," the chairman replied.

"I suppose you do," Englishman said. "Only Mad Dog thought you might be getting a little desperate to get hold of his property. So he deeded it to the state of Kansas a couple of months ago. Gave it to them, free and clear, contingent on that land being put back into native grass and grazed by nothing but buffalo and other indigenous fauna."

"That can't be," the chairman protested.

"Oh, you better believe it can. Mad Dog gets to live there for up to forty years at an annual rent of one dollar. He figures he'll be dead before his lease is up. You might be able to make your eminent domain stick on the other two sections, but you can't seize land from the state."

"But then we don't have ten contiguous sections," Finfrock wailed.

"And, three million dollars or not, you don't have a wind farm," Englishman said.

"Wichita," Chairman Wynn said. "Jud Haines, if he was telling the truth, is catching a jet there this afternoon."

"So, all I'm missing is a connection between our archer and our supervisor, who's become a part-time terrorist and maybe a full-time thief. And he's on his way to Wichita, where I need to go anyway, and our archer is already dead, so there's nothing to keep me here. Well then, thank you, ladies and gentlemen. I'm going after my wife now. And maybe your crook."

"Englishman," the chairman said. "You got to catch him. Get our money back. Otherwise it won't matter what you decide to do about the rest of us. He gets away with that money, this county's bankrupt right now."

The sheriff took his tape recorder off the desk and tossed it to Mrs. Kraus as he headed for the door.

"Hey," Finfrock complained. "Aren't you going to unfasten my handcuffs?"

"You want I should take care of that?" Mrs. Kraus asked.

Englishman turned at the door. "Let him go or lock him up. Put the chairman in a cell with him or let them walk out the door together. Do what suits you. I'll decide whether to level charges when I get back. Just don't let Finfrock near his bar. That way, this community might go bust, but it won't go boom."

Jesus, Wynn Some wondered. What happened if you ate plastic explosives? Was it poison? The stuff couldn't be good for you. His stomach felt like pressure was building up inside and he realized he was sweating a lot more than the balmy afternoon warranted. Was that just nerves, or was something else happening to him? He'd felt a little like this that time he ate all the dried fruit and then got so thirsty. What he drank, of course, caused the mulched fruit in his stomach to re-hydrate and swell. For a while there, he'd looked like he was pregnant and felt like he was dying.

Now, it felt like something was building up in his stomach again, and it seemed to want out in the worst way. If he released it, would it just be a massive burp, or might he erupt like a volcano? Would he belch, or would he explode like that bomb Jud Haines threw into the ditch across from the Texaco?

Deputy Wynn stood perfectly still. If he moved, he reasoned, he might jar the stuff in his gut and set it off. They could be finding bits of him all over Buffalo Springs for years. He fought against the pressure inside, but willpower wasn't enough. The force in his belly was building. He put a hand over his mouth and tried to hold it in. Not possible. He felt it come rolling up his esophagus. His mouth flew open in a rictus of terror. If he could have screamed and burped at the same time, he would have. He squeezed his eyes down tight and waited to die.

The belch rolled out of him. It was the kind of eruption a man who had just polished off four beers might be proud of. It rolled down Main Street.

Wynn opened his eyes. He was alive. He shook his head in amazement and was still shaking it when the earth joined in and shook as well. The echo of his burp came roaring back far louder than when it left him.

The east, where the sides of Main Street merged on their way to an infinite horizon, turned bright as dawn. Then that new sunrise was eclipsed by a cloud of smoke and dust that mushroomed into an otherwise perfect sky.

Did I do that, Wynn wondered. He hoped not, because his gut was rumbling again. Another burp was on the way.

They don't build windows like the ones in the Benteen County Sheriff's Office anymore. As the sheriff watched, he saw the reason for that. The windows that looked out across Veterans Memorial Park toward the east—and the column of smoke and fire that rose from somewhere in the direction of Buffalo Springs' elementary, middle and high schools—were tall and narrow, each half containing a single sheet of glass. On a beautiful day such as this, the lower half could be raised clear up to match the top one and allow languid breezes or escaping supervisors to pass without obstruction.

It wasn't the force of the blast that did it. It was the sound wave that followed and shook the entire town. It also shook a pane free from ancient putty and dry-rotted moldings. The sheet cracked, shattered, and collapsed onto the worn linoleum. Shards flew, glistening daggers to pierce any remaining fantasies regarding the tranquil nature of the day.

"Was that the school?" Chairman Wynn asked.

The sheriff noted Wynn Senior's use of the past tense. He could still see the flag on the pole in front of the school. "Just beyond, I think," the sheriff said, but he didn't pause to speculate about it. He sprinted for the door, motioning Parker to follow. "The girls have my truck. Where's the black and white?"

"Parking lot out back." She dug in a pocket and produced the keys and he took them from her.

The black and white was a twenty-something Chevy with the big-block engine that, despite having traveled three hundred thousand miles, still had enough power to raise a dust cloud to compete with the one on the east side of town as it stormed from the courthouse lot and turned south.

The streets of Buffalo Springs were empty. Just as well, since the sheriff flogged the black and white for all it had. Parker had reached down and started the lights and siren the instant she was belted in. That should have cleared traffic, if there'd been any. They only had to swerve once—to avoid Deputy Wynn, standing in the eastbound lane in front of the Bisonte. He had one hand on his stomach and one over his mouth, his full attention on the towering cloud just east of the city limits.

"Wynn," Parker said, in case he hadn't realized who the fool in the road was. The sheriff switched lanes and never considered stopping.

The cloud had the ominous mushroom shape associated with a nuclear blast, though it was far smaller.

"It is past the school," the sheriff said, relief tinting his voice. Buffalo Springs Day was to be capped off with a dance and banquet in the gymnasium tonight. People were already there. Some huddled around cars in the parking lot while others peered from broken windows in the school buildings or clustered in doorways. He couldn't see anyone who appeared to be hurt, and no one tried to flag them down.

Parker clicked on the radio and told Mrs. Kraus to send someone to check for injuries at the school. It needed to be done, though the sheriff wasn't sure who Mrs. Kraus would find to do it. Wynn Some had looked to be in too much of a state of shock to be of use to anyone. He was the only deputy available. The sheriff needed to be elsewhere. Anything that didn't desperately require his attention would have to get by without him for now.

He was on the brakes before they entered the dust cloud. There was garbage all over the highway—broken branches, clumps of dirt and asphalt, burning weeds. No pieces of shredded metal from a car, thank goodness, nor any human remains that he could make out. He got busy navigating the debris field as the cloud closed in around them, thick and dark as the dregs at the bottom of a cup of Bertha's coffee.

A shape materialized in the middle of the road just ahead. The black and white was pre anti-lock brakes. To maintain any ability to steer, the sheriff had to feather the brake pedal. Some of the debris on the highway was mud and mulched green vegetation. He hit a patch and realized he could aim for the ditch or the car in the middle of the road. He chose ditch, but the black and white had a will of its own. They clipped the rear of the ghostly sedan and spun. The Chevy's rear axle dropped into the culvert and they came to a halt facing back toward town. And just short, it turned out, of a crater that had once been the north side of the blacktop and part of the ditch that bordered it.

"You all right," the sheriff asked, but he was climbing out of the vehicle as he got Parker's affirmative reply.

The sedan had rolled forward several feet and dropped its front wheels into the crater. He couldn't see anyone inside so he scrambled to the door and yanked it open. The car was empty.

"We surrender. We'll come peaceable." The sheriff turned and found a middle-aged couple facing him. They must have gotten out of the Nissan in order to examine the effects of the blast.

"Either of you hurt?" the sheriff asked.

"Oh no. Not hurt. And it wasn't us who blew up that liver, officer. Honest."

The sheriff had no idea what they were talking about. But then, he had no idea why this was happening, or how he was going to get to Wichita in time to stop Judy since it would take a tractor or a tow truck to get the black and white, or this couple's Altima, back onto the highway.

"We just want to go home," the woman said.

The sheriff sympathized. He wanted to go home too. Only his home was a quiet little town in the middle of the continent where nothing ever happened and he lived in peace and quiet with his wife and daughters. Home seemed to be a place that was ceasing to exist even as he watched.

"My husband isn't with me," Judy told the man at the airline check-in counter. She wondered if he ever would be again.

The man looked over the reservation information on her computer printout. "You realize these are non-refundable tickets?"

"That's why I'm here. He's going to try to join me, though. I left a copy of this printout for him and I faxed one to his office, but, just in case, can I leave my copy with you so he can pick up a boarding pass if he arrives without it?"

"There won't be a problem, ma'am," the man said, "as long as he brings a photo ID."

Judy felt herself go cold inside. He was going to ask her for a photo ID as well. She had several, including her passport. She had Englishman's passport as well. She had left his luggage at the house, but she'd left a note telling him she was bringing his passport. He could get by without a change of clothes. They could buy everything he needed there. But he couldn't get into France without a passport. And suddenly, she wasn't sure she could get in with hers, or even get on a plane. She cursed the urge that had sent her to Millie's this morning.

"And I'll need an ID for you, Mrs. English."

Damn, damn, triple damn. She dug into her purse and fumbled between her passport and her billfold for a moment. Neither portrait, with its full head of dark hair, resembled her now. What the hell. She went with the passport.

He did the double take she'd expected. "It's an old picture," she said.

"Uhh," was all he managed by way of reply.

"It's from before I started chemotherapy," she improvised. That might soon turn out to be true, and it was part of the reason she'd decided to see what she would look like without any hair. If she went through with what Doc seemed to think she needed, she might have no choice but to look like this, or worse. So why not make it part of her new, adventurous, Parisian look instead? Besides, she had promised herself she wouldn't think about that. Not until after Paris, if Englishman came. Or when she had to decide if she would come back if he didn't.

"Oh," the man at the counter said. "I'm sorry." He typed something into his keyboard and handed her a boarding pass. "Will you need any special assistance with boarding?" He wouldn't meet her eyes anymore. He didn't want to look mortality in the face. That had rendered the difference between her passport photo and her current looks something he didn't want to deal with. As soon as he could be rid of her, she would become invisible to him.

"No," she said. "I'm having a good day." Only it wasn't as good as she'd hoped. Not without Englishman.

"Just ask anyone at the gate, or speak to your flight crew if that changes, Mrs. English. Have a good flight."

And that was it. His attention was already on the next passenger and all she had to do now was go through airport security and wait for her flight out on the concourse. Judy English was going to Paris, just as she'd always wanted.

That, she remembered, was why they'd gotten divorced. She had always wanted to get out of Kansas. He, once he was back from Vietnam, never wanted to leave it again. He'd lost his sense of belonging, he claimed, when he went overseas, and hadn't found it until he came home. She couldn't understand that. It was just a flat, desolate, empty land people were always quitting. Moving away, because you couldn't survive on a family farm these days, because there weren't any jobs, because there just wasn't any good reason to stay. She'd always been sure, if she could only show Englishman the Paris of her imagination, that he would discover the rest of the world wasn't as horrible as those army bases and that little corner of Southeast Asia he'd experienced. That was all he'd seen, army towns that exploited kids, and a war zone. How could he think anything else?

After the divorce, though, she still hadn't left for Paris. She'd discovered she couldn't take Englishman's daughter away from him. She decided to put off her move from Kansas until Heather was old enough for college. Until about now, actually. Then the other Heather came along and she and Englishman got married again and she'd decided she could spend the rest of her life in Kansas if Englishman would take her to Paris just once. And he'd promised. And he'd probably even intended to do it someday. It was just that she no longer had time to wait.

She had more than an hour before her plane would begin boarding, so she sat on a bench that let her look back through the lobby windows toward the parking lot. Englishman still wasn't there. She was pretty sure he never would be. And if he didn't love her enough to grant her this last wish, what was the point in coming home again? It was his home, not hers. She could die as easily half a world away. More easily, maybe, if she had to do it alone.

◇◇◇

The sheriff found it all pretty confusing. The guy from the Nissan kept insisting it was a human liver, bound somewhere for transplant, that had blown up. He knew it was a liver because they'd somehow knocked it out of the emergency vehicle that was carrying it and a human heart, and they knew all that because the deputy back in Buffalo Springs had told them and it had to be true because he'd been on the verge of taking them in and locking them up until he could find a judge except the deputy had to arrange transport for the liver because of the accident they'd caused even though they weren't speeding, no matter what he said.

The sheriff didn't bother trying to straighten them out. He made sure they weren't hurt, and they weren't, beyond being shaken up and a bit hard of hearing now, because they'd been so close to the blast.

The sheriff had a hard time making the man understand that he needed to hear exactly what they'd seen, but once the tourist got the idea, he proved eager for an audience.

"Well, like I said. We came crawling out of Buffalo Springs, doing no more than twenty-five till we got to that resume speed sign. About then, along came this little silver car with a sticker from one of those rental companies. Woman was driving it. She must have been doing seventy when she went by and she was waving at us to slow down. Well, I didn't know what to do. I mean, after our run-in with your deputy, we wanted to get out of this county in the worst way, but I wasn't going to exceed the speed limit, or even get close to it again until we hit the county line. So here we are, maybe doing all of thirty-five where that sign says the speed limit's fifty-five and this woman passes us and waves for us to slow back down. Well, I did. And she just kept going faster and faster, and then I saw that liver go flying out her window and bouncing down the road and I though Momma was going to have a heart attack. So, I'm trying to decide what to do about it when damn, if that liver don't just suddenly disappear in a fireball. Then, bamo, you come barreling out of nowhere and plow into the back of our car, which I admit, was probably our fault on account of we had parked in the middle of the road and I never thought to turn on the emergency flashers or anything. So, you all just put the cuffs on us and take us in, if that's what you're planning. We'll throw ourselves on the mercy of the court, I guess."

The man didn't stop there. The sheriff just tuned him out and turned his back and started taking in the scene. The dust and smoke were beginning to clear. Even on a perfect spring day, Kansas was not without a breeze. Elsewhere, people might have called it a steady wind.

There didn't seem to be any target for a bomb here. And with the way the woman had waved at the couple in the Nissan, it sounded like she'd been trying to warn them away from the blast. Like maybe she knew it was about to go off and tried to dispose of it safely.

Well, safely was a stretch. They were going to have to set up a detour here because there was a hole where the highway used to be. Or most of it. There was a little stretch of cracked pavement on the south side of the road. The rest was missing, like some alien spaceship had stopped off to take a sample before going elsewhere to create crop circles.

Parker was already on her cell phone to Mrs. Kraus, telling her about the need to set up the detour.

"Have her make arrangements for a place for these people to stay, or get them where they want to go while we fix their car," the sheriff told her. "And I need transportation, or a tow truck to get the squad car out of the ditch."

Parker passed the information along.

Something low and fast streaked toward them from Buffalo Springs. The sheriff stepped into the road and began waving his arms to slow it down. The little red car glided to a stop inches short of the sheriff's knees.

"Hey, bro," Mad Dog said. "Need a ride?"

If the shortest distance between two points is a straight line, Kansas, lacking obstacles such as hills, mountains, valleys, lakes, or points of interest, should be a commuter's dream. There being only the occasional river or stream to contend with, it is theoretically possible to run a highway directly from any point in the state to another—Buffalo Springs to Wichita, for instance.

Theory, however, is seldom translated into reality. Kansas' highways and byways were laid out with grid-like precision, north and south (as the wind blows) and east and west (as the traveler goes), one virtually every mile, from Missouri to

Colorado and Oklahoma to Nebraska. Only later, after cities grew significant enough to warrant it, did Kansans take to the idea of diagonals. These roads, based on risky variations of intersections angled at something other than ninety degrees, run conveniently to and from some population centers. Wichita, for instance, sprouted several diagonals. One, near the airport, goes in the general direction of Buffalo Springs, but sadly stops diagonaling at Nickerson. Still, it's a useful route for those from Buffalo Springs who want to catch a plane—Wichita being the nearest, and one of the few remaining, airports in the state with real-world connections—and it was widely chosen by the day's parade of would-be travelers and those who wished to stop them. Judy English, Jud Haines, the Heathers, Janie Jorgenson, Mad Dog and Englishman with Deputy Parker and Hailey, and finally Brad Davis all aimed toward it. Each chose from among a multitude of roads heading east or south to get there.

Brad Davis was driving south on a paved road when he noticed the truck hidden deep in the row of evergreens. Only the sudden swoosh of tire tracks and the fresh gouges in the ditch indicated something had happened here. Davis was in a hurry, but when a teenage girl jumped into the road and planted herself directly in his path, he hit the brakes.

The truck in the trees was a Chevrolet, a nineties model that might have been in pretty good shape before it went through the ditch and lodged itself in that row of vegetation. It was upright, but from the way the cab was mashed and covered with streaks of rich loam from which bits of grass and clumps of blooming sunflowers hung, it hadn't been that way while it passed through the ditch.

Davis pulled his car over to the side of the road and got out. "Anybody hurt?" he asked the girl with the high cheekbones and bright blue eyes. He didn't want to get involved, or be delayed, but what could he do.

A moaning noise he didn't recognize issued from the truck.

"No," the girl told him. "We're fine. That's just my sister running the battery down."

He recognized the sound, now. A starter, slow and more labored than it should be.

Another head peered out of the mashed cab. Both heads, he discovered, looked remarkably alike. Twins, he thought.

"We had a blowout," the girl in the road explained.

"And survived without a bruise, but our dad's probably gonna kill us when he sees what we've done to his truck." The one still in the pickup supplied this additional information. She did so as she twisted around and pulled herself out through the window. Davis surmised the door wouldn't open anymore.

"Until he gets around to killing us," the first one said, "we desperately need to get to the Wichita airport. Can you at least start us in that direction?"

"Well I..." He didn't have time to come up with a good reason why not because she already had his passenger door open and was crawling in. Her sister joined her in the back and he was suddenly the only one standing foolishly by the road.

"My name's Heather," the first one told him. "Heather English, but you can call me One because my sister's name is Heather, too, or Two, tee-dubya-ohh. If you care, I can explain that on the way."

Sometimes fate smiled, rewarding Good Samaritans for their acts instead of punishing them. This seemed to be one of those times.

"That's not necessary," he said. "You're the sheriff's daughters, aren't you? Mad Dog's nieces?"

"Should we know you?" the first Heather asked from her spot in the passenger's seat.

He introduced himself and explained. "We haven't met, but all of us out at *This Old Tepee* have heard of you."

"Can you help us get to Wichita?" One asked.

"That's where I'm going. But first I've got to meet a friend of yours, Supervisor Haines. He's waiting at an abandoned grain elevator where a town called Harrod used to be. You know where that is?"

"Sure," the Heather in the front seat told him. "It's no more than two miles from here and almost on the way. But why would you meet him there?"

"We're in the middle of one of those limited-time-only business deals. I've got to show him how to tie up some loose ends. Get me to Harrod and I'll take you to the airport," Davis said.

"You're a lifesaver," Two thanked him from the backseat.

He smiled and put the rental car in gear. Maybe, he thought. Maybe not.

◇◇◇

They had to push the Mini Cooper so Mad Dog could get it to climb out of the ditch on the far side of the crater, then it was a tight fit to crowd Parker in the back with Hailey.

"Get me to Wichita in a hurry," Englishman had told him. Mad Dog assured his brother he was just the driver and this was just the vehicle for the task.

Englishman slammed the door and grabbed his seat belt. "Let's go."

"Just a second." Mad Dog turned to face the back. "Deputy Parker, if you check in that sack on the floor, you'll find a pair of leather gloves and a catcher's mask."

"Just because I'm gonna let you break the speed limit, doesn't mean you need racing gloves," Englishman complained. Clearly he wanted them moving, and now.

"They're not racing gloves." Mad Dog swung back, put the Cooper in gear, and chirped the tires as he pulled away from the hole in the highway.

"You mean these," Parker asked. They were thick leather gauntlets that would extend all the way up to Mad Dog's biceps.

"Yeah." With four aboard, the Cooper was a bit sluggish off the line, but the little four-banger came alive as Mad Dog got the rpms up and the supercharger kicked in. "I need you to put those on, please, and the mask." Mad Dog chirped the tires again when he went into second.

"What for?" Parker had trouble getting her hands all the way into the gloves. The gauntlets reached her armpits.

"In case we have an accident," Mad Dog told her. "We're all belted in and this thing's got all kinds of airbags, but you can't belt in a wolf."

"You expect me to hold her?" Parker sounded incredulous.

"Oh no," Mad Dog reassured her. "She wouldn't put up with that."

Hailey wasn't showing any concern about the gloves or the mask. She had her head out the window near Mad Dog's ear, devouring the breeze he was turning into a gale.

"What are you doing with that stuff anyway?" Englishman asked, finally allowing himself to pay attention to what was going on in the back seat.

"I keep it with me in case she gets hurt," Mad Dog replied. "Wolves, they won't put up with much, even from people they love."

Mad Dog glanced in the rearview mirror and saw Parker shaking her head. "I don't expect you to have to use those," he told her. "But keep your eyes open. If you think we're going to hit something, grab her."

"You're kidding." Parker had to speak up now, over the growing noise of the wind buffeting through the open windows and the howl of the engine as Mad Dog redlined it for each gear change. Third now, three to go.

"Just for a second," Mad Dog said. "Probably won't matter. At the speed we'll be going, none of us are likely to survive. But I'll feel better about opening this thing up if you'll try to protect her."

"Oh sure then, why not," Parker shouted.

Mad Dog went into fourth and started easing the windows up. Slow, so Hailey had time to pull her head in. He didn't want her catching a stray grasshopper at more than a hundred. They'd be able to hear each other, too, and the Mini Cooper could go a little faster if he smoothed out its profile.

"How fast will this thing go?" Englishman asked.

"They come from the factory with an electronic chip that shuts them down a little over 130," Mad Dog told him. Fifth gear now, and already some serious speed. He turned on the flashers and the headlights. People could see them a little sooner that way and, fortunately, in central Kansas, there would be no sudden curves or hills or valleys to mask their approach.

"I had no idea something this size could go that fast."

"Faster, maybe," Mad Dog told him. "First thing I did after I got it broken in was find a shop with a computer geek who could bypass the chip."

Mad Dog saw his brother glance at the center-dash-mounted speedometer. It was graded all the way to 150. Conservative, Mad Dog thought.

Doc parked beside the stuffed buffalo. A young man in a pair of shorts and hiking boots came to meet him.

"Doctor Jones," the man said, extending a hand. "I'm afraid Mr. Davis is gone. And Michael's family's, too, to make arrangements."

Doc accepted the hand and gave it the requisite brief, firm shake. Kansas men didn't let other men hold their hands longer than necessary. He struggled to remember this one's name. He was an assistant producer, the man who'd put such an effort into resurrecting the boy that morning—the one who'd confused the issue because his vigorous CPR pumped all the blood out of the body.

"Actually," Doc explained, "I'm not here about Michael."

The man raised his eyebrows. "No?"

Sean. Doc remembered, because the man's name was Irish, like Michael's. "Sean, I've got an unidentified body over at the morgue. I wondered if you were missing any crew members."

Sean shrugged. "Who knows. Since this morning, people have been drifting in and out. Not that I blame them. This production's over."

"Small community like ours," Doc said, "we don't get unidentified bodies much. When we do, someone usually misses them right away. That hasn't happened, so I figure if we got a bunch of strangers out here in this pasture, my body's most likely one of them."

"What's this body look like? You got a picture?"

"Well…" Doc had pictures, but none of them were pleasant to look at or likely to be helpful. "Kid's face was pretty well ruined when she got thrown from her motorcycle."

Sean got a sad look on his face. "A blond girl, nineteen, pretty? I guess you might not be able to tell whether she's pretty anymore. She'd be trim with a good figure—about five six and one twenty with curly blond hair."

"That all fits," Doc acknowledged. "Is there anything else that might help me make this a positive ID? Scars, birthmarks, stuff like that?"

"Nothing I know of," he said. "Except she rides a motorcycle. She's the only woman on our crew with one. And…"

It was Doc's turn to make his eyebrows into question marks.

"She might have been high on something."

Doc nodded. "I found needle tracks on her arm. That sound right?"

"I'm afraid it does."

"Surprises me," Doc said, "that you'd keep someone on your crew who was using drugs."

"Our director, Brad Davis, he's her father. She only answered to him."

That caught Doc by surprise. "Somebody's got to inform him," Doc said. "And I need her name for my records."

"Davis may not be easy to reach," Sean said. "I just tried and he's not answering his cell. But if you need to do the next of kin thing, I hear her grandmother's in town for some kind of reunion."

"What's her name?" Doc prompted again.

"Jackie. That's the girl's name. Her grandmother is a former resident named Jorgenson."

Two surprises in a row and this one a lot bigger than the first.

Sean looked like he was considering something for a moment, then he reached out and took Doc's arm. "There's something I'd like you to look at, Doctor, if you don't mind."

"What's that?"

Sean led him toward the entrance to a Greyhound-sized RV. "There've been some weird things happening around here," he said, opening the door and ushering Doc into an opulent interior. "Not just Michael. Jackie and Mr. Davis, they've been coming and going and there's been this other guy here, sometimes late at night. Last night for instance."

"I don't understand." Sean led Doc past a living room and a kitchen and down a hall.

"That other guy, I think he's some kind of official with the county. Rumors say some bombs went off in Buffalo Springs today."

"Three of them," Doc said, "but what's that got to do…"

Sean opened a door on a small wood-paneled office that made up in luxury what it lacked in size. "Mr. Davis, he left in such a hurry, he didn't tell me what to do about returning this vehicle. So I was looking for the registration or something when I found this. We've got no business having it." He pointed at an empty container lying on the carpet between a cherry-wood desk and a leather recliner.

Doc bent over and tried to make out what it was. There was printing on the side. The first line he deciphered read, "TNT equivalence: 118%."

Whenever something interesting happened, Mrs. Kraus got stuck holding down the fort in the sheriff's office. Minutes after Englishman and Parker left the building, Supervisors Wynn and Finfrock did the same. She had to show Craig Finfrock that the sheriff's handcuffs could be opened by anything you could fit in the keyhole. Then the supervisors ran out and jumped in the chairman's Cadillac and hightailed it toward the explosion and left Mrs. Kraus behind, alone.

On the bright side, phone calls flooded the office and the rumor mill kept her updated on everything. The blast had been half a mile east of town. Nothing more important than a few weeds and Osage orange trees, and a big hunk of highway, had been seriously damaged. There were lots of broken windows, especially at the school and on the east side. A couple of people had minor cuts as a result, but nothing more. When the sheriff reported he and Parker were making a high-speed dash to Wichita in Mad Dog's Mini, she filled him in, then made the calls he needed. Sheriff's offices in the counties they would pass through promised not to impede the speeding Cooper.

Then it got quiet in the office. There were no more explosions or other catastrophes, so the phone stopped ringing. Mrs. Kraus began to get bored. That was why she decided to search Supervisor Haines' office. What else did she have to do? She took along her Glock, not that she expected trouble. All the trouble she knew of had left the county and was somewhere on the road ahead of the sheriff. Still, you never knew.

The door to Haines' office was open. He had departed in a hurry, through a window in the sheriff's office just ahead of that exploding grenade. She didn't think he'd left behind anything incriminating. On the other hand, he might have thought there wouldn't be anything there to investigate, not even a standing building.

The room looked neat enough, though the wallpaper was faded and stained from leaks in the roof bad enough to seep clear through the floor above. But for a phone, a blotter, and a pen set, his desktop was empty. She went through his desk drawers. None contained anything more interesting than the files and memos she expected. Except one file in the bottom drawer on the right.

It was filled with fake ID cards. They had Haines' pictures on them, but other people's names—Chairman Wynn's and Supervisor Finfrock's, and even a couple of Englishman's deputies. And there was another one that hadn't come out right. The county seal and some of the printing was smudged, like the thing had been touched before it dried. It looked like it said sheriff on it, only she wasn't quite sure. She needed her magnifying glass to make it out. She carried it back to her office. She was still trying to read it as she went around the counter, angling it to catch the light from the windows in the west wall. She wasn't watching where she was going and she stepped on a pencil that had been knocked to the floor earlier, along with the hand grenade. It caused her to lose her balance and go over sideways into a filing cabinet.

"Damn, barked my shin good that time," she said, sitting on the floor amidst the glass shards from the broken window, massaging her injured leg. She punched the offending file just hard enough to repay it for her seeping wound without creating fresh ones on her knuckles.

That was when she noticed the fax machine was no longer plugged in. The fax sat atop that file cabinet. Its power cord was still attached, but the phone line wasn't. It lay on the floor beside her. Mrs. Kraus wondered when that had happened. She hadn't thought she'd touched the fax or the cord as she fell. She reached up to restore the connection and discovered a phone line was already plugged in there. Curious.

She cautiously got on her hands and knees and peered around behind the cabinet. It was just a short phone line coming out of the back of the fax machine. It led to a gizmo, to which the loose wire she'd found apparently needed to be plugged.

These newfangled contraptions had to go and be so complicated. Why on earth did the fax need a phone line to pass through a funny-looking box with some wires leading to…What was that back there? She brushed some glass aside and sat on the linoleum and stretched to reach behind the cabinet so she could pull the wires and see what they were connected to. Sweet Jesus, they went to what she thought was a blasting cap, stuffed into a roll of dough-like material and duct taped to a pint of lighter fluid.

Haines must have hooked this up when he went through the faxes just before the incident with the grenade. Either he hadn't made a good connection or someone had tripped on it and pulled it loose while they were trying to save themselves. Otherwise, she thought, it would have exploded when the next call came in on the fax line. And with the lighter fluid as an incendiary device, turned her into a crispy critter in a matter of seconds.

Mrs. Kraus felt herself go all wobbly. She would have had to sit down if she wasn't already doing so. This was the second time today she'd come whisker-close to being killed by one of Jud Haines' weapons of terror. That was scary.

A phone rang. Since it didn't trigger an explosion, she reached up and answered it.

"Just a second, Doc," she said.

A stray thought nagged her memory and she had to concentrate to snag it. When she did, it raised the hair on the back of her neck. She'd remembered one of her mother's favorite sayings. Third time's a charm.

"Pull over!"

Mad Dog hit the brakes and guided the Mini Cooper to the side of the road. Before he could ask why, his brother had thrown the door open and vaulted across the ditch. That was when Mad Dog noticed the truck among the evergreens, and the way the ditch had been torn up as the truck found its way there. He and Hailey tumbled out as well while Parker tried to figure out how to move the seats so she could do the same.

"They're not here and there's no blood," Englishman said, looking worried all the same.

"Who..." and then Mad Dog realized that the truck with the crumpled roof was Englishman's, the one the Heathers had been in when they left Buffalo Springs after encountering that couple in the Nissan. Mad Dog and his brother and Parker had been updating each other and comparing notes on the road.

"Somebody must have picked them up," Englishman said, worrying it over in his mind. "But they should have called to let me know this happened before it got reported to the office.

They ought to know how much I'd worry, under the circumstances."

He came back across the ditch, stuck his head in the Cooper, and asked Parker to call the office. "They wouldn't be able to get me on my cell," he reasoned. "Not since the battery ran out. Maybe Mrs. Kraus has heard from them."

Parker's phone began to ring before she could fumble it off her belt with the gauntlets on. She punched a button and told it, "Parker."

Mad Dog looked around, trying to picture how the accident had happened and what might have become of his nieces. Hailey was standing just a few feet ahead of the Cooper, front leg lifted, nose and tail extended. She looked like a bird dog pointing a covey of quail.

"Is that Mrs. Kraus?" Englishman wanted to know.

Parker told him it was, and handed over the phone.

Mad Dog had never seen Hailey do anything like that before. "Whatcha got, babe?" He couldn't see anything where she was pointing, just a footprint on a patch of bare dirt at the edge of the pavement. He bent and looked at it closer. The print had an unusual pattern. He'd never seen one like it before, not until about an hour ago over where they were filming *This Old Teepee*.

Mad Dog thought he knew who the girls had gotten a ride with. It left a bad feeling in the pit of his stomach. He wasn't sure why until Englishman turned the phone off and handed it back to Parker.

"Mrs. Kraus discovered a bomb in the courthouse, and Doc's found something that confirms Jud Haines is one of our bombers," Englishman said. "But he's not alone. He's had at least one partner it this."

Mad Dog nodded. He said the name at the same time Englishman did. "Brad Davis."

They hadn't managed to peg the speedo. The Mini was heavily loaded, and there were too many little towns to pass through, each with its traffic light or hard-to-see intersections. That succession of hamlets came every five to eight miles, so much alike all of them could have been labeled Slow-Place-In-The-Road, Population Declining.

"Jackie's dead?" Mad Dog said. "My granddaughter?"

The sheriff tried to stop himself from reaching a foot for the brake pedal that didn't exist on the passenger's side as Mad Dog threw them around a couple on a Harley.

"She's dead," the sheriff agreed. "And she's probably Janie Jorgenson's granddaughter. Whether she's related to you, that's another question."

Mad Dog dropped well below the Cooper's top speed to pass a horse-drawn Amish buggy. "Yeah, not if what Davis said is true. Then he couldn't be my son, but who else could he be if he's mixed up in this thing?"

"Well, Haines could be Sam," the sheriff said. "He might be forty, and I've never met or heard a thing about his family."

"If it's Haines," Parker said from the back seat, "he's taken his sweet time getting around to killing you, Mad Dog."

"Look," the sheriff said, "it's obvious Haines is a crook. He had those faked identity cards Mrs. Kraus found. He most likely put that device on the fax. It's all but certain he planted the bomb at the Texaco. Then there's the money and the grenade. But that's all we know for sure."

Parker ticked items off across her leather-clad fingers. "Mrs. Jorgenson says you have a son. Mr. Davis says it isn't him. Mr. Davis says she's his mother and the head of Windreapers. We've got no independent proof of any of that. But Davis and Jackie are linked to Haines and the explosives and now, maybe, Davis has the Heathers."

The sheriff nodded. "Yeah, that last part scares me. But right now, we don't know who any of these people really are. Or if any of the stuff they've told us is true. It's a tragedy about Jackie, but she was involved in this somehow—the arrows if not the bombs."

Mad Dog blew by a tractor pulling a piece of farm machinery and avoided the eighteen-wheeler headed in the opposite direction with less margin for error than Parker approved, judging by the way she started to grab for Hailey. "The Janie I saw today hardly seemed bent on destroying me or Buffalo Springs."

The sheriff agreed, to a point. "She stopped and took that bomb from Wynn Some, then tossed it safely outside of town. She may not want anyone to get hurt, but she knew what was in that sack. That makes her part of the bombings."

"Maybe," Mad Dog said. "But I don't believe she wanted to hurt me, or that she was lying about us having a kid."

The traffic was getting heavier as they closed in on Wichita. At least they had a divided highway to work with now.

"Janie was in this car with me while it was rigged to explode," Mad Dog said. "She sure wasn't acting like a suicide bomber."

"No," Englishman said, "Haines gets my vote. It's like he was following a plan to scam the county until he realized all that money could be his alone. The first few bombs were set so they weren't likely to hurt anyone—except the bomb in your car. Then things changed. He'd squeezed the money out of the supervisors and he was ready to make his getaway. That's when he decided he was willing to kill people, other than you. The grenade you found, that was convenient, otherwise he must have planned to set off the bomb on the fax to insure the supervisors wouldn't wise up before he skips the country and wires himself the money. Think about it. If Doc hadn't stumbled on a curious assistant, and that grenade had been the real thing, why would we suspect him? We might still be sifting debris to find out who was in there. He could have been long gone by the time your car exploded."

Mad Dog skimmed by an RV on the right as a cement truck lumbered along, blocking the passing lane.

"Ah, Hell," the sheriff said. "I don't have a clue about any of this. We'll find out soon enough…or we won't. But I've got to find my daughters and catch Judy before she gets on her plane."

◇◇◇

Mrs. Kraus relaxed in the comfort of a window booth at Bertha's from which she could keep an eye on the courthouse in case it suddenly erupted in smoke and flames. Bertha had taken pity on the stressful day she'd undergone and slapped down a big glass of sweet iced tea with lemon and a massive chunk of fresh-baked apple-crumb pie with the terse and unheard-of comment, "On the house." It hadn't been that long since the judge brought her lunch, but Bertha's pies were to die for, and nearly dying in the line of duty was thirsty work.

After the last bite, she picked up the cell phone one of Bertha's customers had loaned her and punched in Parker's number again. The phone sure had a lot more thingamabobs on it than she could imagine uses for, but if you just hit the right buttons, you got the party you wanted, and heard them better than she'd expected.

"Another update," she told the deputy.

"It's Mrs. Kraus," she heard Parker inform the occupants of Mad Dog's car. Then she thought Englishman shouted something like "You can't fit through there," and Mad Dog reply, "We just did."

"We're just outside of Wichita," Parker said. "What's up?"

Mrs. Kraus had already told them about the bomb wired to the fax machine and the stuff she'd discovered in Jud Haines' office. And she'd passed along what Doc had found out at *This Old Teepee*.

"I closed up the building," she told the deputy. "Put danger signs on the front doors since you can't bolt them shut. I got Chairman Wynn organizing county security. The crater in the highway already has a detour around it."

"Good," Parker said.

"Greatest thing," Mrs. Kraus continued, "is a highway patrolman stopped in here at Bertha's. He was sent to check on us. Minute he came in, everyone started telling him about the bombs. We finally got someone who believes us. He's called for back-up. Just went to check out the courthouse a few minutes ago. I gave him your number. When he gets a minute, he's gonna call to ask the sheriff what's going on. I wasn't sure what I should tell him, so I didn't."

Parker relayed the information and told Mrs. Kraus that was terrific.

"And I heard from Doc again," Mrs. Kraus cackled, saving the best for last. "Most serious bomb-related injury he's discovered was Deputy Wynn. The chairman's son was idiot enough to eat some of that plastic explosive. He thought it was a sack of dough. Doc says he'll survive, but he won't be available for duty this afternoon."

"Why's that?"

"Well, Doc hadn't run into this problem before. He called poison control and reassured himself the stuff won't kill you. Then he improvised. It ain't gonna be the way Wynn Some feared, but that boy's still got an explosion to look forward to when Doc's most powerful laxative takes effect."

◇◇◇

They were off the diagonal on the west side of greater Wichita. Mad Dog could see his brother fidget when they got stuck and had to wait out a traffic light on Ridge Road. The airport was just ahead. They should make it with a little time to spare.

But traffic poked, staying tightly packed and stubbornly resistant to letting Mad Dog slip the Mini through. They caught two more red lights before Mad Dog made a space where one hadn't seemed to exist and squirted around a van and onto the airport's entrance road.

"Long- or short-term parking?" Mad Dog asked. "Or do you want me to drop you in front of the terminal first?"

But Hailey was fussing behind his ear, her attention on something off to their left, along the stretch of aircraft businesses and hangers that paralleled the easternmost of the runways between which the airport feeder road led.

"I think that's Jud Haines' car," Parker said as Hailey jumped in and out of her lap and made insistent nose prints on the window. A red Buick sat in a parking lot that served the airport's executive terminal, as well as charter and private aircraft storage and service facilities.

"The girls are probably at the main terminal," Englishman tried to persuade himself, "unless they're hostages." He checked his watch and Mad Dog knew there wasn't much time left if Englishman hoped to catch Judy.

"Your call," Mad Dog told his brother as they came up on the last place to turn before negotiating parking or drop-off zones. "Might not be Haines' car. Who knows where Davis is. Maybe they're all in the terminal."

"That's where I'll go," Englishman decided. "The girls would have gone after Judy, so that's what I'll do. You two check out that car."

Mad Dog infuriated a security guard who thought he was moving too fast. Englishman pointed to the badge on his chest as he jumped out to join the parade of tourists, dumping his .38 and holster on the Mini's floor before Mad Dog tore away, back toward the lot where they'd seen what they thought was Haines' car.

There were several big lots, and it took Mad Dog a moment to find the entrance to the right one. Hailey finally convinced them to turn in and check the far corner, away from other vehicles.

"I wonder why…" Mad Dog said, but he threw the Mini to the end of the lot and into a nearby slot.

Hailey was the first one out of the Cooper. But she didn't bound over to the apparently-abandoned Buick. She approached it warily, preceded by a rumble from deep in her throat. Once he was out of the Cooper and on his feet, Mad Dog discovered why. Two figures lay in the car, hastily bound with duct tape and strapped down on the seats to which they were confined by their seat belts—the Heathers.

"Damn," he said, and stepped forward to tear a door open and get them out of there.

"Don't touch it." The panic in Parker's voice made a non-existent ruff of hair stand up along his back. It matched the one Hailey was showing as she growled at the car.

"Why?" he asked. But he already knew because he could see the wires.

J udy had to take her shoes off to go through security. She thought that was silly. There were plenty of better places in her clothing—slacks, a white blouse and a blue blazer—to hide a weapon. So, why strip everyone of their shoes? At least she was wearing the cute sunflower-printed socks the Heathers had given her last Christmas.

She went through the metal detector without a problem after carefully removing all her jewelry and putting it in one of those containers they offered you. She'd dressed with the idea of passing these security checkpoints. Plastic buttons on this blazer, not metal ones, and a belt that tied and had no buckle. They found nothing wrong with her carry-on luggage, or her purse, so she was soon offered a seat where she could put her shoes back on. She had a bad moment then, sitting there, looking at those cheerful sunflower socks the girls had given her. Would she ever see the Heathers again? And, if she did, would their lives be ruined by having to care for a mother who couldn't care for herself? Would she survive to see them marry? Ever see a grandchild? She felt herself tearing up until she realized a young soldier was in front of her, waiting for one of the chairs so he could get back into his own shoes. Lord, they were even checking soldiers. Absurd!

She pulled her flats on and made way for him and he smiled at her. He was Hispanic, maybe. He had a dark complexion and high cheek bones and he reminded her a little of Englishman. With a shy smile and eyes that swept across her figure before going to hide beneath his long lashes, he bore an amazing resemblance to the Englishman she'd seen, all those years ago, across the gym at the Bisons' basketball game. Englishman was still in his Army uniform then, a wounded war hero, and everything Judy had dreamed of. After halftime, she'd squeezed into the seat next to him. He'd noticed her. She made sure of that, making a big deal of slipping past him in the bleachers and sticking her mini-skirted tush in his face. Even then, he hadn't talked to her. Just an occasional glance out of the corner of those surprisingly blue eyes. Glances that took in her efforts to fill out her already tight sweater by throwing her shoulders back and taking deep, chest expanding breaths. His smile seemed to mock her and so, when the game was close and the crowd's attention was riveted elsewhere, she'd slipped off a shoe and rubbed one of her feet up the side of his calf. He hadn't been able to ignore her after that. Only a few hours later, before he discovered the girl who had picked him up was only a high school sophomore, they were lovers. The only lover she'd had in her life, and she didn't regret the absence of wider experience one bit. Not even now.

Teary eyes and fond memories caused her to take the wrong concourse. She was almost to the end of the gates before she discovered her error. She turned around at the sign on which Wichita State basketball legend Dave Stallworth welcomed visitors and informed them he was a Shocker. The team's nickname had been Wheat Shockers before urban snobbery shortened and altered the meaning. Not that taking the wrong way was a problem for Judy. Her plane wasn't even boarding yet. She was retracing her steps, passing the security checkpoint when she heard one of the guards saying, "Thanks for your cooperation, Sheriff English."

She turned with a wide grin and searched the crowd for a familiar face. The one she found wasn't Englishman's, even though the man was the one the guard had been addressing. He combed blond hair off his forehead and took his badge and ID case back from security, stuffing them into a pocket as he fumbled for his western cut boots and carry-on luggage. She almost went over and demanded to know what he was doing, passing himself off as her husband. But he might know about the alleged blond bomber at the Farmers & Merchants.

In the end, she let it go. With all these real law-enforcement types around, she decided she might be better off if Jud Haines didn't spot her.

◇◇◇

The sheriff looked around the lobby and didn't see Judy or his daughters anywhere. Not Haines or Davis either. He didn't know Mid-Continent Airport well. He'd only been there once since Nine-Eleven, a favor, picking up Doc Jones when he returned from a family funeral. The last time the sheriff had flown into Wichita himself was when he came home from that military hospital in Hawaii. In those days, you climbed down stairs from the plane and your friends and family could come out and greet you on the tarmac, just like his mom and Mad Dog had.

Even though he'd known he should expect additional security, the reality had stunned him. He'd felt like he was in an alien place. Maybe you needed security like this at airports in LA and Washington and New York, but in the heartland's heart? He'd felt then like he'd felt in Buffalo Springs this morning. Like home wasn't really home anymore.

He had a badge and he had ID proving he was in law enforcement, but he was out of his jurisdiction here. He wasn't sure they'd let him through to the gates without a lengthy clearance process he didn't have time for. But, it occurred to him, maybe he wouldn't need to do that. He was ticketed for a seat on Judy's plane.

He used his badge to bypass the line waiting to check in at the airline's counter. "I'm supposed to be on a flight that's leaving for Atlanta in a few minutes," he told the clerk.

The clerk started entering his name from his ID onto her computer and agreed, not letting him finish. "I'll say you are. Why are you here? You're checked in. You're supposed to be at your gate. They're boarding right now."

She looked at him accusingly and he said, "Well, I need a pass."

"Oh my, you lost it." She punched more keys and a printer buzzed and she handed him a ticket and a boarding pass. "You better hurry," she said. "I can't ask them to hold the flight for you."

Since Nine-Eleven, it's not a good idea to run in an airport. But if you do, having a badge pinned to your shirt makes it a lot more acceptable. They even waved him around the line waiting at the metal detector. He almost bypassed security completely. Almost. He would have but for the man doing random checks with a wand.

"I passed Sheriff English through here a few minutes ago," the man said. "You're not him." That was when the armed security guard stepped between the sheriff and the concourse and things got seriously complicated.

"I love what you've done to your hair."

Judy was in the waiting area, hunkered down behind a magazine where she'd been sure Jud Haines would never notice her.

"Oh, thanks, Jud." She reached up, flustered, trying to comb her fingers through her curls. There weren't enough left. "What are you doing here?" She also wanted to ask why he was using her husband's name, but Judy had other concerns on her mind, too. Haines might connect her with the robbery of the Farmers & Merchants and prevent her from flying to Paris. Paris had become an obsession.

"Family emergency," he said, turning off his perpetual smile and looking briefly solemn. "I've got to make an international connection in Atlanta, same as you."

"You know about my trip?" That surprised her.

"Yeah, Englishman told me. You know, you're a lucky woman. He's a really special guy."

Judy didn't understand and said so.

"I just found out I had to make this trip this afternoon. No problem with reservations out of Atlanta, but I couldn't find a flight from Wichita. So Englishman offered me his ticket. Since he's in the middle of a full-fledged crime spree, he couldn't use it."

Judy's heart froze. It no longer mattered how perfect the day outside the windows might be, or that a regional jet waited to whisk her to an Air France connection. "Oh," she said. It was hard to believe Englishman would do that without telling her first. And hurtful. Of course, her cell phone had been turned off since she left home—avoiding calls from Englishman and the Heathers. Still, it didn't seem right.

"Englishman wouldn't do that," she said, though she wasn't sure that was true. The ticket was in his name and you couldn't transfer it. Given the current security level at airports, Jud was taking quite a chance flying under a false identity. Englishman might even get in trouble for helping him. "I don't think it's legal."

"You're right," Haines said, eyes flashing sincerely beneath his blond thatch. "But since it was an emergency, Englishman made me this ID card." He flipped open the leather case. His picture stared at her above Englishman's name on a Benteen County Sheriff's Department identity card. "And he loaned me one of his badges," Haines said, indicating the five pointed star on the opposite flap.

It was just the kind of selfless thing Englishman would do if someone needed his help—and it got him out of going to Paris. She sighed. Somehow, she'd known all along he'd find a way not to go with her.

"You look surprised," Jud said. "I'm sorry. I figured Englishman would let you know."

"My cell's off," Judy explained. She felt a rush of embarrassment. It was bad enough for Englishman to abandon her, worse for him to give his ticket away and let the recipient come tell her about it. Couldn't he have gotten word to her somehow?

"Probably a good idea," Haines said, turning his smile back on. "Leaving your cell phone off," he explained when she showed her puzzlement. She'd lost the thread of their conversation.

"Long goodbyes and all that," he said, "and they'll make you turn it off during the flight anyway."

Judy nodded. She just wanted him to go away so she could feel sorry for herself without interruptions. He didn't do that, though. He dropped into the adjacent chair.

"This'll be nice," he said. "We can look out for each other, chat and keep our minds off our troubles, all the way to Atlanta."

"Yeah, great," Judy muttered. She'd just decided Paris was probably a better place than most in which to die.

The breeze was no longer soft, nor the sun gentle—not for Deputy Parker. In her head, it had turned hot and arid and the asphalt beneath her feet had been transformed from a parking lot on the outskirts of Wichita to a street in the middle of a Tucson summer. The Buick wasn't a dirty old Chevy truck, but she was certain it contained the same demon. There was a bomb in there, with two girls, this time, instead of one. Her mistake had cost a life in Tucson. Here, the price would double.

"What should I do?" Mad Dog asked.

She didn't know. Hell, she wanted to turn around and run until she'd gone far enough that she wouldn't hear the explosion. She couldn't face the responsibility. It was too much.

"Don't touch it," she said. "Don't touch a thing."

"There's a bomb in there with the girls, isn't there? Can you defuse it?"

"No," she said, but not loud enough for him to hear. Her feet were stuck to the pavement. She couldn't run and she couldn't help. She couldn't do a thing but wait for the eruption that would be followed by a rain of wreckage and shredded body parts.

"I'll go look for Haines and Davis," Mad Dog said. "One of them's my son, I know it, and it's me he wants, not them." She heard him. She'd heard everything they'd discussed about the events of the day as they slipped between eighteen-wheelers at a hundred miles an hour. Mad Dog's comment might have made sense to her if she'd been able to concentrate, to think of anything but the look in that woman's eyes in the moment before she died on that blistering hot street in Arizona.

Mad Dog turned. "I'm going after them," he said. "Get the girls out of there."

"Be careful," she said, loud enough for him to hear this time. "There might be a remote detonator."

"Right," he called over his shoulder. "So it'd probably be good if you get them out before I find anyone." Hailey spun and followed him.

Mad Dog was right, she supposed. But first she'd have to make herself move.

It finally hit the sheriff. The woman at the airline counter, she'd told him he was already checked in. She'd assumed he'd lost his gate pass and ticket and issued him new ones. Now, this guy at the security gate said a Sheriff English had already gone through. Probably Jud Haines, he supposed, considering what Mrs. Kraus found when she was searching the supervisor's desk.

"You sure about that other guy," one security guard asked another. There were four of them, now, gathered around discussing his fate. "This fellow's got all the right IDs to go with that badge. He's even got a membership card to the Kansas Peace Officer's Association. He looks legit to me."

"I am legit," the sheriff said, looking around for his daughters. "The other guy, I think he's the one who's been setting off bombs and leaving terrorist threats all over my county today. Robbed the bank, too."

"Aw jeez," the ranking officer said. "If this guy's for real, we gotta shut this place down, clear the terminal, and sweep it for explosives. I don't wanna do that unless I'm damn sure. Last false alarm I know of cost the man who called it his job."

"Why don't we just phone this guy's office," the one with his hand on the butt of his gun said. "They can tell us whether he's who he says he is."

Great idea, the sheriff thought, but not this afternoon. Not after Mrs. Kraus had found a bomb in the courthouse and cleared the building. If nobody answered at the number on his business card, they were going to get more suspicious. It would take even longer to persuade them that the other Sheriff English had to be prevented from boarding a plane. And he wasn't going to get a chance to talk to Judy. By the time he persuaded them to check with the Highway Patrol and he cleared things up, her plane would be gone. Hell, he wasn't even sure he could convince anyone who mattered before they got to Atlanta. Then Haines could disappear under another assumed identity and stopping Judy would require the sort of actions he'd promised the Heathers wouldn't happen. And where the hell were the girls, anyway?

Some of the security people around the sheriff had been working the line through the metal detectors and carry-on x-ray and things there had slowed to a crawl. More than a couple of loud grumbles had been raised in complaint, but one voice, with a serious Panhandle twang, turned suddenly threatening. It drew the attention of the men around him and the sheriff seized the opportunity. An incoming flight must have just disembarked, because the concourse leading to the gate he wanted was suddenly flooded with humanity.

One step, two steps; he was in the crowd and the guards still hadn't noticed. He turned and ducked and sprinted toward Judy's gate. "Hey!" somebody shouted behind him, and then he was around the corner and in no danger, for the moment, of taking a round in the back. They would sound the alarm, and stop him soon enough, but not, he hoped, before he found Judy and the Heathers. And best of all, once they sounded that alarm, no commercial flights would leave this airport for hours.

He spared a moment to wonder how long he might cool his heels in a cell, victim of the Patriot Act and some seriously pissed security people. They wouldn't even have to charge him, or bother letting anyone know where he was for a few months, since he was about to cost the government and the airlines a lot of money. But then he saw her, and recognized her in spite of the hair, just as she was ducking through the gate to board her flight. Jud Haines was right behind her. No sign of the Heathers, but he had to deal with Judy right now, persuade her not to go. Getting her cured, that was worth any price.

◇ ◇ ◇

"Mmmm!" Parker could hear one of the girls trying to talk through the duct tape and closed windows of the car. And then, though her feet wanted to flee, they began carrying her toward the Heathers and the bomb instead. Slow and awkward—like wadding through the mucky bottom of a farm pond—but she got there.

One Heather lay stretched across the front seats. The other was in the back. A cat's cradle of wires linked them and the Buick's four doors. They weren't bundled with duct tape like the woman in Tucson. Each had a strip wrapped over her mouth. Other strips bound their ankles and held their hands behind their backs. The rest tied them to the seat belts, fastened to keep them below window level so it was unlikely they'd be discovered in this empty corner of the parking lot.

Parker had to put her hand on the roof of the car to keep from falling over. She was hyperventilating, she thought, but she didn't have any paper bags to breathe into, or time to pause for a panic attack. If there was a remote on the device, Mad Dog might encounter the bomber any second.

She had to start this. She knew it and it terrified her. But she could get help. There'd be a bomb squad at the main terminal. They could take over as soon as they arrived. She grabbed the cell phone off her belt and fumbled it with the leather gauntlets she'd forgot she was wearing. It hit the parking lot and came apart in a hundred pieces.

She was alone, now. There would be no help. She had to do this by herself. If she made a mistake they might die like that woman in Tucson. But they'd die anyway, if she waited.

Before she could spend too much time thinking about it, she stepped back and put a fist through the driver's door window and pulled the honeycomb of shattered glass back out onto the pavement by her feet.

They were still alive. That meant he hadn't used a trigger that was sensitive enough to be set off by her blow to the window. None of the wires were attached to glass. It had been a chance, but…Well, she didn't have time to think about it or not take chances.

She peeled off the gauntlets and doffed the catcher's mask and stuck her head in the window above the Heather in the front seat. Big eyes locked onto hers and, for a moment, she almost froze as they transformed into the ones from Tucson. She shook it off. She reached in, carefully avoiding the wires that led to the doors and to something under a patch of tape on the girl's bare midriff. She worried the strip of tape over the Heather's mouth—Heather English, she knew which was which by now—until it was clear.

Heather said, "It's on me. There's nothing on Heather. Get her out before you try to disarm it."

Parker examined Two's situation. It wasn't as bad as it could have been. The doors back there, they were wired too, but the wires hardly covered the second Heather the way they did the first, and weren't attached to the girl. Parker thought she could go in through the back window, cut her loose, and get her out without much risk.

"Do you know what it is? Whether it's got a timer or an antenna?" she asked One while she retrieved the catcher's mask and the gloves.

"I don't know. It's something malleable," the sheriff's daughter explained. "Other than that, no."

C4, but Parker had assumed that. She leaned over the trunk and took a swing with the mask. The back glass imploded. Square-edged shards of safety glass, unsplintered and not apt to cut you, littered the inside of the car. Just the same, she used the gloves to clear the worst of it away before she climbed onto the trunk, stuck her head in, and began disentangling the second Heather from the seat belts. She used her pocket knife, then sliced Two's hands and ankles free. She didn't bother with the tape across Two's mouth, and neither did the girl, not until she was scrambling off the trunk.

"Run," Parker told her. "Get behind a car and stay down."

"No," Two said. "I can help."

"You can help more by doing what I say."

Reluctantly, the second Heather obeyed.

Parker went back through the rear window. It was awkward as hell. Her legs stuck out and her body angled down into the car. Gravity tried to slide her in further where she'd make contact with the wires. She got her toes down on the edge of the trunk and stopped herself just in time. Her face was inches from the gap between the front seats, and the patch of tape that was the focus for all those wires crisscrossing the car.

Parker took a couple of deep breaths. How had they found time to do this? She hadn't thought they could be that far ahead.

"You ready?" she asked. Not that it mattered.

"Sure," Heather told her. "I mean, maybe there's no detonator. Maybe this is all just an elaborate fake."

"Probably," Parker agreed, knowing it wasn't, and knowing Heather also knew that.

She held her breath and reached out and began peeling back a corner of the tape with her pocket knife. If she screwed up this time, she comforted herself, she wouldn't have the opportunity to fret over her mistake.

It was a large metal building without indications of luxury on the outside. Mad Dog entered through wide doors that swung open in anticipation of his arrival. They revealed unexpected opulence—lush carpet, expensive and comfortable furniture, paneling with framed art that looked like originals rather than prints.

A beautiful young woman in an elegant suit that showed off her long legs came through a door across the room. "Good afternoon, sir. How can I help you and your gorgeous animal?"

If he'd had time for it, Mad Dog would have been slightly awed. There was a small restaurant to the left of the lobby—cloth napkins and fresh-cut flowers on each table—and a lavishly decorated waiting room on the other side where half a dozen people read magazines or watched news or weather on plasma screen TVs.

He was reminded of the first time he visited an airport with his mother as a child. It was in Hutchinson, and the facility had a technological elegance that both awed and welcomed. He'd been able to go out and watch the single commercial flight that came and went while they dined. One of the crew members had given him a pair of shiny wings to pin on his shirt. No one made him stand in a line or submit to being searched. He'd thought those days were gone. Apparently not, if you could afford your own plane.

"I'm looking for Brad Davis. I think he just came in." He didn't know why, but he was sure it was Davis he was looking for, not Haines.

She shook her head. "I'm sorry, sir. I don't know anyone by that name." She seemed genuinely regretful and anxious to be of assistance. He wondered if her patience would disappear when she discovered he wouldn't be parking his Learjet here.

"He couldn't have been five minutes ahead of me," Mad Dog persisted. "Good looking guy, about my size, dark hair turning silver on the sides. He was wearing a pair of cargo pants and a beige polo shirt and fancy hiking boots."

"That sounds like Mr. Haines," she said. He was amazed that she hadn't said anything about heeling his dog or getting her out of the building. Hailey had trotted down a hall that led toward the other side. Maybe he should simply follow her, but if he did, this young woman would undoubtedly call security and have him removed. And then it hit him. Haines! She'd said Haines.

"Jud Haines?" The description didn't fit, but maybe Haines and the director had switched identities.

"Yes," she said. "Ms. Jorgenson and the Windreapers jet have been waiting for him."

Janie. What did that mean? Was she waiting for her son? Had they planned to revenge themselves on him together? Or was she at risk, expecting Jud Haines and about to get her violent son instead?

But Haines was violent too. He'd been setting off bombs, had stolen money. Did Janie know that? Mad Dog started edging toward Hailey's hallway. "I've got to catch him," he told the woman. "Family emergency. Urgent." He bolted down the corridor after his wolf.

Restrooms opened off it, and a variety of offices. At the end was another glass door where Hailey stood, peering intently. He reached her before any guards arrived to escort them from the premises. He tried the door and it didn't budge. There was a numerical key pad just above the handle. The young woman appeared at the end of the hall behind him.

"I'm sorry, sir. You have to have the access code to unlock that door. We only give it to our customers."

"Really urgent," Mad Dog tried again. "Life and death."

"It's too late anyway," she told him. "Look, you can see they're already rolling." A sleek white corporate jet was indeed pulling away from the building toward the runway beyond.

"Come back to the office," the girl said. "I can get you patched through to their radio."

Mad Dog seethed in frustration. What to do? Should he try that? Would his son want to kill him badly enough to come back? Not likely, he thought. Too many witnesses. Should he go back and help Parker with the Heathers? Might Englishman need him at the main terminal? He needed spiritual guidance. He let his hand slip down to the little sack of ochre Bud Stone had given him and closed his eyes in silent supplication. The door swung open and Hailey shot through.

"Oh dear, I'm sorry," a man said. "I just wanted to come see your wolf."

"It's all right," Mad Dog said, wondering whether his natural shaman's powers or Hailey's spooky ability to get through locked doors had guided the man to them. It was miraculous either way. He slipped through and followed her.

Hailey surprised him. She didn't follow the plane. She turned south where the hallway ended and raced past a series of hangers where all manner of private aircraft were being serviced. Maybe she knew a shortcut. Mad Dog didn't. He followed the jet, hoping Janie or his son might glance out and see him and stop. And then he could…Well, then he could hope for a little more aid from the spirit world—with a plan, say. Yes, a plan would be nice.

◇◇◇

The sheriff heard people yelling behind him. He didn't look back. He had an advantage. They hadn't taken his badge, and he held it up so the crowd parted ahead of him instead of making an effort to restrain him. Two airline personnel, who looked like they might pay more attention to the shouts than his badge, let him go when he looked them in the eye and added a shout of his own. "Police business! Stand aside!"

The woman behind the desk at Judy's gate was telling a microphone that this was the last call for the flight. He showed her the badge and tossed her his papers as he flew through the gate. He was a little surprised to find himself at the top of a flight of stairs that led down to the tarmac. Apparently this flight didn't generate enough passengers for something as big as a 737. This regional jet looked like one of the big guys, only scaled down to subcompact size. Room for maybe forty passengers, he guessed, as he scrambled down the steps. Then he stopped thinking about stuff like that because Judy and Jud Haines were near the back of the line waiting to climb more stairs and board their flight.

"Judy!" he called.

His shockingly blond wife turned. There was such a look of joy on her face that, for a second, he felt like everything should slow down and turn into one of those slow-motion scenes in which lovers run across a field into each other's arms. Only Haines turned his way too, and his look had nothing to do with joy.

Judy took a step toward the sheriff and was brought up short when Haines whipped a cord out of his jacket and looped it around her neck. People around them scattered. The flight attendant at the top of the stairs got wide-eyed and the sheriff slowed to a jog.

"Stay back!" Haines warned him. "I've got nothing to lose."

The sheriff held his hands up so Haines could see they contained nothing more dangerous than his five-pointed star. "Nobody's been hurt yet. Don't make a mistake and spoil that."

"That's bull, Sheriff, and you know it," Haines replied, backing toward the plane's stairs. "I blew up your office while Mrs.

Kraus and Chairman Wynn and Supervisor Finfrock were in it. I heard the grenade go off, saw the smoke. No one could have survived in that confined space."

"All of them did," the sheriff said, still advancing. "Finfrock got screwed when he bought that grenade. It was some kind of fake. Lots of noise and a bunch of smoke, but no shrapnel. No one even got burned."

Judy was making little gurgling sounds and trying to get her fingers under the cord. It looked like something that might attach a cell phone to an earpiece. They'd seize a pair of nail clippers or a miniature pocket knife at the security checkpoint and call them weapons. A cord suitable as a garrote, however, had passed without a thought.

"I don't believe you," Haines said. Behind him, the flight attendant at the door began trying to close it. It took Haines a moment to notice over the roar of a 737 backing away from a nearby gate.

The sheriff used the opportunity to narrow the gap. He might have closed it altogether but the security guards cleared the gate above him at that moment. One of them shouted, "Halt or I'll shoot!" The sheriff thought *he* was likely the one being addressed, not Haines. They might not have even taken in what was going on just beyond the sheriff. But Haines didn't know that.

He pulled Judy around so she was between him and them. Haines must have had the garrote pretty tight. Judy's struggles were getting frantic, wild and panicky in her need for air. The sheriff was getting panicky too. She might die right there in front of him. Desperation, not logic, persuaded him he could make it. He launched himself, went for Haines' arms and missed and heard the explosion of the pistol and the whine of a bullet singing past his ear. He got tangled up with Haines' feet and lost his balance and went down on his hands and knees as Haines managed to back onto the bottom of the stairs. Judy wasn't struggling anymore.

"Move again and you're dead," the security officer yelled. The sheriff believed him. It wouldn't have mattered if he'd had a chance of knocking Judy free from Haines in the process, but Haines had gripped both ends of the garrote in one hand and grabbed the stair rail with the other. He was pulling the two of them up and there was no way the sheriff could get to him before the idiot from security put a round in his back because he hadn't noticed a murder taking place a few feet beyond his suspected terrorist.

Options. The sheriff flashed them through his head. It didn't take long because he couldn't come up with any. What he needed was one of Mad Dog's miracles.

Parker had to pee. She wondered why. She couldn't remember when she'd last had time to take a drink. She was so soaked in sweat it seemed impossible that anything could be left over for her bladder. But there it was. And the condition was aggravated by the way the back seats pushed into her lower abdomen in just the wrong place, and because she had to wiggle around and add still more pressure as she traced this wire and that, and began peeling away the next layers of tape over what she assumed was the bomb on Heather's belly.

Well, she didn't have time for a restroom break. If she wet her pants, she thought it was less than fifty-fifty anyone would ever know. The fireball would probably dry them out, and when they scooped her up with a spatula and a sponge, or found her torso a hundred yards from her foot, and maybe never found the other foot at all, they wouldn't notice a little thing like a bit of damp uniform.

"How's it going?" Heather asked. She must be really uncomfortable, lying across that armrest. She was sweating too, and Parker would wager she'd want to visit a bathroom as well, as soon as this was over. Fear does that to you. That, she realized, was the source of her own need.

"Slow, but good, I think." Parker had unpeeled enough tape so she was almost there. She could feel where the ends of the wires were twisted. They couldn't be under more than another layer or two. But she had to be extra careful getting to them. Letting one touch the other might complete the circuit.

"Keep me posted," Heather said. "Unless it's bad news. Then, I suppose I'll be the first to know."

"Probably wouldn't feel a thing," Parker said, hoping that was true for both of them. "But that's not a problem because I'm gonna have you out of here in a minute. Count on it."

She got the edge of the next layer started and realized this was the one. There was bare wire right beneath her fingers. She held it down as she removed the tape, making sure it didn't budge until she uncovered it completely.

Nothing! The wire was fastened to nothing. She made sure it didn't ground against anything as she pulled the tape away from the second one. It wasn't attached to anything either, except the end had been stuck through the corner of a Windreapers business card. On the back, someone had written. "Bang, you're dead."

The wires, the elaborate spider web that linked all the car doors, had simply been for show. There was no bomb attached to them. But there was still something under another few layers of tape. Two possibilities, Parker told herself. A transmitter activated device or a timer. The possibilities those conjured made her begin ripping tape away.

And then, there it was, staring her in the face. Small and digital, two zeros followed by a colon after which two numbers flashed at her in threatening red. As she watched, they changed from twenty-four to twenty-three to twenty-two. She ripped the rest of the package off Heather's stomach. Too many bits of tape still attached it to the car. She had twenty seconds to back her butt out the rear window, get to the door, and drag Heather far enough before what was maybe a kilo of C4 tried to send them to eternity. She didn't think twenty seconds was enough.

◇ ◇ ◇

Since a balmy breeze was blowing out of the south, unusual only in that it was just a breeze and not a full-fledged Kansas wind, Mad Dog had expected Windreapers' jet to turn left and head for the north end of the nearest runway. Instead, it turned south. For some reason, the jet was being diverted around the main terminal to the parallel runway on the west side of the airport. It was the kind of thing that made him think Hailey must have known that from the moment she cleared the executive terminal.

The jet wasn't moving very fast, not much faster than an aging former jock could run after it. And it had to stick to the taxiways. Now that he knew where it was going, he could head cross country, maybe cut off a couple of hundred yards before they got to where they were going.

Mad Dog concentrated on his breathing. He'd have to pace himself if he was going to chase them that far. Besides, concentrating on his wind kept him from thinking about what to do if they saw him and stopped.

Had Janie been straight with him? Or had Brad Davis? Or neither one? He tended to believe Janie because he'd been in love with her once, and the bomb with the Heathers wasn't a pro-Davis argument. But even if he was evil, that didn't mean she might not have turned evil too. Which was better, trailing a psycho whose presence put Janie's life in danger, or a mother and son team involved in an elaborate scheme to fleece Benteen County and maybe kill him and his nieces?

Inquiring minds, he told himself. But the answers would make a huge difference in what he had to deal with if they saw him, or whether they'd stop if they did.

And then another complication occurred to him. To go around the terminal, they had to pass it. That meant Mad Dog would have to run by all manner of airport personnel. Some were bound to be security types. The woman from the private terminal had probably called in a report about him by now. Mad Dog wasn't likely to get past the main terminal. Knowing that inspired him to an extra burst of speed.

A 737 was leaving one of the gates ahead. The Windreapers jet slowed a little and for a moment he was nearly parallel to it. He thought he saw faces at the windows. He raised his hands and waved madly and stepped in a hole and went tumbling.

Mad Dog bounced up quickly enough, at least for a man his age. He got his feet under him and discovered he'd hurt his knee again. He could still run, sort of, but it had turned as weak as wheat futures and he was a lot slower than only moments before.

It didn't matter. The Windreapers jet stopped. Someone opened the hatch and a dark head with a hint of gray protruded. It was Brad Davis, or the man he'd thought was Davis. He had a gun and it was pointed at Mad Dog. The gun made a popping noise and one of the blue lights near Mad Dog's feet shattered.

Well, Mad Dog thought, at least Janie hadn't lied about everything. The man who'd claimed he was her son wanted to kill him. On the other hand, it was sad to realize he wasn't likely to live long enough to find out whether she had been honest about the rest of it.

The second shot plucked Mad Dog's sleeve. His boy was getting his windage. And Mad Dog was ready for that plan to occur to him.

The third shot probably would have done him serious damage, except a massive concussion rolled across the field from back in the parking lot and spoiled junior's aim. The detonation didn't do Mad Dog's imagination any good either.

◇◇◇

Sometimes, the miracle department is open. The problem, the sheriff later decided, was that it must be part of a bureaucracy. You needed one very specific miracle. You got something else, not built to your specifications.

The sheriff got three—bureaucratic triplicate, perhaps. The first was an explosion. Considering his experience with explosions today, he had every reason to think this was related to the ones in Buffalo Springs. That meant it had probably been directed at his brother, his daughters, or his deputy. Still, it was loud enough to be heard over the roar of the departing 737, and it drew the attention of the armed security guard as well as Jud Haines.

The armed guard glanced toward the blast and Haines looked at his watch. "Shit," Haines muttered. "Bastard promised me twenty minutes."

It was the chance the sheriff needed. He scrambled up and threw himself at Haines.

The second miracle got in his way. Maybe Judy had been faking it, or maybe the blast pierced her diminishing consciousness and drew a reaction. In either case, she swung a vicious elbow into Haines' groin. It must have missed, because he didn't double over in helpless agony. But it had been close. Haines lost his balance on the stairs and dropped back to the concrete. That put Judy directly between the sheriff and his target. Still, the sheriff managed to get an arm around her and a hand on the cord. He yanked it away from Haines.

At which point, the third miracle arrived. Like Mad Dog, the sheriff had often wondered at Hailey's ability to appear in unlikely places from which she should have been securely barred, and at the most unlikely times. Here she was again, sudden and improbable, with her teeth firmly imbedded in Jud Haines' butt.

Haines screeched. He tried to turn and kick at Hailey, and ended up on his hands and knees because Hailey was just as suddenly and improbably gone, tearing back between the wheels of the jet Haines and Judy had been about to board.

The Marquis of Queensbury might have objected, but the Marquis hadn't watched Haines strangle his wife. The sheriff tore the cord from Judy's throat, stepped around her, and kicked Haines in the same spot Hailey had bitten. Haines let out a second shriek and went down face first, in a manner that did his boyish good looks no favor and would require the efforts of a dental surgeon to reconstruct his winning smile.

The sheriff might have done more, but Judy threw her arms around him and said, "You came." Her voice was hoarse, but it was obvious Haines hadn't seriously injured her.

"I love you." The sheriff couldn't think of another way to explain it.

"I know. And I knew you wouldn't let me go without you," Judy said.

That's when the miracle department shut down. One of the security people shoved a muzzle in the nape of the sheriff's neck. "Nobody's going anywhere," the man said, "except into a windowless cell until Kansas gets oceanfront property."

Mad Dog fancied himself a natural-born shaman. Sometimes. Sometimes he thought he was a fraud. Just now, he was leaning toward shaman. After all, his son had taken three shots and missed him with every one. He felt like one of those Native American warriors the cavalry's bullets couldn't find because they'd purified themselves and donned their ghost shirts. Mad Dog didn't have a ghost shirt, but he did have a little sack of earth from the Cheyenne's sacred mountain.

He can't hit me, Mad Dog told himself. If I focus my spirit on him, I'll cause his aim to be untrue. This holy earth and my shamanistic powers will protect me.

As if to prove him right, his son popped off another round that whined close by, another miss.

That was four bullets. He only needed those powers and his talisman to work twice more. Mad Dog let out a war whoop that would have done his ancestors proud. Like a Cheyenne Dog Soldier of old, he contemptuously charged his enemy. And rattled him in the process because the fifth shot went wide as well. As did the sixth, wild and way off target because someone in the plane was grappling with Davis, or Sam, or whoever the man with the gun really was.

It was Janie, coming to his rescue. He couldn't see her, but he knew it. He reached out with his mind to give her strength. The pain in Mad Dog's leg was gone—healed as he drew on his powers and pulled them about him like a cloak. I am strong, he told himself. I am invincible.

Somewhere in the back of his head, he heard Helen Reddy chime in with the next line, and the title to her career-defining song. *I am woman.*

It was one of those loss-of-focus moments that had tripped up this master shaman throughout his career. He had to maintain his concentration to control the forces of the universe. One little slip, and they weren't his anymore. They were random, or acting on their own agendas, and he was back at risk like any other mortal.

The hatch on the side of the plane swung open just before he reached it. Sam or Brad or the mad bomber of Benteen County stood there, one arm around Janie's throat, the pistol to her temple.

"Daddy," the man said. "How nice that we can have this brief family reunion."

He swung the gun to point it at Mad Dog.

"Please don't shoot him," Janie pleaded.

"He can't," Mad Dog reassured her. "He hasn't got any bullets. He's fired six shots. I counted."

"Jesus, did you really mate with such a moron?" Their son turned the gun sideways for a moment and let Mad Dog see it. It was a semi-automatic, not a six-shooter.

"Oh," Mad Dog said. Well, he could stand there and take a bullet or he could do something about it. He was still too far away to do anything physically, but maybe he could recoup his grasp on those universal forces he'd been wielding only moments before. But he had to concentrate. He had to banish everything else from his mind. He closed his eyes.

"And too much of a coward to watch," his son said. The words hardly registered. Mad Dog had been in situations like this before. He needed to find some psychic weapon and hurl it. So he did.

Mad Dog didn't realize Hailey had already been part of another family miracle. But his mind sensed her and knew she would be part of his. And he suddenly understood what Bud Stone, the old Cheyenne, had meant—Hailey, she was his *nisimon*, his guardian spirit. He opened his eyes in time to see her leap into the doorway. It was a long way up there, but he'd seen her clear higher fences. She set her teeth in his son's leg.

The man tumbled down onto the taxiway as Hailey and Janie tangled with each other and fell, inside the plane. Before Mad Dog could stop it, his son reached up and slammed the hatch shut, leaving Hailey inside. And he threw a punch at Mad Dog. Mad Dog had slipped many a punch in his time. That was why he was so surprised when this one caught him in mid-charge and sparked a nova behind his eyes.

Mad Dog found himself sitting on the tarmac. His son had bent and picked up the gun Hailey caused him to drop. He turned and shoved the muzzle in Mad Dog's face.

"Sorry, Dad," he said. "If you'd given me a b-b gun, I might have shot my eye out. You didn't, so I'll shoot out yours."

He pulled the trigger.

Nothing happened. He pulled it again, and still the pistol wouldn't fire. Mad Dog rolled woozily to his feet. Pieces of the gun's mechanism lay scattered on the yellow concrete. It wasn't jammed. It wasn't a misfire. The pistol was broken, another miracle Mad Dog would gladly accept.

His son looked around wildly. Mad Dog thought he considered the Windreapers jet, until he remembered Hailey. He seemed to consider killing his father with his bare hands, too. Mad Dog might be getting old, but he was still a big man, and a strong one. And he was back up, ready to defend himself.

"Give it up," Mad Dog said. "There's no way out. Your daughter's dead. Let it end here."

"You think I care about Jackie? She was just a tool. And she nearly screwed it all up this morning. Whatever happened to her after that, she deserved."

His son reached into a pocket and pulled out what Mad Dog realized must be another bomb. "I'm tempted to use this and make it a clean sweep of the whole family," the man said. "But I'll bet this and the gun will buy me a way out of here. Then you and I, we'll finish this another time."

Mad Dog's son turned and sprinted, limping from Hailey's tooth-work, toward the main terminal, toward where the 737 was taxiing to a runway. He got in front of the plane and waved the gun so the pilot could see it, then leveled it at the Boeing's cockpit.

Mad Dog followed. It took him a bit to get up steam, but he was determined. His son couldn't be allowed to hurt anyone else.

Sam planted himself square in the 737's path. The pilot didn't know that the gun pointing at him had been damaged. He had to assume it was a real danger. He had to act accordingly.

The 737 pivoted to the right with surprising agility. The pilot must have slammed on the brakes on one side while he gunned the engines. The big plane didn't spin on a dime, but it roared into a turn far more rapidly than Mad Dog would have expected. Or than Sam had.

But Sam had something else to worry about. Maybe he'd inherited some of his father's ability to sense what he couldn't see. Or maybe he was just smart enough to realize there was nothing to keep his old man from pursuing him. He turned far faster than the plane, just in time for Mad Dog to lower his head and lead with a shoulder—the way he had when he and Janie were young and he was the star of the Buffalo Springs Bisons and mammoth linemen were between him and a goal line.

Sam slipped him, and caught him with another roundhouse that crashed into his chest just below his chin. It hurt like hell, but Mad Dog spun and got ready to throw a punch of his own. Only he couldn't pivot as easily as he'd expected because something was attached to his neck. Sam had caught his fist in the thong that held the sacred Cheyenne earth. It threw both of them off balance before Sam tore his hand free. And then they were dodging the 737's fuselage. A great wind plucked at Mad Dog. It ripped at Sam's hair and whipped his clothing. And then Sam seemed to vanish into thin air. The howling engine under the wing brushed by Mad Dog and changed its note as it began throwing pieces of itself, along with a crimson mist, onto the tarmac behind. Mad Dog knew where his son had gone.

The FBI agent returned the phone to its cradle. "I'll be damned," he told Sheriff English. "All your stories check out. Including the bomb in your courthouse."

"All?" The Chief of Security for Mid-Continent Airport—the only other man in the room and the guy whose day the sheriff had ruined—still appeared to want English put behind bars indefinitely.

"Yup! We had a call reporting bombs and terror threats from Benteen County. The agent who logged it asked the Highway Patrol to check it out. Of course, by then, the festivities had moved here. It even turns out the guy who went through that jet engine had plastic explosives and a gun on him. Pieces have been found and identified."

"Shit," the security chief muttered.

"We'll hang on to Mr. Haines, of course," the fed continued from the seat he'd appropriated, along with the security chief's desk. The sheriff considered objecting, but thought he was about to get out of this a lot easier than he'd expected. He buttoned his lip and nodded.

"You'll be relieved, Sheriff, to know he's already admitted everything. He blames the guy he knew as Davis for talking him into changing this from a simple con into a deadly ripoff. He's confessed to setting some of the bombs, and told us where we'll find a few more he says Davis left for your brother. He wired your county's funds to a bank in the Caribbean. He gave up the access codes, though. We'll be getting it back to you, when we get around to it."

The sheriff pocketed the badge and wallet the agent tossed across the desk to him. "What made Haines so chatty?"

"We showed him that leather badge case his partner fixed him up with. Turns out it was another bomb. Davis persuaded him to use it to get on that flight with your wife. That way, he could eliminate his partner, and maybe kill another member of the family as well."

The agent paused for a moment, pursing his mouth as if what he had to say now would leave a sour taste. "The only remaining member of your wild bunch who may be involved in a crime is Ms. Jorgenson, but all that took place on your turf. If you and your posse, including Chief Crazy Horse's Ass out there, hadn't come charging into this airport, she would have just flown off to somebody else's jurisdiction. I'm letting you take her with you. You've put too big a hurt on several budgets already."

They had indeed. It was three hours since the sheriff had been taken into custody and Mid-Continent Airport was only now beginning to let passengers return to the terminal as arrivals and departures were rescheduled. It was a big building to cover, even with the aid of every bomb dog in the Wichita area.

"We'll let Benteen County decide what to do with her, and pick up the tab if you prosecute," the man said.

The airport's security chief protested. "You mean you're not going to charge this hick lawman with anything?"

"Well," the agent said, "I suppose we could charge Sheriff English with violating your security, but then he'd have to defend himself by explaining how you failed to heed his warning that your security was already breached. I don't see where telling the public how you let the bomb in a badge case slip through will do anybody any good."

The chief sputtered, but he didn't argue.

"Does that mean I'm free to take Ms. Jorgenson, my family, and my deputy and go home?"

"All of them. Your punk-rock wife, your twin daughters who conveniently share the same name, your space-case brother, and his pet wolf. Take the whole crazy lot. Except that deputy of yours. You can leave her." He turned and glanced at the airport's security chief. "I might know where there'll be a job opening."

The sheriff got to his feet and went to the door. Just before he reached it, the agent made one last request.

"Sheriff."

The sheriff turned and looked back.

"Do us both a favor. Any of you want to fly somewhere in the future, don't come through security in my jurisdiction."

◇ ◇ ◇

Heather English rose as her dad entered the room. "We're all going home," he told them. They had been waiting in a windowless area to which access was rigidly controlled after they'd each been questioned. She and Heather had been hovering protectively on either side of their mother, regaling everyone with testimony about the heroism of a pleased but embarrassed Deputy Parker.

"Start sorting out who's going in what vehicle," Englishman said. "That includes you, Ms. Jorgenson. I'm not charging you with anything yet, unless that's what it takes to get you back to Buffalo Springs. But you've got a lot of explaining to do."

Janie Jorgenson sat beside Mad Dog. Her eyes were red and her makeup a mess, but she'd stopped crying. "No excuses, Englishman," she said. Heather knew her dad must kind of like the woman, since he didn't interrupt to insist she call him Sheriff or English. "I'm responsible for most of what happened in Buffalo Springs today. I wanted revenge on the town, so I bought one of your supervisors to help me get it. And I arranged to have my granddaughter, Jackie, be there to help with our little scam."

"How'd you do that?" Englishman wondered.

"I'm a big contributor to PBS. I just gave a little more…" She shrugged and Heather thought the woman might lose it again. She didn't. "We planned to force you into selling Windreapers exclusive rights by setting up a fake terrorist attack. Jud told me he could trade for all the explosives we needed if I'd get him an antique rifle. I made one available where Jackie could get it to him.

"But no one was supposed to be hurt. Jud was going to get a nice commission and come work for me, and I was going to make sure neither Windreapers, nor any other company, ever built a thing or created a job in Benteen County. I was going to sit back and enjoy watching you collapse into bankruptcy."

"What about your son?"

She sighed and Mad Dog reached over and took one of her hands. "Funny," she said. "I didn't have a clue he was there. Not until Jackie hinted at it. And I never knew he was a film producer or that he'd finagled his way onto *This Old Tepee*. I think it was a coincidence that we decided to take our vengeance at the same time. Then he played long-lost daddy. Persuaded poor Jackie to let him in on my plans and piggy-backed off us. No, Sam's part in this came as quite a shock."

"You better tell him about Jackie," Mad Dog prompted.

Her voice started to break and she had to stop for a moment before she answered. "Jackie was a troubled kid. Drugs, sex. I actually thought she'd be better off in Benteen County, but what a role model I turned out to be. What Mad Dog wants me to tell you is that our granddaughter killed that boy this morning."

"We know she was the archer," Englishman said.

"She'd been sneaking out and meeting Michael. They'd had a sexual relationship since shortly after she got there. She was jealous. She told me when I talked to her this morning. She only meant to scare them, then Mad Dog and Hailey came jogging down the road and surprised her and she flinched—shot Michael in the back. She would have shot the girl, if she'd meant to hit one of them."

Mad Dog took his hand back and put it around her shoulder. Heather thought she didn't look entirely comfortable with it there, but she didn't shrug him off.

"We think she shot at me at the courthouse," Mad Dog said, "to make it look like I'd been the target all along. Janie had told her to get on her motorcycle and come over and wait here in Wichita. She planned to consult her company's lawyers before she decided how they should handle the boy's death."

"So, no," Janie continued. "I couldn't fly out of here tonight, anyway. I've got to make arrangements for my granddaughter." She paused and a tear slid down her cheek before she continued. "Mad Dog and I, we've got things to work out and grieving to do, and I need to pay some penance to my old hometown."

Englishman nodded. "You saved the life of one of my deputies. Grabbed the bomb that was supposed to blow Mad Dog across most of the state and dumped it out in the country. That counts for something. And you've paid a heavy price today. Find a way to make good on a deal that benefits Benteen County and compensate folks for the damages you caused—maybe we won't need to file charges. I'll let you, and what's left of our supervisors, work that out before I make up my mind. Now, let's get saddled up. We've got more than two hours on the road before we can call it a day."

They rose from their chairs, slowly, wrung out, squeezed dry of spare energy by all they'd been through. All but Judy. She was up before anyone else. She went across the room and took Englishman by the arm.

"No," she said. "I still want to go to Paris."

"But you've got to see doctors. There are tests, treatments."

"And they'll still be here when we get back. Or they have doctors and treatments in Paris, if we need them.

"Englishman, you know how much I want to go. Maybe I'll have lots of years and lots of chances. But maybe I won't. Indulge me. Let me see the City of Lights while I can enjoy it. Two weeks. Our insurance company has to approve those tests Doc says I need. It'll probably take that long before I can start them anyway."

Heather put in her two cents. "Doc said it might be good for her."

"Yeah, Dad," Two agreed. Heather couldn't remember Two ever calling him Dad before. "We've decided you should take her."

"But it's too late. I mean, we're in Wichita and it's eight o'clock, three hours after we were supposed to fly out of here. The plane is still here, maybe loading soon, but that flight from Atlanta will be long gone."

"You never looked at our tickets, did you?" Judy chided. "We had quite a layover in Atlanta. Our Air France jet doesn't leave until eleven-thirty."

Englishman shook his head. "We still might not make it." Heather thought he was less trying to talk himself out of it than simply doubting things could fall into place.

"Have you got your passports?" Janie Jorgenson interrupted.

"Right here, in my purse," Judy replied.

"Then you've got time. My jet's fueled and ready. My pilot will just have to file a new flight plan."

"That's mighty kind of you," Englishman said, "but I can't do that. It'd be like taking a bribe."

"Don't give me that," Heather said, punching his shoulder to emphasize her point. "You practically promised her you weren't going to charge her with anything. That working this out is between her and the supervisors. So where's the bribe?"

"If you think it's about money," Janie said, "give me your tickets to Atlanta. After my lawyers get through with the airline that ticketed and provided boarding passes to two sheriffs named English, I'll make a profit on getting you there."

Heather's dad was out of arguments. All he had left was a complaint.

"But look at me," he said, gesturing at his mud-splattered clothes. "And I haven't eaten all day."

"We'll take care of that," Judy said, "on our way."

"It's the right thing to do," Mad Dog said. "My spirit feels it."

Englishman shrugged. "Okay, but no dancing in the rain."

The Windreapers jet was fast and comfortable and private. The pilot and the cockpit were sealed off from the intimate little dinner Judy and Englishman shared. They poured a second glass of wine after they finished their gourmet meal. It had been provided by the people at the executive terminal, along with a change of clothes for Englishman, small things, the pretty manager told them. Not nearly enough to make up for letting a killer pass through to the plane earlier.

"You'll love Paris," Judy said. She could see by the look in his eyes that he wasn't convinced. She slipped off her shoes and gave him a wanton look as she rubbed one of her feet up the inside of his leg under the table.

"You'll love it because I'll love it."

"You're probably right," he admitted. "You usually are. It's just…"

She interrupted him. "I know, but I don't want to talk about death and dying right now. I only want to think about Paris, and how going benefits you."

He raised an eyebrow and she slid her foot a little higher.

"Do you know what the mile high club is?"

"No," he said.

Before they got to Atlanta, she showed him. Then he napped. It was, after all, the fourth time today.

Afterword & Acknowledgments

I remember Kansas bombings. I witnessed many and took part in others. Our bombs, however, were leftover Fourth of July fireworks, and our targets, friend's rural parties. You knew you'd thrown a successful party when someone drove by and launched a few firecrackers and maybe a Roman candle your way. I was reminded of that, and the fantasies of our youth, when I attended reunions of the Partridge Rural High School Class of '62. That's where the idea for this story was born, and why I associated the name of an old friend with the explosives in this novel. Apologies. The Finfrock I know is more like Englishman than the namesake who inhabits these pages

Bad things happen to good people like Judy. The older I get, the more I encounter that fact of life, and that's where another element of this story originated. Bad things took two special people out of my life while I wrote this book. One of my dearest friends died of breast cancer. Kate was among the first to read my fiction and take it seriously. She helped me persevere. Just over a month later, the same terrible disease claimed my sister Charlie. At least I had the pleasure of giving her a copy of the predecessor to this volume. *Prairie Gothic* was dedicated to her, and our surviving sisters.

As I finish this, I've just learned my sister Jodi faces a crisis of her own. It's more evidence of bad things happening to good people. The best. Prayers, pixie dust, and good thoughts for her will be appreciated. And, any small miracles.

I've mentioned how difficult it is to go home again in each of my Kansas books. That task will be harder now that Charlie is gone. She was the last of my family still living in Reno County. Reno, of course, depopulated, bumped a little north and west, then exaggerated for effect, is the model for Benteen. My Kansas connections are down to cousins in the eastern part of the state, my sister Kita, in Salina (Kansans pronounce Salina with a long "i"), and my nephew Eric and his family in Mulvane. And friends, of course, lots of friends.

The prairie wind still whips my hair and sings in my ears, but it does that in my memory. I left Kansas in 1968 to continue my education. I spent one terrible summer (1969) struggling to write a thesis in my parents' basement. Beyond that, I've only been back to visit. I know the land. I know the people. I love both. But I don't know the realities of daily life there anymore. I hope I haven't done my former state and its residents an injustice in these pages. Those friends and that family who still live there, they help keep me grounded, as have the residents of Kansas-L. I thank them all.

For those who may wish to write a novel one day, I promise you two things. It's much harder than you expect, and every bit as rewarding. Even if you never publish.

The process takes lots of help. First, and always most important, is my chief publicist, editor, partner, and wife, Barbara. Karl Schlesier kindly spent hours talking to me about the Cheyenne Way. If Mad Dog and I are on the right course, we owe it to him. I am part of a very special critique group. They point out my flaws, glaring and otherwise, and keep me from stepping on my best lines. This novel is much better than it might have been because of J. Mark Brown, Sheila Cottrell, J.R. Dailey, Margaret Falk, Elizabeth Gunn, Mary Logue, E.J. McGill, and Susan Cummins Miller. None of them should be blamed, however.

Kimba and Hailey (yes, there really is a Hailey—sort of), our German Shepherds, give their constant support and never suggest I should have told the story differently. Doctors Thomas Lindow and Ray Malone kindly answered medical questions. They aren't responsible if I failed to ask the right question or misinterpreted information they supplied. Dorothy-L, Nick Wolfe Garcia, Sid Jackson, and Vic Amos helped me learn about foreign object debris and jet engines, and more. And Doug Pope gave me a look at an executive terminal. There's one in Wichita, roughly where I put mine. Otherwise, they bear no resemblance to each other. I've flown in and out of Mid-Continent's main terminal enough to know it well. The real one has far better security. In fact, only a few of the places I describe are real. And none of the characters or events.

Bloodlines is real, though. If you love folk rock, search out a John Stewart album. The man is an American poet of the first magnitude, his music, the history of our lives. On bloodlines, you can learn more about him, see an occasional request for prayers, pixie dust, and good thoughts, and meet a lot of good people—perhaps, even, angelbravo and lordfrench.

Mad Dog's Mini Cooper, that's real too. He had so much fun with his, he persuaded us we should get one of our own. He was right.

Barbara Peters and Rob Rosenwald are the people who make Poisoned Pen Press such an extraordinary place. But for them and their marvelous staff, many fine writers and great stories might not have been published, or might be out of print. I thank them for balancing those successes by keeping me aboard.

Many others had a part in this. Marilyn Pizzo at Poisoned Pen, for instance, helped me find and fix some loose ends. She, and those others, listened, told, tolerated, and inspired. They all deserve personal thanks, and might have gotten it if I were being paid by the word.

Finally, I need to credit this book's title. John Orr of the *San Jose Mercury News* wrote a kind review of *Prairie Gothic*, my last Mad Dog & Englishman novel, under the title "Plains

Crazy." I was unable to resist the urge to borrow it for their latest adventure.

For any flaws or errors that remain, I alone am responsible.

JMH
Tucson, by way of Hutchinson, Darlow, Partridge,
Manhattan, Wichita, Sedna Creek, et Tabun,
Albuquerque, and a yellow brick road
www.jmhayes-author.com